MW01222620

Gray Masters: Alliance

ॐॐ

Darin Castalds

KRIS

My silent wish

Part 1

She sat in a far corner, demurely, her hair pinned elaborately, with curls playing about her face and tripping on her shoulders when she moved. Her back was straight, her shoulders back, a perpetual shade of a smile touching her cheeks. No doubt she was raised a lady.

He strode across the room, confident others would make way for him, and so they did. As well they might, with his ten thousand pounds per annum and estates from here to Kent. That same wealth protected him, and her, as it happened, from speculations as he approached and then sat with her.

"Miss ...?" He bowed before her, begging her name.

"Chambers. Althea Chambers."

"Miss Chambers. I am George Hamlin. May I have the pleasure of your company?"

"I should be honoured, Mr. Hamlin. Do sit down." She indicated the open space on the bench beside her.

He sat.

She continued to watch the party with that same air of being just ready to be amused, as though he were not even there. He watched her, the party, her again. She said nothing.

"You should be honoured, you said."

"Hmm?" She answered, her eyes on the dance floor.

"You should be, but you are not."

She turned to face him.

"How very observant you are, Mr. Hamlin."

"Not half so much as you, I'm afraid."

"Whatever do you mean, sir?"

"I have been here near fifteen minutes and you have all but ignored me. Not the actions of one who is honoured. You are enraptured with watching others

5

mingle and dance and make merry, yet you make none yourself."

A bold statement, even from one such as he.

Althea put on one of her most brilliant smiles as she turned to him. "They make more than enough for all here and beyond. They certainly don't need my help." Her brilliance of feature was wholly insincere, though none yet, in her one and twenty years, had discerned it.

"Why not partake of it?"

"I?" She paused. "No, thank you."

"You disapprove then?" He shifted to face her fully, leaning in, suddenly engaged.

"Not at all. Far be it from me to judge how they behave."

"I think you just have."

Althea opened her mouth, astonished, then closed it with a sigh. She pursed her lips.

Hamlin laughed aloud. "A word to the wise, Miss Chambers, never play at cards. Your magnificent expressions are an open book."

She looked at him out of the corner of her eye. She lifted her chin. "It is not for me to decide what others should or should not do. Only what I should or should not do."

"You said yourself, you should be honoured."

"And so I am." She turned her brilliantly insincere smile on him again. It never failed to distract and disarm even the most ardently stupid.

"Don't flatter me, Miss Chambers. I know well how you shun company of any kind."

Althea raised an eyebrow.

"Why then risk the wasted time? Surely there are partners enough to amuse you."

"You amuse me. I would never think even a moment with you as time wasted."

"Who is flattering whom, now, sir?"

"Do you know this is not the first gathering I have watched you at?"

"Watched me?" She turned her gaze back to the party. "Whatever for?"

"Indeed I have. No one guessed. I always stood in line of sight of you, making sure to have conversation such that I could always gaze upon you."

"That could hardly have gone unnoticed, sir." Althea barely repressed rolling her eyes.

"Many overlook the eccentricities of those such as I."

"As well they might. One ought not give offence to a man of your considerable consequence."

Hamlin snorted. "My consequence, indeed."

"Lower your voice, you'll shock the whole room, speaking so."

"But not you."

"Surely not. I am of so little consequence, I have no claim to the pretense of being offended."

"Your carriage says otherwise."

"A dance, like any other, I'm afraid. You of all people should not be fooled by it. I daresay you grew up with as much and more of it than I."

"I have."

Althea smiled indulgently, seeing a romance budding between a man her foster father would have deemed infinitely worthy and her foster sister. They would get on well enough. She'd hear of the wedding plans before little Mary was tucked in bed.

Hamlin followed her gaze. "What amuses you, lady?"

Althea did not answer, only kept watching.

"She is your sister?"

"Of a sort. As very like one as I should ever know."

"Pardon?"

"I am but a ward, Mr. Hamlin. An odd body, grateful for the charity of others."

"But not their pity."

"Surely not."

"Yet you are raised up with them."

"We all dance our steps."

"Is that why you do not partake?"

"I do partake. From a distance. Their wine is too strong for me."

Hamlin surreptitiously looked her over again, seeing now the way the gown was a hair out of date, the fabric just the wrong side of worn. Althea felt his gaze.

"You might as well take your eyes fill, Mr. Hamlin. No one but I will notice."

"I apologize."

"No need, Mr. Hamlin. I know what I am, and am not ashamed. Look all you like."

"You are rare."

"As a penny." She continued to gaze into the crowd, unperturbed by his attention, neither preening nor fidgeting. She chose not to gage his reactions to her words, for surely he would not approach her a second time.

Best to be honest, that she might not reproach herself later for saying what she did not mean.

"I should like to see you in another setting, Miss Chambers."

"Should but don't?" She inquired, a teasing light in her eyes as she stared ahead.

"I mean, I would like to."

"Ah. Well, I daresay, Mr. Hamlin, if you wish it, all the world would leap to make it come true."

"You mock me."

"I do not." Althea smiled. "I mock others." She paused. "And I shall pay for that in due time. Forgive me. That was ill said and unkind. Neither of which are deserved."

"On the contrary, it was too well said. You are right. Many would seek to win favour with me."

"Indeed, sir. Many would," she replied.

"But not you."

"I have read that happiness should be sought only where its attainment is possible. Wishing to fly, for instance, as a butterfly does, is impossible. Therefore wishing it is only a study in frustration. But, when you wish for what is possible, well then, happiness is virtually assured."

"What has that to do with this?"

"I could no more win your favour than become a butterfly, sir." She looked at him then. "Your family and connections would forbid any such alliance, as well they should, that you might not disgrace your House."

"You would not disgrace any man with sense."

"Even men of sense must abide by the general rules of society."

"You have been slighted," he deduced.

"Not at all, sir, not at all. I speak from observation alone."

Men with sense and without had not even noticed her enough to slight her, as she was always introduced as the ward of a fine house. Instantly she was dismissed in favour of her foster sisters.

"They must believe you wish for their lives. The wealth, the attention from worthless young suitors."

"They might, but they would be mistaken."

"Do you never wish to trade places with the -" he couldn't finish the statement, too daunted was he by her steady gaze.

"One ought not say 'never'. I have far more freedom than they, than you do, sir."

"Living on the charity of others? This is freedom?"

"The world is far greater than this small island, sir. Equip me with a sturdy pair of well-fitted shoes and I could find my way. But others, they can easily become trapped in the dance, like a child in that hedgerow labyrinth out back." She almost seemed to shrug, but the movement was so slight, Hamlin thought he might have imagined it.

"You are too polite to say that I am trapped."

"I am not so polite as that. I do not say what I do not believe. Your choice to slight others by paying such attention to me proclaims to all that you do not feel bound by the steps others would encourage you in."

"You are most singularly forthright, Miss Chambers."

"What good could come from dissembling?"

Months passed before the next ball was announced. Althea's foster sister had indeed snared the worthy young man in question, for he appeared almost daily with gifts and invitations for both Mary and the family. Dinners, shooting, picnics, whatever he could contrive of to tempt her into his company, he did, much to the satisfaction of Mary's father, Mr. Henry Wentworth.

To his credit, the young Mr. Davies included Althea in the invitations. She brought both book and embroidery to amuse herself with, keeping out of the way as much as possible to allow Mary every potential moment with Davies.

Mary commented on it one night as they prepared for bed.

"You are so good, Althea, truly. Always willing to chaperone us, yet never so closely that we cannot have a private moment. Mary hugged her with enthusiasm and planted a wet kiss on her cheek.

Althea laughed, pushing Mary away. "Take your sloppy kisses and be gone."

Mary made a puckered face and danced from the room.

When the day of the ball arrived, Althea helped Mary with her ribbons and hair. The maid might have done it, but for Mary's insistence that Althea added a touch of artistry no other could emulate. Again, Althea smiled indulgently on her foster sister. *May she never have to grow up. May she always have someone to watch over her,* she prayed as she carefully pinned Mary's tresses.

"There. I think that should do." She patted Mary's shoulders and stepped back to allow Mary to admire herself.

"Oh, Althea, I look like a fairy princess. You work magic, you do."

"Don't tell the vicar that, or we shall have no peace until he has exorcised me," Althea warned, only half joking.

Mary giggled and traipsed out, leaving Althea to manage her own cast-off gown and freshly-washed hair without help. Althea glanced down at her shoes. *Worn thin and nowhere near so lovely as they had been when Mary first got them. Thank goodness for long-hemmed fashions.* Althea wiggled her toes then pulled together both hair and attire in moments.

As they settled into the carriage, Mr. Wentworth wagged a finger at Althea. "Now, you will *try* to have some fun this time, won't you, my dear? You may be just a ward, but there is no reason you must sit in the corner and sulk."

"It is not for a mere ward to take attention away from the worthy ladies in search of suitors, sir." Althea spoke the words lightly, taking the sting from Mr. Wentworth's insult, surely unintended.

Wentworth laughed heartily. "You? Take attention away from noble ladies? Fear not, my dear, *that* is not possible."

Althea bowed her head. "As you say, sir."

As before, Althea found a comfortable bench with a good view of the room and watched. When Colonel Fitzgerald and his wife proposed a game of cards, Althea smiled at the memory of Mr. Hamlin.

"Miss Chambers, come join us, we are in need of a fourth."

"You are very kind, Colonel, but I must decline. I have been told I haven't the face for it."

"Shocking!" Exclaimed Mrs. Fitzgerald.

"Come now, Miss Chambers. Too much modesty is most unbecoming."

"On the contrary," interrupted Wentworth. "A ward cannot be too modest." He looked at Althea significantly.

Althea dropped her eyes. "You see, Colonel? Truly another had best take that chair."

Wentworth nodded approvingly, and, crisis passed, removed himself to an adjoining room.

The card players found their fourth in Mr. Hamlin, who sat facing Althea. She raised an eyebrow when she caught him looking at her, and turned to face the dancers in the hall, leaving her face in profile to Mr. Hamlin.

As the game progressed, Mr. Hamlin proved to be an excellent conversationalist, dancing his steps perfectly for any observer to see, up until the cards took a singular turn in his favour. As he won yet another trick he commented loudly enough for Althea to hear.

"The rules of this game must be flawed. Indeed they must."

"Come now, Mr. Hamlin," Fitzgerald objected. "That is usually the protest of the loser, not the winner."

"That is precisely my point, Colonel. The game seems conspicuously skewed in by favour, when I have done nothing to earn such good fortune."

Althea risked a glance in Hamlin's direction, only to find him looking directly at her, with significance. He looked away quickly enough to conceal his attention from the others, but not so quickly that Althea missed his meaning, nor that he was indirectly speaking to her. She returned to watch the hall, amusement lurking just beneath her skin.

Another trick, another win for Hamlin, and again he exclaimed. "See here," he played his card. "I have no more wit than the next man, yet that ace appears in my hand as though brought by some supernatural guardian. The game is decidedly skewed."

Althea's stomach clenched. She feigned intense interest in the dancers as she sought to control her features, suspecting Hamlin's wit was greater than he claimed.

The game came to an end, Hamlin protesting the unfairness of chance, despite winning the game by a considerable lead.

"I say, you are a sore winner," remarked Colonel Fitzgerald as he cleared the table. "Never in my life have I heard a man lament his good fortune as you do."

Hamlin bowed to Fitzgerald. "You are absolutely right, Colonel. Please accept my apologies. I was a perfect boor."

"Tut, Mr. Hamlin. A man of your consequence need not apologize to Her Majesty's humble servant."

"I do when I behave abominably. Forgive me, Colonel."

Fitzgerald sighed. "Very well, Mr. Hamlin. If you insist. Certainly, you are forgiven."

The card players left the room and Hamlin took the opportunity to approach Althea.

"Good evening, Miss Chambers," he bowed, keeping back from the doorway to avoid being seen.

"And to you, Mr. Hamlin. I trust you are enjoying yourself?"

"What, I? Winning every hand whether I willed it or no?"

Althea smiled, the first genuine smile Hamlin had seen. "To borrow from the Bard, the winner doth protest too much."

Hamlin followed her gaze to the dancers. "Will you not dance, Miss Chambers?"

"Thank you, but I cannot."

"Their wine is still too strong for you?"

"Indeed, Mr. Hamlin. Indeed."

"Who is that there, with the white branch on her head?" Hamlin indicated one of the dancers.

"She is one of my foster sisters, sir. Miss Janice Wentworth, and that is not a branch, it is a flower, sometimes called Baby's Breath."

Hamlin made a face. "I see now why you shun the revelry."

Althea's eyes widened. "Do you indeed?"

"Miss Chambers, it cannot have escaped Wentworth's notice that you are easily five times as pretty as his progeny. I suspect he would lock you in a cupboard and throw away the key rather than bear the insult of having a 'mere' ward outshine his daughters."

Althea turned to look at Hamlin then, her mouth agape before she remembered to shut it. "Mr. Hamlin, you are truly shocking."

"When we last spoke, you asked 'what good could come from dissembling'. I am only following your own advice."

"Perhaps I should guard my words more carefully in future."

"Oh, I do hope you don't, Miss Chambers," he bowed again and left the room, allowing Althea to resume her observations as the revellers made merry.

While Hamlin could not openly pursue Althea, he could attend every social occasion for miles around in hopes of seeing her there, which he did, even going so far as to sponsor events, to create opportunities for them to meet. At every one, he approached her, sparring with her verbally, despite her protests.

"Surely your family has made known their feelings about such an alliance," Althea said to him on one such occasion.

"Indeed, they haven't, for they've no notion I seek to make one," Hamlin grinned like a schoolboy who hasn't yet been caught in a prank.

For her part, Althea did guard her words more carefully, literally biting her tongue at times. Those moments of silence seemed only to spur Hamlin to greater lengths to shock her into speaking.

While she was flattered that such a man should take an interest in her, she feared his growing recklessness. Should his relations, or hers, discover his intentions, there would be a scandal. He might recover from such, but certainly she would not. Her freedoms were all too rare, even now. How much fewer and farther between, if Wentworth should discover that Althea claimed the attentions of a man easily ten times the fortune as Mary's Mr. Davies? Add Janice's utter dearth of suitors to the insult, and Althea would never be let out of the house again.

No hope that Hamlin would rescue her, either, for his family would have him shipped off to France to reclaim his senses sooner than they would allow such an alliance.

Besides all of that was the geas. Whatever Althea did, it was within the confines of Wentworth's will. She could not so much as cross the threshold if it was not his wish that she do so.

As a child she had tested the boundaries repeatedly, unable to understand why she could not join her foster sisters outside to play until Wentworth gave her permission. Nor could she understand why the desire to do so fled quicker when her wish was stronger. The more she wanted something, the faster she forgot her desire.

'Twas certain strange. A combination of invisible barrier and twist of desire that kept her from disobeying. As she grew older, more able to order her thoughts, the latter became less powerful, less able to leave her wondering what it was that she had wanted.

Mary commented on it more than once, when they were small, how Althea would be on her way to join them in a game and then suddenly stop, a blank look on her face, to wonder what she was about to do, and then declare she wanted no part of the game when Mary reminded her.

Time, and Wentworth's harsh words, taught them to leave these mysteries unremarked.

All this preyed upon Althea as Hamlin made his appearances, yet she could not speak of it, for that, too, was beyond Wentworth's will for her. So she demurred or remained silent, deflecting Hamlin's comments, subtly encouraging him to abandon his hopeless cause.

Her efforts were lost upon him. The more she retreated, the more ardent he became, until one day, while she was walking the path on the edges of Wentworth's estate, Hamlin came upon her. Presumably, he'd been lurking nearby, hoping for just such a 'chance' meeting. It was at that meeting that Althea refused him as directly as she dared.

He complained of her confinement, of the extraordinary measures he'd been forced to take to contrive meeting with her, and of the blatant way Wentworth demeaned her in company.

Althea let him speak, not daring to interrupt his soliloquy. When he finished, she answered as truthfully as she dared.

"I am humbled, when it suits them," Althea explained. "Else I am treated well enough. I serve. I am allowed to exercise my pleasures in some few hours of the week. I was allowed lessons with my foster sisters when tutors were employed, that I might not be wholly ignorant." She turned an unnaturally bright face to Hamlin. "Do not pity me, sir. Indeed, I am well enough."

"It will not do!" Hamlin exclaimed with vehemence.

Althea froze, fearing he might strike her in anger. The blood drained from her face and her heart stilled, barely beating. Seeing her reaction, Hamlin cursed himself a fool, stepped back from Althea, and held himself still.

"I apologize, Miss Chambers. I did not mean to frighten you. I am not angry with you, though your calm acceptance of the situation baffles me utterly."

Althea took a breath then, a look of serenity settling on her features. "I beg your pardon, Mr. Hamlin. I can only imagine what you must think of me, alternately cowering and quipping with you." She longed to explain, to tell him the whole of it, that he might abandon his clumsy attempts to win her. The geas forbade it. Even now, she could feel it tightening around her, making it impossible to draw a proper breath, worse than the tightest corset. "Please, sir, may we sit down?" She nodded towards the low stone wall that lined the lane.

"Certainly, Miss Chambers. Are you quite well?"

Althea nodded as they sat. "Thank you, Mr. Hamlin, for your persistent concern. Indeed, I cannot fathom nor repay the honour you do me. A man of your consequence is not easily denied. Yet I cannot allow you to continue this way."

"Miss Chambers, it is not for you to decide where best I should spend my attentions," the Hamlin authority crept into his voice then, making Althea sit up straighter, attentive to him. The difference in her stance was minute, barely perceptible, but to Hamlin it was as obvious as a trumpet blare. He closed his eyes, again cursing himself silently. "I will, of course, respect your wishes, Miss Chambers. I ask only that you give me some explanation, for my company has never repelled you before. Have I unknowingly committed some unpardonable offence?"

The geas clenched Althea's stomach, a warning. "No, Mr. Hamlin, nothing of the sort. As much as two people from so wildly different stations can be, we are friends, and remain friends." Althea thought carefully, searching for words around the geas. "I cannot disclose my reasons, Mr. Hamlin, I beg you not to press me for them," the geas cinched her breathless for a moment. She'd strayed too close to its boundaries.

Hamlin saw, something. Perhaps more accurately, he felt something, some intuition, that warned him. "Even here, on a country lane, with no one but you, and I, and the birds, to hear, you dare not speak it."

The geas squeezed tighter, painfully, and Althea could not hide the wince. *Let me deflect this,* she willed to the geas. *Give me breath to divert him.* The geas relaxed marginally.

"Apart from any other concerns, Mr. Hamlin, your family would rightly wish for you to find an alliance with someone who is your equal. Every minute you spend with me, you are not spending with your peers. You must see this," she pleaded. The geas relaxed still further.

"I do see this, Miss Chambers, but recognizing it and abiding by it are two separate things," he persisted. "If it is your wish that I leave you to your observations of the living, if you do not care for my company, then I will honour your wish. Just tell me this, so we are perfectly clear: do you care for me?" In that moment he dropped his worldly mask, sitting with her, just a man with a woman, not a lord and a geas-ridden Ward.

"I cannot tell you that."

Hamlin was buoyed up and crushed at once. On the one hand, she made it clear she did care for him. On the other, something other than societal guidelines prevented them from being together. He vowed, suddenly, that he would do whatever was necessary to free her.

"Dearest, loveliest, Miss Chambers," he took her hand and kissed it. "I understand, as best I can. Forgive my intrusion. I am heartily sorry for the pain it has caused you." He stood and offered his arm.

The geas loosened to its usual state, allowing Althea to move and breathe freely. She took a deep breath, and stood, grateful for his arm, his support.

"You are too kind, Mr. Hamlin, and do me much honour. I am exceedingly grateful," she said sincerely.

Hamlin put his hand on hers, caressing it with his thumb.

They returned to where he'd found her, in the woods behind the Wentworth house. "I will cherish our time for as long as I live, Miss Chambers. Never doubt it." He kissed her hand again.

Althea cast her eyes downward, humble. "You are kind and generous, Mr. Hamlin. I am honoured."

"Not 'you should be honoured', Miss Chambers?"

"Be well, Mr. Hamlin. I wish you all that is good in life, with every expectation that hope will come true." She curtsied low then, turned from him, and made her way to the house.

Hamlin watched her go with both sorrow and determination in his heart. She would be free.

છ⭑ଓ

The Wentworth's annual shopping trip took them into London, leaving Althea to spend her time as she saw fit. She retired to the music room while the they were away and looked at the various instruments in the room. Her mind flooded with memories of the lessons with Mary and Janice. The tutor declared both of them hopeless after little more than a month. Althea concealed her talent after watching how they struggled. The lessons ceased after a year, Wentworth insisting the tutor keep trying, despite his early prognosis.

Althea used that year to learn as much as she could, while never letting on that the lessons were not wasted on her. She suspected the tutor knew, but guarded her secret. Even the tutor could not miss how Wentworth felt about his ward, and rightly feared for Althea, should she outshine Mary or Janice.

So, when the Wentworths left the house, Althea often found herself drawn to the music room. She sat at the piano and began with scales and arpeggios to warm up. When she was limber, she rolled into some simple, flowing melodies, soon adding her voice over top, playing and singing from memory at times, making up both notes and lyrics at others.

The servants silently stole into positions within earshot of Althea's playing, also sharing her secret, though Althea knew it not. The music moved through the range of human emotion. Sometimes serene, sometimes angry, fearful, happy, longing. Everything Althea felt flowed through her fingers to the piano, and the staff was enchanted.

"'Tis magic," one of the maids whispered to her neighbour.

"Hush," her co-conspirator hissed, not only to keep from disrupting the music, but out of caution. This was a good Christian home in a good Christian town. Words like 'magic' could bring the church's wrath down upon them. Althea's musical talents were known among the servants, but not among any others. She never played at parties or when the Wentworth's were at home, save for a fiddle hidden in her room. That she played with an un-rosined bow after the family was asleep, the strings sounding barely loud enough for her to hear without carrying through the walls.

If only, Althea sighed as she finished the song on the piano. She started another, in mind of a great wide world. *If only I could have a pair of well-fitted shoes. I would be free of this place.* The song crescendoed, fraught with dreams of 'one day', of glory, of freedom. *Whatever it took, I could make my way, free to laugh, to love, to sing, as I chose.* The melody fell into a minor key. *No geas to suffocate me. No strange power stifling me. No Henry Wentworth demeaning me at every opportunity.* The music grew dark and thunderous.

In the hall, some of the younger servants shivered in fear at the dark power that thrummed through the house. The elder ones nodded, some even smiled at Althea's determination not to succumb, her disinclination to simply lie down and accept her fate. Silently they rooted her on, willing her to fight through the oppression they saw and understood only half of.

They were her silent allies. They saw how Wentworth treated her, giving her only second-hand clothes, second-hand books, personal items, all well-used and now beneath the quality suitable for his noble daughters. Althea was in that in-between. Neither servant nor family. Yet the servants claimed her for their own when they saw that Wentworth would not.

Althea's anger wore itself out, and the music shifted to something lighter and more delicate, sounding like rain plunking in the chimney, and wind chimes in the softest of breezes. It mimicked the chuckle of the stream that tripped through the woods behind the house, and the calls of the little birds.

I should be grateful, Althea mused. *All this, I have to enjoy. There may be a great, wide world out there, but this is a fine place, full of beauty and peace. If one must be captive, surely there are worse prisons.* Her music wound down slowly until she grew restless for fresh air. She ended on a major chord that fell into place one note at a time, and she sat for a moment, letting the chord carry through the air until it faded away into nothing but a memory. She looked on the instrument with love and closed it up, pushing the seat back.

15

The servants melted away, resuming their duties as though they'd never left them, Althea none the wiser to their silent support. She selected a book from the library and took herself outside to read in the afternoon sun. She sprawled unladylike on a blanket, and as she read, idly played with a flower growing beside her. Her book spoke of great gardens, mended and tended with care. She read on, not overly practically concerned with tending the grounds around the Wentworth estate, but diverted from her own thoughts and situation.

When she grew hungry, she closed the book and stood to collect her blanket, and that was when she noticed that all the flowers around her had grown considerably since she'd sat down to read. She blinked, staring at them, reaching for the sun, every bud blooming, their faces open and beaming with life. Again she blinked. *How odd,* she mused, then shook her head. She simply must not have noticed how fine the flowers were before, or chose the spot unconsciously for its beauty.

She bent and gathered up blanket and book and headed for the house, rolling her eyes at her foolish fancy.

Hamlin began his quest by searching the peerage records for Althea. Not finding her specifically, he searched for any Chambers, hoping to find mention of some unnamed offspring, as occasionally happened when a house fell into decline. He found nothing.

Deciding his volumes were far from comprehensive, he began a series of correspondences with some of his more unusual acquaintances. They were, well, odd. Accepted in polite company, surely, but distinctly odd.

His own family, rigid in their sense of propriety, were dismayed by his continued association with them, but could do little to prevent the connection without violating that same propriety, so they endured in relative silence.

Mr. Hamlin let the request for information lay among the inquiries after the health and welfare of his friends and their families, making it seem idle and unimportant. Some unnamed sense warned him not to make his search obvious, that raising suspicion might draw attention to her that could cause her harm. For that same reason, he'd not asked around locally about Miss Chambers, certain that not only would word of his inquiries reach Althea's ears, but those of Mr. Wentworth as well, who might not look kindly upon the attention.

He rounded out his letters to his friends with news of the Hamlin household, recounting events, passing on any information they might find useful or diverting. His letters written, he dispatched his man to the post.

He sat back in his chair and thought about his extraordinary friends. Like he, they did not cling to protocol and form the way his family did. They were by no means uncouth, they simply accepted more of the world, more of society, more readily than others. Among them, he would never hear the words "as well as she should be", implying that the lower born were more inclined to certain evils. Among them he would never see a servant treated poorly, indeed, the servants were often free to speak their minds, as trusted and respected advisors, more like a slightly lesser rank in a military command, than as the silent ghosts the Hamlins, and too many others, demanded they be.

Hamlin thought fondly of a time when he'd dropped in on Peter Croft, unannounced. Hamlin hadn't expected to be in the area, or he would have sent ahead. As it happened, a storm blew a tree across the highway, blocking the road, causing him to detour into Croft country. The detour took him hours out of his way, into the teeth of the storm, forcing him to beg hospitality of his old and rare friend.

Peter welcomed him with nary a word about being put out. The staff hustled with dry clothes, warm food, and building up a fire. Hamlin, George, had been so dazed by his travels, it wasn't until he was fed, dry, and warm, that he noticed the state of dress they all were in. Nobles and servants were dressed alike in loose-fitting pants, and shapeless smocks, their hair hanging loose in a most immodest manner. What struck George was how very comfortable they all looked, and how grateful he was to be bundled in a generous robe and slippers.

"Honestly, George, what were you thinking, traipsing about in this weather?" Peter asked jokingly, his eyes dancing with merriment. "Thank you, O'Dell, we can take care of ourselves tonight. Go to your sweet Adelaide until morning." Peter dismissed the man with affection.

George stared, surprised by the familiarity.

Peter only laughed. "Shocked you, have I?" He picked up his tea and settled more comfortably into his chair by the fire. "Well, you'll find much and more of that here, old boy. We don't stand on ceremony among ourselves, and I've always thought you more flexible than most about such things. Perhaps I over-estimated your tolerance." He sipped his tea, looking over the rim of the cup at Hamlin.

George sat quiet a moment before a slow smile spread across his face. "I think you'll find there is some difference between surprise and disapproval, Peter, at least for my part. I cannot speak for others."

Peter nodded in approval. "Ah, you exceed all expectation, as usual, George. I daren't ask how you find our modest part of the world. I can guess at your answer."

"Wet," they said as one, and chuckled.

"It has been far too long, Peter."

"Agreed, old boy. Though some in your circle might say it has not been long enough," referring to the Hamlin Mater and her court of followers.

George snorted. "We both know my opinion of that. She'd be shocked speechless at tonight's events, then eaten up by a desire to tell her friends, while bound by the same etiquette you flout, not to repeat it. She'd give herself an ulcer. I am certain of it."

Peter laughed, then said, "then I am glad she did not travel with you. I would not wish such an unkind state on anyone."

Hamlin shook himself out of the memory with a smile. Peter would reply quickly, with or without information on the Chambers woman. The others, he was less sure of, as they always seemed to be travelling, one never knew where or why, for they always seemed clandestine about it. But he felt confident that if his letters reached them, he could expect something in return, if not as soon as he would like.

Left with nothing to do about Miss Chambers but wait, he threw himself into his familial duties in earnest, vowing not to violate Althea's request that he keep his distance.

The Wentworths returned from their trip in a flurry of chatter and orders for the servants. The amount of luggage they brought home was truly alarming, the servants forming a brigade to pass in box after crate of new clothes and new personal items for the family.

Selfishly, Althea mourned the loss of music their return would mean, and wondered what of Mary and Janice's previous wardrobe would be considered worn or unfashionable enough to be handed down. She knew better than to ask if any of the boxes were meant for her, knew better than to even hope for a gift from the Wentworths.

Not once in all her years with them had they ever given her a present. Cast-offs, surely, but never something new, never something made expressly for her. No matter how much Mary might love her, even she would not risk Mr. Wentworth's wrath. The one time she'd tried to make a gift for Althea, when they were just children, the gift was confiscated by Mr. Wentworth, and Althea hadn't seen Mary for a week. Mary never made the same mistake again.

Althea wondered at that, now, as she helped Mary put away all her new things, piling up the old, to-be-discarded items in a corner to be taken away when they were done. She knew there was a distinct difference between being a ward and being a nobleman's daughter, but the extremes Wentworth went to in pointing it out to her and any other seemed all out of proportion. Even the severity over the giving of gifts seemed out of step with reality. *Perhaps,* Althea mused as she smoothed out a dress, *being my Guardian is some sort of punishment to him. Burdened with a ward he does not want, but cannot put out. Perhaps it is payment for some unspeakable transgression.* Althea continued to ruminate while Mary babbled about all the sights and sounds of London. *Did they know it would be just as much punishment for me? Being an unwelcome and daily reminder to him of whatever his crime was? Surely, whomever placed me in his care must have known.* Just then she was drawn out of her reverie by Mary's words. "I'm sorry? What did you just say?"

Mary huffed. "Honestly, Althea, sometimes I think you are touched, the way you blank out everything, in a daze." She opened a trunk. "I said, we met a Lieutenant Chambers at dinner with the Blakes. He was fiendishly handsome. If it weren't for my Mr. Davies, he might have tempted me to stay in London. As it turned out, 'tis better I hadn't, for Father acted very strangely when he was introduced. You'd think he'd seen a ghost. We left London the next day and father wouldn't hear a word spoken of him." Mary gasped and covered her mouth. "Lord, I wasn't to tell you of it. Oh please, Althea, don't say I told you. You mustn't let on you know." Mary's eyes were wide, the whites showing in fear of her father.

Althea set down the gown in her hands and hugged her foster sister. "Be at ease, Mary," she rubbed Mary's back. "I shan't breathe a word of it." She held the girl out at arm's length, projecting reassurance in her face. Mary calmed and smiled weakly.

"You are too good, Althea."

"We are none of us 'too good', Mary. You know I love you as my sister, and I could never wish you ill." Althea turned back to the discarded gowns. "Now, tell me more of your adventures in London."

"You won't find her in the peerage, old boy," Peter wrote, affecting the same tone in his letter as he did in person. George always marvelled at that. Anyone else sounded stilted and scripted in correspondence. Peter wrote as if he was as comfortable on paper as he was anywhere else. "She comes from a long line of mariners. HRMs Navy boasts generations of Chambers, including a lost Captain who may have been her father. It seems there was some to-do over his choice in wife, I haven't got all the details, but your Miss Chambers could be his only offspring."

"Weather's much finer than the first time you graced us with your presence. You should come out again, and see the county in her glory."

George Hamlin hardly needed more incentive to accept the invitation. He dashed off a hasty reply, sending it to the post that same day and following only two days behind.

"You have gotten yourself caught up in something," Peter deduced immediately upon George's arrival. He waggled his finger for not being included sooner.

"I am not sure what I am caught in, Peter, but it is more than my meagre talents can unravel."

Peter snorted. "Even were your talents meagre, your consequence is not. Why not use those fabled resources of yours to do your hunting."

George raised an eyebrow at his old friend.

"Oh ho, so I am now a fabled resource of the great George Hamlin. I see." He paused. "Perhaps you should tell me the whole of it." They settled into a sitting room with a glorious view of the lands surrounding the state.

"There's deuced little to tell, Peter."

"Save the Lady's immeasurable charms, no doubt."

George choked on his tea.

"Come now, even tossed in lightly among the bric-a-brac you call correspondence, your query leapt from the page."

George shared what he knew.

Peter sat back and looked at George with a measuring gaze, as though trying to decide something. "Tell me again of the ball. Every detail."

George's brow knit together. "But I told you already."

"Every detail, George, please."

George recounted the event again, closing his eyes to envision the scene more vividly. When he was through with the retelling, Peter bore the look of one who had come to a decision.

"I can't recall," Peter led in, "how you felt about Hamlet."

"Alas, poor Yorick, and all that?"

"I was thinking more along the lines of 'there is more in heaven and earth', actually."

"What has that," George began the question that would have ended in "to do with this", if Peter hadn't interrupted by putting up the palm of his hand.

"Bear with me."

"Surely, more in heaven and earth," George shrugged. "How can anyone help but believe in more than man can perceive?" He looked inquiringly to Peter.

"And the Scottish play?"

"Mac-"

Peter hissed.

"Right. The Scottish play. I suppose you mean the 'toil and trouble' bit, and not 'out, out damned spot'?"

Peter nodded.

George sat back to ponder a moment. "A bit overdone, but a worthy device of the Bard."

Peter rolled his eyes and smiled. "The great George Hamlin would offer the greatest poet who ever lived, advice. I should live to see it."

"You did ask."

"I did indeed. Let us stick with 'more in heaven and earth' then, shall we?"

George nodded.

"Would you believe that even mere mortals can call upon that 'more'?"

George smiled, remembering another play. "Surely, but will it come?"

In answer, a great wind swept the room, moving curtains, papers left on table tops, even pushing furniture about.

George sat stunned as the wind left as quickly as it came, and all once again settled to rest.

"It comes," Peter said softly. O'Dell pushed open the door, concern written on his features, a slight sheen of sweat on his brow.

"My lord?"

"I do apologize, O'Dell. I might have warned you beforehand, but I had no idea it would be necessary," referring to the tempest.

"Very good, sir. Will you be needing anything?" O'Dell resumed his affable air.

"I think Mr. Hamlin may be in need of something rather stronger than tea,"

Peter surveyed the shock in George's stillness.

"Very good, sir," O'Dell repeated, and began to bow himself out.

"No, wait, please," George suddenly snapped to attention. He looked from O'Dell to Peter. "I'd rather not have anything stronger. I shall need all my wits for whatever might follow." Peter nodded to O'Dell, who left promptly.

"A regular occurrence, I suppose?" George asked.

Peter chuckled. "I am usually less dramatic."

George nodded. "I see."

"You do not. You also have the gift. But yours is so minute, we never thought it necessary to bother you about it."

"We?"

"All your eccentric friends and I. The Guilds."

"You all command the wind?"

"No. Some Fire, some Water, Earth. Only I have Air among us."

"I shouldn't like to see a demonstration of fire, thank you."

Peter chuckled again. "Yet again, you exceed all expectation, old boy. How quickly your mind races to accept what you could not imagine only moments ago. Truly, you are a marvel."

George snorted, dropping the manicured etiquette his family so cherished.

"All my staff, actually, are gifted in one way or another. At the very least, they are sensitive to magic, which is why O'Dell came so quickly. He feared I might be under attack."

"All?"

"All, old boy. It makes things simpler. No hiding the gift, no making up stories when the world does not behave as most people think it should."

George sat stunned. Finally he returned to the reason he'd come. "What has this to do with Miss Chambers?"

"What indeed?" Peter grinned. "I would guess that she has rather more of the gift than you do, old boy. Your card game alone was rather more than chance."

George blinked. "She did that?"

"I suspect so." Peter took a long pull of his tea. "We will have to look into her. I am surprised she has escaped our notice up until now."

George looked sharply at his friend. "Why would she? She's a ward to a low-ranked noble, kept out of public view more oft than not."

"We, the Guilds, watch for people with the gift. It is important they are taught how to use it rather before furniture goes whizzing about the room."

"What havoc you must cause as children," George wondered aloud.

Peter laughed heartily. "Rather less than you might imagine, old boy. The gift is hereditary. Usually our parents manage us until a proper tutor can be found."

"Then my Mater?"

"Not a drop. 'Twas your Da that had the gift."

"Rest his soul."

"Indeed. Your mother never knew, and since you didn't show any signs of your gift causing trouble, we never bothered her or you about it."

"Miss Chambers?" George brought Peter back to the reason he was here.

"Right. Well, it is not unheard of for our mariners to be gifted. Air and Water are both handy elements to call in their line of work. There was a powerful Chambers a few generations back, but the gift seems to have faded from their line."

"You mentioned a Captain who might have been her father?" George prompted.

"Ah, yes, Captain Edward Chambers. If he was gifted, we certainly never knew about it. Seemed as exotic as dirt, that one, the very model of HRMs servants, as is his brother, a Lieutenant Matthew Chambers."

"But why is Miss Chambers stuck with the odious Wentworth, if Lieutenant Chambers still lives?" George asked.

"The odious Wentworth? Really, George."

George snorted. "I should be grateful. Had she been raised by her uncle, I might not have," George stopped himself with a sip of tea.

Peter chose not to tease his old and rare just then. "We might not have known about Captain Chambers at all, but for the to-do over his wife."

"His wife?"

"I should say, his intended wife. There was an understanding between he and a Miss Catherine Aldergrove. Her family has also been among the gifted, and she no little amount herself. Then one day, Captain Chambers returns home from a voyage and announces he's married and has a bairn on the way."

George grimaced. "I imagine the Aldergroves did not receive the news with joy and congratulations on their lips."

"They did not. Catherine least of all, and she is known in some circles for her temper. Coincidentally, the Aldergroves and the Wentworths have some connections."

George's face grew dark, imagining some sort of cruel conspiracy. Peter noticed, surprised by George's intensity.

"You *are* in trouble, aren't you, old boy?"

"What?" George's voice was sharp, angry.

"Save your bark for the deserving. I wonder how this Chambers girl has gotten under your skin so quickly."

"Not quickly at all. I have been nearly a year in watching her. She is enchanting. For all that Wentworth treats her poorly, she still looks on his daughters with nothing but kindness and a kind of protectiveness. Gatherings amuse her, but not as they do others of her sex, for the gossip and gowns, rather for the observation of behaviour. She calls their manners and social conventions a dance."

"And so they are," Peter agreed.

"Her wit is without equal. She speaks as though she is not quite a woman at all, but some other creature, watching, with a longer and broader view of man.

22

Her depth can steal all thought away from me." George turned pleading eyes to Peter. "Can you help her?"

"We shall try."

That season brought exotic strangers to Briardowns. Althea had never heard of nobles wintering in her town in all her one-and-twenty years. She, like her foster family, was curious to the point of distraction, yet the newcomers seemed reluctant to show themselves.

Servants came to town to purchase goods for the households, but the Masters were not to be seen. Soon rumours began to spread through town, each more fantastic than the one prior. Finally, when the town could bear it no longer, one of the newcomers appeared, at Sunday service.

She was one of the first to arrive, looking splendid in her London finery. She apologized to the Vicar on behalf of her friends and for herself, for not making an appearance sooner. The estates they'd taken for the season required much more work than they'd anticipated, and none had noticed the passage of time until now.

"I am little use in such matters," she demurred, "and I am the only one who could find suitable clothes for church, all our Sunday best still packed and waiting," Mrs. Weatherby blushed. The Vicar excused them all graciously, and repeated Mrs. Weatherby's explanation as he greeted the rest of the parish.

When the Wentworths arrived, they took their usual pew near the front of the church, Althea on the outside edge. Mrs. Weatherby looked sharply at her as they walked up the aisle then ignored them all for the remainder of the service. Althea wondered at Weatherby's attention, but said nothing, as the geas clenched her chest tight. She would not even be allowed an introduction, it seemed, to this fine lady in her large hat. Althea paid as little mind to the sermon as always, looking attentive, but observing those in front of her instead, never one to miss an opportunity to note human behaviour.

It wasn't until the service was over and the Wentworths were home again that the geas released Althea. She retired to her room, feigning a headache when Janice and Mary began gossiping about the regal Mrs. Weatherby. Althea felt the geas squeeze her once, warning her away from the conversation, and fled as gracefully as possible.

Wentworth sat smug in his chair seeing the distance Althea was placing between herself and the exotic stranger. He need not fear interference from that quarter, at least.

The following Sunday brought an invitation from Weatherby, to a gala, so that she and her companions might introduce themselves to the local nobility. The Wentworths were delighted to accept, Althea's invitation notwithstanding.

Althea dressed soberly, putting no elaborate ribbons or curl to her hair, hoping not to excite any attention from their hosts whatsoever. She spoke not at all on the carriage ride there, much to Wentworth's satisfaction. However the receiving line when they arrived made Althea's continued silence impossible, despite the restrictions of the geas. She was introduced as a ward, and that should have been the end of it. The hosts should have nodded, perhaps murmured a welcome, and moved on. Alas, Mr. Weatherby lit up like a firefly at the introduction, and pried at the particulars of the Wentworths and how they'd come by such a charming creature.

Althea could barely take breath around the geas, and fanned herself to keep from passing out as sparkles appeared at the edges of her vision. Wentworth deflected the inquiry as politely and quickly as he could and they made their way inside. He pulled Althea into an alcove, a grotto made by the architecture, with a warning.

"Not one word, you understand me?"

Althea nodded, still pale and oxygen deprived.

Satisfied, Wentworth left her alone. She found a seat out of the way, and did as she always had, she watched the room, with an eye on her foster sisters, to make sure they were enjoying themselves.

And so they did. Delighted by the novelty of their hosts, and the grandiose rooms elegantly appointed, Mary and Janice were like small children in their wide-eyed wonder and delight.

Althea's tension eased as she watched from her corner perch. The geas eased its hold on her as she assumed her usual role. The light danced in her eyes again as someone struck up a tune and the dancers took to the floor.

"Don't turn around," Hamlin's voice came from behind her, soft, inaudible to any but her. The geas clenched again. "Do not be afraid, Miss Chambers, none can see me behind this curtain. You should know that our hosts mean you no harm. In fact, they may be able to help you where I cannot."

The geas wrapped around Althea's throat and squeezed, making her claw at it, suddenly terrified. It squeezed tighter until she ceased her struggles, afraid of the attention she might attract.

"I am sorry, Miss Chambers," Hamlin whispered and departed.

"Deuced vicious," Peter commented when Hamlin returned to his side, having seen the whole exchange. "Whoever spelled her had no love for her, that's certain."

Hamlin was ashen, guilty for the pain he'd caused Althea.

"You saw?"

"Aye. Even someone only sensitive would have seen the poisoned purple glow that enveloped her when you approached. You chose your time perfectly, old boy. When it tried to strangle her, only the dance kept all eyes away from her."

"Can you do anything for her?"

"Hard to say, old boy."

"Say it anyway," growled George, his tone betraying his joking words.

Peter turned to face his friend, a gentle smile on his face. "We shall try, George, but consider how much harm we might do her by bumbling into this thing head on. You will have to be patient."

Hamlin stood mute, angry at whomever put this spell on Althea. He nodded then left the room to find some better spot to watch her from.

Althea recovered quickly, taking deep breaths once the geas unclenched. She fanned herself as her eyes sought Janice and Mary. There, Mr. Davies found Mary once again and they were off the dance floor and deep into conversation. Althea was certain that Michaelmas would bring a wedding, if only Davies would pluck up the courage to ask Wentworth.

She scanned the room again, watching all of Briardowns' nobility jockeying to meet the newcomers. Mr. and Mrs. Weatherby were gracious hosts, all smiles and politeness. Their companions, the Durstons, no less so, which Althea found pleasantly surprising. Mrs. Durston was a tall angelic blonde, her skin porcelain, her features delicate. She was just the sort, Althea observed, who was like to snub her lessors, yet she invited conversation, laughing readily at a joke, commiserating with all sincerity at someone's troubles. Mr. Durston was more sober, earthy, with chestnut hair and brown eyes. He was clearly comfortable in life, and wore it in some extra stone, yet he moved with the grace of a dancer, light on his toes despite his bulk.

From her peripheral vision, Althea spotted the fifth of their party, a Mr. Croft, approaching. He was swarthy, his hair seemingly perpetually windblown and unkempt, but his rich green eyes were kind. The geas twinged as he sat down beside her and gazed out at the party, but did not constrict any further. *A warning, then,* thought Althea as she kept half an eye on Mr. Croft while watching Janice turn and turn again, passed from one partner to another.

"I say, your people certainly know how to enjoy a party," Croft kept his eyes ahead as he spoke quietly to Althea.

"We are all much honoured by the hospitality of you and your friends," Althea mouthed the dance words smoothly.

"Who is that, dancing, with the blue ribbon at her waist?"

"My foster sister, Miss Janice Wentworth."

"I see." Peter pondered how to come at the geas sideways. "You are not a Wentworth, then?"

"No, sir. My name is Chambers. Althea Chambers." The geas didn't even flinch.

"Indeed? I knew a Captain Chambers. Good man of the sea he was. Could he be a relation of yours?"

"I have no idea, sir, though likely enough."

Peter nodded. "Why do you not dance, Miss Chambers?" He turned to face her then, hoping to take in the expressions George boasted about.

Althea's countenance twitched as the amusement so often lurking just beneath her surface, made a ripple in her formerly anxious countenance. "My lord, the floor is full of dancers with no need of one more."

"Tosh. Two more. There's always room for another pair."

Althea looked slyly at Peter, a lightly scolding look in her eye. "I cannot, sir, as I am sure your friend Mr. Hamlin informed you."

"I haven't the faintest idea what you are talking about, Miss Chambers." Peter feigned ignorance with the conviction of an actor.

"Come now, sir, it is unseemly for a man to dissemble so. Anyone who chose to look would have seen you, thick as thieves, a short time ago, and Mr. Hamlin none-too-pleased by the end."

"You fear his glaring at us?"

"You are mistaken, sir. It is not 'us' he is glaring at, it is you." Althea raised her brow as a smile dared twist one side of her mouth. She took a deep breath and looked straight ahead at the dancers.

"You are forthright, aren't you?"

Peter sat shocked by Althea's bluntness and her accuracy.

"I should wish for a shorter tongue. I humbly apologize, sir, for any offense."

"I've heard how you use that word 'should', Miss Chambers, to mask your meaning from the ignorant."

Althea's eyes went wide, her jaw dropping as she fought to close it.

"I assure you," Peter continued haughtily, "I am neither ignorant of your language or your condition, so you need not mince words with me."

Althea sat up straighter, her posture already a fine example of worthy upbringing, and faced Peter. "My lord, I sincerely apologize." The geas cinched her chest tight, preventing her from drawing breath.

Peter saw the geas react to his words and her next intended response, but his offended pride overruled any sympathy he might have felt for her.

"Now you see that your intellect is not unsurpassed, Miss Chambers. Others may have noticed but were too polite to correct you. I am not so encumbered. If you want the help that I and my friends came to give, I suggest you keep a civil tongue in that pretty head of yours." Peter took advantage of her breathlessness, got in the last volley, and vacated his seat to find Hamlin.

Only when Mr. Croft was halfway across the room did the geas relax, allowing Althea breath once again. *Three times in one evening is quite enough,* Althea decided, and took herself outside to the empty gardens where she hoped to remain unnoticed for the duration of the festivities. If anyone came out, she could hide herself in the hedges.

Alas, her luck was decidedly out. Hamlin followed moments after her. She ducked into the bushes and hoped he would turn back to search for her inside. *If only these were denser,* she wished, fearing the moonlight would illuminate her pale dress behind the branches. To her great astonishment, the bushes, rose bushes, suddenly burst into growth, the blossoms growing and opening their white blooms in moments.

"Miss Chambers?" Hamlin called softly. "Are you - good heavens!" he exclaimed as the rose bushes flourished. He came to peer at the flowers, spotting a glimpse of her between the branches. "What magic is this?"

"Please, Mr. Hamlin, do be quiet. Words like those," Althea left the rest unsaid.

"Yes, of course," he peered in at her, his eyes dancing in suppressed laughter, "but however shall we get you out?"

"Oh, Mr. Hamlin, I am so glad to amuse you, truly," Althea bit off the words. The thorns would tear the dress to shreds. She would disgrace the Wentworths. Mr. Wentworth would not forgive her. No change of clothes would do either. One simply did not arrive wearing one thing and leave in another.

I don't suppose you could let me out? She thought at the roses, looking mournfully at the thorns, with a sigh. Nothing.

I rather thought not.

Just then Mr. Durston came out, looking about as though for an intruder. His surprise when he saw Hamlin was plain on his face.

"George?"

"Aye, John. We have a bit of a muddle here."

"I'd say. There's an Earth working around here, and it's not me."

The geas clenched around Althea again.

Hamlin glanced back at Althea, seeing her immobilized. "John, please, don't speak of it."

"Why ever not? It's just you, me, and the rose bushes."

Althea would have laughed if she could have.

George grimaced. "And what is in the rose bushes, trapped."

Durston approached then and peered between the blooms. "What have we here? Miss Chambers, isn't it?"

Althea nodded, unable to speak.

"Got you tight as a swaddle, it does. Hum." John looked thoughtful.

"John," George warned.

"Aye. I have eyes, don't I? Not another word of it. Though she didn't make a favourable impression on Peter, I'll tell you."

"John," George warned again.

John pulled up his sleeves. "All right, Missy. You'd best close your eyes, no telling what might happen."

Althea looked alarmed, her eyes going wide.

"Fear not, I know what I'm about. You're safe as a babe. Just be a good lass and shut your eyes for me."

Althea graced him with a look of disgust then let her lids drop shut.

She heard the rustle of leaves and branches, then felt herself get yanked out by her arm. The geas still held her tight, so she didn't even have breath to exclaim at the sudden pull. Obediently, she kept her eyes shut tight, even when she heard someone brushing themselves off.

"It's all right, Miss Chambers," Hamlin said. "You can open your eyes."

Althea blinked then saw Durston, his clothes torn and frayed where the thorns had caught at him. He'd parted the branches, ruining his own attire holding them back, to pull Althea through unscathed. The geas finally released it's terrible hold, allowing her to breathe once again.

"Sir, I am so very sorry," she began, looking terrified.

"Think nothing of it, Dear Lady. A host may change his clothes as often as he likes. Especially a stranger, who might be willing to bear the reputation of an eccentric, or a clothes horse." He winked at her then. "Peter may not have been impressed, but I am. Not one in one hundred could have coaxed those roses into such a state, especially at this time of year."

The geas cinched her stomach, making her flinch as though she'd been punched.

"Still too close, eh? Well, never mind, Missy." He patted her shoulder and went inside to change.

Althea turned to Hamlin. "I owe you an apology as well, Mr. Hamlin."

"Not by my lights, Miss Chambers. You have endured much and more this evening. I daresay you deserve a rest. I will send Mrs. Weatherby out to take you to one of the rooms away from the guests." He bowed and took his leave before Althea could find her tongue.

Althea stared up at the night sky, wishing she could fly away to the stars, where there were no Wentworths, no suffocating strangeness, no dances of manners. Her vision blurred as her eyes welled up with tears. She rubbed them away angrily.

Mrs. Weatherby appeared in the doorway, her silhouette outlined on the ground by the light spilling out from within.

"Miss Chambers?"

Althea turned. "Mrs. Weatherby, you are very kind."

Mrs. Weatherby made a face. "Not many of your set would find social exile a kindness," she observed. "But then, none of your set," she pursed her lips then, careful not to say anything about the geas or magic. "Come along, my dear." Mrs. Weatherby beckoned as she turned into the house.

"I have been treated to the company of all my hosts."

"Not quite."

"Yes, ma'am. Still, with a houseful of guests I know the inconvenience I have caused, and I sincerely apologize."

"Don't say 'sincerely', dear, it makes people believe the opposite."

I am forever stepping wrong with these people, Althea gritted her teeth.

To Althea's surprise, Mrs. Weatherby led her to a music room. "This old barn seems to have at least two of everything." Mrs. Weatherby explained. "The sound does not carry, I promise you. Both Elizabeth and I play, and never hear one another."

"But madam,"

"Even if you don't play, no one will think to look for you in here." Mrs. Weatherby went on as though Althea hadn't spoken. "Except me, of course. When your family looks ready to leave, I shall come get you." She announced, the matter settled. Then she left the room.

Althea looked longingly at the piano forte, truly a treasure and a superior specimen of its kind. Guilty, she glanced around to make sure no one was near and pulled the bench out. Her fingers caressed the keys in silent appreciation of their beauty before she launched into tune after tune, trying to purge her troubled soul with the notes.

Just as they did in the Wentworth house, the servants who could, gathered near the music room. Althea's playing held a pounding heart, an ever-tightening geas, and confusion. It held heat and shame, and wild surprise, and underneath it all, a longing. That longing carried on for line after line, leaving the pounding and confusion behind. The notes soared, flying away to some oft dreamt of place, yet anchored to safety. She hovered there, high above it all, twisting, gliding, looping, diving and banking, only to climb again, until a minor key crept into the chords that tripped their way through, a cruel wind, and she descended, remembering, coming to ground, saddened, exhausted by an unseen burden, her hope weak, barely a wish she believed would never come true.

It was then that Mrs. Weatherby could be heard in the hallway.

"What's this then? A break for everyone in the household?" She sounded cross as she appeared in the doorway.

Althea shot up from the bench as if stung. "You Ladyship, I apologize."

Mrs. Weatherby waved a hand, dismissing Althea's words like a bad odour. "Don't waste apologies on me, Child. They grow cheaper with their quantity. I see I was told correctly of your esteemed talents."

"I don't know what you mean," Althea confessed.

"Your cook is my housekeeper's sister. She said you've the voice of an angel, and a gift with a piano your foster sisters decidedly lack. She did not exaggerate, much to her credit." Mrs. Weatherby declared, approving of the woman's character. "Half my staff have been huddled in earshot, perched upon every surface that would hold them, like birds on a wire, for who knows how long. The better part of an hour at least, as I was perched only slightly behind them that long." Mrs. Weatherby smiled then, the first Althea had seen directed at her. The smile transformed the woman's face from a sour crone to a warm and welcoming matron. "A shame we had to put you through these trials, but if the better half of the local guild is going to help one lowly ward, we need to be sure it will be worth it."

"I appreciate your candour, Mrs. Weatherby."

"I rather thought you would, though I half expected you'd be upset by our mercenary ways."

"Is there any other?" Althea's voice held a bitter edge, thinking of the dances to form advantageous alliances she saw so often.

Mrs. Weatherby's eye grew wide, then she blinked. "A bit young for such cynicism," she shrugged, "very well. Your Guardian will be looking for you shortly. You lot," she called over her shoulder at the doorway, "Back to work. Music hour is over." She turned back to Althea. "Give them a moment to scatter, and we shall return you to the guests."

As it turned out, Mrs. Weatherby had impeccable timing depositing Althea in an isolated corner and gliding into the crowd just before Wentworth's head swivelled to find Althea. He approached, a wide smile on his face. "I trust you kept out of trouble?" He demanded.

Althea tilted her head wordlessly.

"The girls are saying their goodbyes, you might as well wait in the carriage."

Althea curtsied, Wentworth hardly noticed, then stepped outside to the box.

"Ma'am," the doorman tipped his hat as he bowed and held the door open for her to step in.

Tommy had been ceaselessly kind to her all the years she'd been with the Wentworths. Althea smiled gratefully at him and stepped up.

"'Twas a rare delight to hear you play again, Miss Chambers," Tommy said as he passed her in. "All of us that wait tend to gather near the servants' wing to pass the time while our Masters are inside. The mistress placed you just above us, perhaps to give us a rare treat. Good Lady that, not often one such as herself would think on us small folk." He gave Althea a wink and a broad smile just before he shut her in, leaving her astonished as she sat waiting for her Guardians.

Mary and Janice chattered amiably all the way home. Althea stared out the window, lost in thoughts she could neither hold nor articulate. Mr. Wentworth spent the trip eyeing Althea suspiciously.

Finally having their house to themselves, George, Peter, the Durstons and Weatherbys gathered around the fireplace to discuss the Chambers situation.

Peter fumed silently, knowing that raising even one word against Miss Chambers would only harm his friendship with George, which he valued above all others.

Mrs. Weatherby, Edna, sat down beside him. "This profound passion she has raised in you, Peter, is unnatural." Her husband sat down on her other side and patted her knee.

"Or perhaps wholly natural, elemental, even." He nodded to John sitting across from them.

John bowed his head in acknowledgement. "Her gift is beyond anything I've ever seen. Even despite the spell on her, magic is drawn to her as surely as water flows to the sea, and accumulates, unused, until it overflows whatever chains she is bound by, and the world changes around her."

Elizabeth Durston got a hunting look in her eye. "If she's earned that much of your admiration in so short a time, perhaps I ought to pay her a visit and warn her not to poach."

John kissed his wife soundly. "Not a soul could poach me away from you, my love."

Elizabeth blushed.

Edna diverted attention back to Peter. "There, you see? It is not her you dislike so, it is inimical elements, and her profound strength in it that has set you on edge."

Peter glowered.

John laughed. "Now, Peter. You and I manage well enough, despite being opposing elements. I call you a flake, you call me a garden gnome, we have a drink, and part as friends."

George Hamlin had sat silent until now, understanding little of what was being said, until the last, when he piped up.

"See here, Peter, you'll not be calling names or having drinks with Miss Chambers."

Peter sat back, dislodged from his animosity by George's intensity, and chuckled. "She really has roused your protective instinct, hasn't she?"

George just stared meaningfully at Peter.

Mr. Mark Weatherby, like Elizabeth Durston, hadn't the chance to interact with Althea, outside of the receiving live, but was surprised by the passion she'd aroused in those of his companions who had. His was the most minor gift among them, save Hamlin's, and so didn't suffer from the same friction from opposing elements as those with greater gifts did.

"Before anyone gets ahead of themselves," he glanced between Peter and George, "we first need to break this curse on her, and the only way to do that is to learn more about her, without setting it to strangle her, or raising suspicion in town."

One of the maids came in just then with refreshments.

"Beg pardon, my lords, ladies," she curtsied. "But we small folk might be of some help."

Peter smiled, glad to have brought enough of his own people to give the others courage. "Go on," he said.

"Missus already guessed at it, with the girl's love of music. We've already got ties into that house. Servants hear things, see things."

"Say things." Mrs. Weatherby interrupted, the way she had with Althea.

The maid blushed.

Edna Weatherby continued, "and I am very glad you did. It twisted me up to see her suffer our worthy gentlemen's clumsy attention. It was a relief to give her sanctuary."

"Aye, ma'am." The maid curtsied again.

"Very well, what do you have so far?"

"She's treated poorly, ma'am. Nothing obvious, no beatings, but she's more like an unwanted pest one cannot get rid of, at least to Mr. Wentworth. The oldest daughter, Mary, loves Miss Chambers like a sister, but Janice is her father's daughter. They belittle her and demean her, and all the while she smiles and says nothing, never an unkind word from her to anyone."

Peter snorted.

"Now don't you malign her, Mr. Croft. She's nothing but kind to Eva's sister, and every other servant in that house. Why, when the family is away to London, all the staff have a holiday, Miss Chambers dresses herself, draws her own bath, eats cold cuts and leftovers, so's not to trouble anyone."

"The grass still grows," Peter muttered.

"An' she, as like to help with that as anyone." The maid stood up for Miss Chambers, fearless beyond reason.

"Lilly," Mark caught the maid's attention. "You seem unusually fond of Miss Chambers."

"Aye, sir, and I'm sorry if I forget my place. But she's a rare one, and when she played for us, well, you couldn't help but feel everything she feels. All torn up and hurting, and brave. She could make a stone weep with joy, if she were so minded."

"Thank you, Lilly, that will be all for now. If you or any of the others find out more, come to me."

Lilly curtsied and left.

"Well," Mark faced the group, a little stunned. "We've a small army of people to gather information on that front. Let's to bed and see what our talents and connections may uncover on other fronts, tomorrow." He leaned over and kissed his wife on the cheek. "Come, Mrs. Weatherby, we've all had a full day."

❧❦

"My dear Lady Aldergrove," Wentworth wrote. "Newcomers to the village seem particularly enamoured of our mutual friend. I wonder if you'd be so good as to advise me of your wishes. Also, with my eldest daughter near married, and my second not long to waste in her shadow, I should like to discuss other nuptials with you, as per our understanding."

Catherine Aldergrove rolled her eyes at Wentworth's presumption. Truly, she'd said nothing of the kind. Saying it might have made her culpable. She only chose not to disabuse him of the notion, neither agreeing or disagreeing. If, in his foolishness, he imagined that as consent, that was his own folly, and no affair of hers. She reread the letter and sneered. 'Mutual friend' indeed. That mongrel was no friend of hers. Whelped on some nobody Chambers bedded in port while she waited at home for his next commission.

Catherine glared at the letter. Thank heavens Mr. Wentworth, then Corporal Wentworth, had served with Captain Edward Chambers. When she bargained for that storm to sink the ship, the admirable Chambers got everyone else off and away in time, but was unable to get himself away before the old girl sank to the ocean's floor. His last act, last request, was to ask Corporal Wentworth to take certain papers, last wishes, to a London lawyer. They bequeathed his wealth to his daughter and her to his brother, a Lieutenant Matthew Chambers.

Catherine smiled, reliving Edward's destruction, and how she continued her revenge upon him even after his death. How his soul would twist in the ever-after, knowing his daughter was an unwanted ward. The bitch that birthed her died shortly after the girl was born. Edward so soon after that no arrangements had been in place. How fortuitous that Wentworth had been sniffing around her family for years. Knowing how Edward had snubbed her made him long to avenge her. But Chambers was his superior officer, superior in every way, really, and so Wentworth kept his mouth shut, obedient in all things. But when Edward entrusted his final wishes to Wentworth, Wentworth went to the Aldergroves first, before seeing even his own family. He'd obviously hoped for vows in exchange for this opportunity. What he got was a squalling mutt.

Thank the fates that his mother hushed up his sudden child with a wedding and the new bride didn't protest. The Mathers were approximately Wentworth's equals and bore the burden tolerably well, though it took Vivian another four years to produce Mary, and another two for Janice. *Who would have thought that only two would wear her out completely?* Catherine mused, shuddering, wanting no part of the dangers of childbirth herself. Vivian died shortly after Janice was born, leaving Wentworth no heirs, and a ward whose father he loathed for the crime of capturing and breaking the heart of the woman he loved.

"If you love me," Catherine had said, "you will take her home with you. You need not love her as your own. In fact, I'd rather you didn't."

Trapped by his own confessions, he took Althea in, vowing that she never know the love of father or mother for as long as she lived. Catherine cast the geas on the child. It hadn't appeared as though Edward had any magical gifts, but the mother was an unknown. Catherine could not take the chance that the girl had enough magic to ensure revenge, so she wrapped the babe in a spell to keep her magic, if she had any, buried. It kept her bound to Wentworth, unable to leave his grounds without his permission, and prevented any talk of magic or teaching of magic to her. She would be ignorant and afraid all her life, living only by the grace of Wentworth's hatred for her father.

Catherine smiled again. *Oh, Edward, how you must churn, seeing how low your choices have brought your filthy whelp. Our children would have had every privilege, been beautiful, talented, Masters of the world. For you, I would have braved the chamber of birth and death. Not now, though.* Catherine decided it was time for her to see what sorrow the girl had come to, and to confirm the strangers were no threat to her complete revenge. She rang the bell for the maid.

"All's quiet on the home front," Mark reported to the guild and Hamlin, weeks later. The servants gave him regular updates, naming the slights done to Althea, and the kindnesses she did for them. The only news, such as it was, could have been gathered by reading the post. Mr. Alan Davies and Miss Mary Wentworth joyfully announce their impending nuptials, etc. "Have we heard anything from our little birds?" He asked, looking around at each of them.

Peter cleared his throat. "I have." He paused. "I looked into Captain Chambers."

"You've got over your dislike of her, then?" Edna goaded him with a smile.

"How could I not? With daily proof of her nature and her situation, who could help but pity and admire her?"

"She won't thank you for your pity," warned George.

Peter raised his gaze to meet his friend's. "Perhaps not, but she has it all the same. All the more so, now that we know her family."

"*We* don't. *You* do," prompted Edna.

Peter scowled at her. "Her father, Captain Edward Chambers was one of the finest seamen HRMs Navy had ever seen. Better even than his forefathers, also in service, who were none of them slouches. Chambers looked to be forming an alliance with the Aldergroves, which both consented to, on condition of Edward being awarded a ranked ship, which he was sure be. Miss Catherine Aldergrove was smitten, beautiful, and spoiled, with a temper no few people had commented on. Temper aside, Chambers bowed to the will of his family."

Peter continued, the guild listening raptly. "Until the Reliant, Edward's ship, put in at a port in Falmouth, where he met the enchanting Miss Fairchild. Angelina Fairchild stole his heart on sight, so his former shipmates claimed. In the time it took to outfit the Reliant and make whatever repairs had forced her to dock, they courted, wed, and consummated. Captain Chambers came home married, forfeiting the Aldergrove alliance."

"The Fairchilds, some of you might know, are steeped in magic, and head of the guild for their area. The gift runs strong in their blood. Based on his shipmates' accounts, I'd say Edward's own gifts were considerable, though he kept them hidden from family and guild, presumably out of a desire to earn his accomplishments by more mundane efforts, though that's pure speculation on my part. Whatever his reasons, their only child would have a double dose of already considerable gifts."

"Alas, Angelina died soon after Althea was born. Edward was at sea. No provisions had been made for her. A terrible storm took Captain Chambers to the grave, though he managed to save everyone else on board. His dying wishes were never known." Peter shook his head. "Edward and Angelina were new parents, Edward hadn't even laid eyes on his only child before the sea took him. Who can blame them for not having provided for Althea? They imagined they'd have more time."

John coughed. "I don't know, I think George here might."

George glowered. "Is that all?" He demanded.

Peter nodded. "I have a few more birds out looking for bread crumbs. Perhaps one of them will turn up something." Peter shrugged. "The fates have been unusually cruel to her, but she has not learned cruelty in response. Bit of a wonder, eh, old boy?"

George snorted. "You only say that because you do not know her."

Mary and Janice waited anxiously in the sitting room for Lady Aldergrove's arrival. Though she couldn't name why, Althea awaited the woman's arrival with only dread. Rather than spoil the girls' good humour, she took herself outside, despite the cool of autumn that was full upon them. The trees, lately radiant with their orange, red, and gold, now stood barren like wraiths. They did not even boast their lovely skirts, for the gardener had raked like a fiend, every fallen leaf an affront to his well-tended lands.

Althea longed for the joys of spring, of hope, and grew ever more desolate as she trod among the trees, all of them easing into their annual slumber. She might have poured her unsettled feelings into the music room, but for her secret. No balls had been hosted since that last where she was set upon in the rose garden. She was both relieved, not wanting another bout with her geas, and disappointed, for it meant no music and no Hamlin to relieve the oppression of the Wentworths.

Althea shook herself. *Do not be unkind. Mary has been a joy in her wedding plans, neither too fussy nor too obtuse in her bliss.* Althea smiled then, recalling how just yesterday afternoon Mary had pleaded with Althea to arrange her hair on her special day.

"I am sure Mr. Wentworth would be happy to provide you with a true hair dresser, my dear."

"Pooh on a hair dresser. I want you, Althea."

Althea smiled indulgently on Mary, touched. "Then you shall have me," she assured the girl.

Now, walking through the spindly wood, Althea sighed, still smiling at the memory. *No help for it,* she chafed her hands, grown icy without gloves, *I must go in and prepare for the great Lady's arrival, and Mr. Wentworth's inspection.* She trundled through the yard and into the house to clean up in her room as best she could.

That august Lady arrived in a coach with six black horses, a perfect matching set. She made no small impression, driving through town, and at about the same time as she pulled up to the Wentworth's, news of her reached the guild.

"Master Mark, you should have seen it, fine black carriage, fine black horses, only a great house could afford such a thing," Lilly reported dutifully.

"Did you happen to find out whom this fine carriage was carrying?" Mark asked, amused.

"Aye, sir. Butcher said it was Lady Aldergrove, to see the Wentworths, sir. Cook mentioned it when ordering roasts for her Ladyship's visit, sir."

Mark smiled. "Good lass. Thank you for coming to tell me. If you hear anything more, let me know." He pressed a coin into her palm before he dismissed her.

He found the guild gathered in the sitting room, huddled close to the fire. *No wonder. This fall has grown too cold too fast,* he mused as he joined them. They all looked towards him expectantly, his air betraying that he had news.

"Well, we're in it now," he began. "Lady Catherine Aldergrove is paying the Wentworths a visit as we speak."

Silence prevailed as they considered what that could mean.

"It could be a simple social call," offered Elizabeth.

George snorted.

Peter looked askance at his old and rare then said, "not likely." All eyes turned to him.

"More little birds of yours, Peter?" Edna inquired.

"In twenty years she hasn't come to the village. It is no coincidence that she is here so soon after our arrival. Between our little gala and today, there is hardly time enough for the post to carry a missive to her and her time to pack and travel. No," he shook his head. "She is here because we are here."

"Don't you think that is a bit presumptuous, Peter?" John offered gently. "Much as we may be accustomed to, well, the world working as we deem it ought, not everything revolves around us."

Elizabeth put her hand on her husband's knee with a warm smile. "The delights of an Earth, they always take a broader view."

"Why that should be Earth's trait and not, say, Air's or Water's, I don't understand," claimed Edna, all Fire.

"Fire is just as far reaching, my dear," Mark pointed out.

"Only when it is wholly free, which we generally guard against, Love."

They shared a look then, and lingered in it until Peter cleared his throat.

Mark looked at the group then. "I'm afraid Peter is right. The servants tell me that Mr. Wentworth sent post the day after our soiree. The two events are linked, whether we wish it or no."

George stood then. "I know I have no gift worth speaking of, and my inclusion in the guild is honourary at best, but what, pray tell, are you, we, you, going to do for Miss Chambers?"

"Old boy, do sit down," Peter begged. "We must know the precise nature of her visit before we decide on a course of action. Which," he held up his hand as George opened his mouth, "we will take measures to find out." Peter looked at his friends again. "Did any of you feel her coming in?" Heads shook all around. "Well, I did. Might be safe to say she's Air, which might mean something, later."

They remained huddled around the fire, planning elemental spies, and mundane methods of drawing Lady Aldergrove out.

Wentworth greeted Catherine warmly, inviting her to take the most comfortable chair in the parlour, where he introduced his two daughters.

"And our ward, Miss Chambers," he added as an afterthought, cleverly concealing Catherine's acquaintance with the girl.

Catherine observed protocol, asking after their health, and Mary's coming wedding.

"And you, Miss Janice? Have you a young man to lose your heart to?"

Janice blushed. "No, my lady. But then, there are two years between Mary and I."

Catherine nodded. "I am sure your suitors will pour from the woodwork once your sister is safely married."

Janice cast her eyes down in deference to the lady's opinion.

For her part, Althea remained mute and still, sitting to the right and a bit behind Janice, at the small table tucked into the corner of the room. She listened and watched as best she could, feeling very much like a mouse beneath the gaze of an owl. A hungry owl.

"How lucky you are, Miss Chambers, blessed with not one, but two beautiful sisters. I should have liked a sister myself, when I was younger." Catherine watched Althea closely.

"Yes, my lady," was all she uttered, meeting the precise etiquette of the moment, if not providing sparkling conversation.

"Shall we prepare for dinner?" Wentworth suggested. "I am sure, Lady Aldergrove, that you are tired from your long journey and would like some time to rest."

Catherine turned her gaze on Mr. Wentworth with disgust. "Thank you, Mr. Wentworth. That is a delightful idea." The maid appeared to escort her.

"Whatever is the matter with you, Althea?" Mary asked. "You're white as a ghost and hardly said two words. You are never daunted by our betters at the balls, surely you aren't afraid of Lady Aldergrove?"

The truth was that the moment Lady Aldergrove entered the room, the geas threatened to squeeze the life out of Althea, but she could hardly say so.

"Leave her be, Mary," warned Mr. Wentworth. "I will address Miss Chambers' manners later. For now, dress for dinner."

Both Miss Wentworths fled the room at their father's tone.

"Now, you listen to me, Miss Chambers," Wentworth turned to her with a savage expression on his face. "You will be polite to Lady Aldergrove, you will answer promptly, you will be modest, and you will not be sullen. Do you understand me?" His face was near purple with rage.

"Yes, sir," Althea breathed, her heart pounding for want of oxygen and fear of both Lady Aldergrove and Mr. Wentworth's wrath.

"Good. Now help Mary and Janice dress. After your performance just now, I think you will be excused from dinner. I shall tell Lady Aldergrove that you are unwell. You will be fully recovered come morning." His heavy tone was unmistakable.

"Yes, Mr. Wentworth." Althea carried herself upstairs to help Mary with as much dignity as she could muster considering she'd been sent to her room without supper like a small child.

The servants heard, of course, and they conspired where the family would neither hear nor see. Dinner was carried off smoothly, and while family and guest were in the dining room, cook's helper ducked up the back stairs with a tray for Althea.

"We heard you were feeling poorly, Miss Chambers, so cook put together some of your favourites to tempt your appetite." He winked and backed out the door, leaving Althea stunned speechless.

The next morning, Lady Aldergrove took a keen interest in Althea's delicate health. Althea's geas wrapped her like a boa constrictor forcing her to take only the most shallow of breaths.

"But listen to you," exclaimed Lady Aldergrove. "You scarcely draw breath. Not enough exercise, I wager. Come, we must go for a good, brisk walk," her eyes gleamed in malice, knowing Althea could not deny her, and imagining the girl might just pass out along the way. *Lovely excuse to leave her out there, lying in the cold, while I come back here in search of a doctor. Delicious!*

"Yes, Lady Aldergrove, I am sure, that's just the thing." Althea's face was pale, but she put on the most amiable face she could. "How kind of you to think of it."

Wentworth nodded his approval.

Once Althea and Lady Aldergrove were in the gardens, the Wentworths staying inside, Lady Aldergrove took pleasure in nudging the geas.

"It would take magic to make the flowers grow this time of year."

The geas cinched Althea's stomach.

"Such a pity the grounds are so desolate." Catherine looked away, having noted Althea's sudden tension as the geas constricted.

"But what an old maid you are," she insulted Althea. "Has no one taken an interest in all these years?"

Althea put on her sweetest smile, "no man with sense or without sets his sights on a ward when not one, but two noble, and eligible, daughters are about, Lady Aldergrove." Althea bowed her head. "I am content here, for as long as Mr. Wentworth's good Christian charity permits me."

They'd walked some distance from the house by then, and Catherine turned, enraged, on Althea.

"Content, are you?"

Althea stepped back.

"Content was not part of the plan at all, my dear." She purred, her demeanor changing with the wind.

"I don't understand, my lady."

"I knew your father, you know," Catherine continued in that same silky voice. "Loved him. I never knew the bitch who whelped you, though."

Althea stood stunned, a longing to hear more of her father, never before spoken of, clawing at her, though she didn't want to hear even one more word of him from this woman.

Lady Aldergrove stepped closer and called the wind. The geas wrapped around Althea's throat, strangling her while she clutched at the unseen bonds around her neck, Catherine leaned in close, her lips almost brushing Althea's ear as the storm whirled around them.

"Magic, my dear, magic all around you."

The geas squeezed tighter and Althea's eyes bulged as she clawed more desperately at her throat.

"I know just what this does to you, you mongrel, I put it there. No magic for you, not around you, not spoken of, without the geas trying to suffocate you. No new things for you. No warning from you to others. No revealing your terrible secret."

Althea's vision began to gray at the edges, her struggles getting weaker.

"You were to be miserable for all your days. Not content." The wind continued to twist around them in a cyclone. "Just to add one final touch to your wretched existence, you are never to have a well-fit pair of shoes. Ill-fitting footwear is the most painful of irritants, don't you agree?"

Althea's vision narrowed until Lady Aldergrove's face was all she would see.

"Henry has been careful, I can tell. One pair of shoes could have undone the whole spell."

Althea's world faded to black.

She awoke freezing cold, on the ground, her head resting uncomfortably at an odd angle, between some tree roots. Lady Aldergrove loomed over her.

"Oh good, you're awake," she purred.

Althea cringed.

"Ah, that's much better. You should be afraid , my dear. Henry may have made your life comfortable. I am here to ensure it is not. After today, he will not fail to follow my example. Now get up. You were out so long the others will believe we went on quite the stroll, you and I."

Althea got to her feet clumsily, still dizzy, her heart hammering and her whole body trembling. The geas still smothered her, keeping her from taking anything more than the smallest sips of air.

When they came in the house, Lady Aldergrove released the geas enough for Althea to take a full breath, which she gulped down greedily.

"Careful, my dear," Catherine warned knowingly.

Althea promptly vomited just as Janice came to the entry way.

"Vile," was all she said, staring with disgust at the mess on the floor.

"I think Miss Chambers has had enough for one day. Ring the servants to clean this up." Catherine turned up her nose and strode to the parlour.

"Mary may swoon over you, but I shan't," declared Janice and left Althea doubled over at the door.

She wanted to weep, she wanted the shaking to stop, she wanted her head to stop pounding. Instead, Althea stumbled to the kitchen to get a pail and cloth.

On seeing her, Cook insisted she sit while he sent someone to clean the mess.

"I am so very sorry," Althea apologized.

"Tut, Lovey. Think nobbut of it." He rubbed her back briefly then brewed chamomile tea.

"There you are, Miss. Sip on that till you've got enough strength to climb upstairs to bed.

Althea savoured the honey he'd sweetened it with.

Peter suddenly sat rigid in his chair during breakfast.

"Peter?" George peered into his friend's face. "What's taken you?" George looked around the room at the rest of the guild.

"Some powerful air magic, I reckon," said John. "Felt much the same to me when your Lady shoved them rose bushes into bloom." John blushed as he realised he'd fallen into his home dialect. Elizabeth patted his hand in reassurance.

Peter blinked then seemed to come to himself. "If that's what it feels like when someone of your element works, then I am suddenly very grateful to be the only Air among us."

Mark grinned. "The more powerful your gift and theirs, the more it affects you. Since my gift is such a trifle, my Edna could call a fire rain, and I'd hardly blink."

"Well this one is a monster, if this reaction is any indication," Peter groused.

John took a sip of tea, looking thoughtful.

George stood, anger and haste in the movement. "What are we waiting for? We must do something!"

Edna turned her hot gaze on him. "What would you have us do, Mr. Hamlin? Run out and start elemental warfare?"

George opened his mouth to shout again, took a breath, then closed it and sat down.

"Quite right," Edna nodded. "What has you so captivated, John?"

John took another bite of his eggs before answering.

"She's Earth. Bound by Air, it appears," he pointed his fork at Peter. "Peter is going to have to be the one to unlock the enchantment while we keep the Air Master busy. But," he took a swig of tea and swallowed. "Since Fire and Water work equally well allied with Air as with Earth, it is even odds that they will be for us, rather than against us."

☘❧

Lady Aldergrove continued her ministrations on Althea every morning, taking her out for a stroll to keep the others from bearing witness. Mr. Wentworth continued the torture at night, stealing into her room, crawling into her bed, alternating between whispering words of magic in her ear and telling her there was no sin, she was just a ward, not a daughter, after all.

Althea was sickened by what her life had become, dreading each day, each moment. Janice joined in the torments with petty snipes and insults, though nothing more. Mary remained silent, fearful of her family and their guest, secretly counting down the days to her wedding, when she could get away and would not have to see Althea's pale face, bruised eyes, and constant flinching and tremors.

It wasn't until the invitation to the Durston's midwinter fete that Althea's torment abated. Leaving her at home under pretense of illness would only attract attention. Taking her with, in her current broken state would arouse more. So they let her reclaim enough of her health and wits to be presentable.

As usual, it was Althea who fixed Mary's hair before the outing. As she worked at pinning the curls 'just so', Mary caught her wrist, making her flinch.

"I'm sorry," Mary whispered, "for everything, for leaving you to them. I don't know why they are doing whatever they are doing. But I'm sorry for not being able to help you."

Althea looked indulgently on Mary, touched by the gesture. "It's not your fault," Althea patted her gently on the shoulder and resumed pinning the curls. "Now hush and be still, or you'll go to midwinter with your hair half up and half down."

Mary giggled. "What a fashion statement that would be."

"Yes indeed. It says 'my maid is too slow'." Althea's smile was a shadow of its former self, as though it, too, was afraid to come out.

The fete was decided upon in response to the magic ripples that put Peter on edge every morning.

"I've no idea what that woman is doing each and every morning, but she's not the least bit subtle," Peter complained.

George was beside himself with worry and anger at his helplessness to save Miss Chambers, and had ceased joining the guild for breakfast, though he could not bear to remove himself from the house entirely to return to his own estates.

Edna's suggestion of a ball was received poorly at first, until she explained that it was the only way to bring Miss Chambers into their sphere of influence again, as the Wentworths were not extending any invitations to anyone to visit.

"I can occupy the Lady while one of you smuggles Miss Chambers into the music room again. Peter can see what he can do about unlocking the spell around her, and if he's successful," she looked at Peter pointedly, expecting no less than success, "that shall be the end of it."

"Save the Lady's wrath, of course," John muttered.

"Don't you have a hole we can throw her into?" Edna fired back. "The Earth elementals, even without your encouragement, would like to torment an Air if one should fall into their hands. Especially an Air as foul as this one."

Peter shuddered, recalling a childhood trauma of falling down a well. His saving grace was that the well had water, a friendlier element, and so the Earth elementals let him alone.

"Before you get all shivery and remorseful, recall how your breakfasts have been ruined for weeks by this woman's choices, not to mention what her victim suffers daily." Edna scolded Peter.

"I didn't say a word, and wouldn't have. But you cannot blame me for not relishing in her punishment. I would surely go mad in her place."

"It is a wonder Miss Chambers hasn't gone mad by now, the way the servants tell it," George interjected. "All this time, sick and wounded, with no help she can see, no hope of an end to her suffering. Don't you fret over that beast of a houseguest." His words were acid, silencing the guild.

"Quite right," Elizabeth whispered. "Who knows, Peter? Maybe there is another way to release the spell than head-on magic. At least consider it when you speak to her."

As guests began to arrive, every member of the guild took their places and danced their social steps beautifully. Mark whisked Aldergrove off to Elizabeth, claiming she could not abide a mystery, and Lady Aldergrove was at least that. John stayed well clear of Lady Aldergrove and focused instead on the musicians, making sure there were plenty of dance sets to keep the Wentworth daughters, and hence Mr. Wentworth watching them, occupied.

Edna escorted Althea to the music room once the fete was in full swing, and George watched the hall entrance leading to it, guarding Althea from any visitors, save Peter.

This time Althea didn't hesitate to sit down at the beautiful piano. She poured all the anguish and fear and loathing out onto the keys, then shifted to howling laments, in minor keys, that wailed like something other-worldly.

Peter stopped mid-step as the music reached his ears, frozen by the perfect agony held in the sound. He shuddered before forcing himself to step into the room, and into Althea's line of sight.

She lifted her hands from the keys the moment she saw him, letting the unfinished chord hang in the air, adding to the tension in the room.

"Lord Croft, I beg your pardon," Althea flung herself from the bench and dropped into a low curtsy.

Peter waved his hand as if shooing a fly. "Forget that nonsense, Miss Chambers, we haven't the time."

Althea stared at him, confused.

"I am sorry to put you through this again, Miss Chambers. I know your last visit with us was a trial for you, but I am going to attempt to unravel that which binds you."

The geas cinched and released in warning, Peter's words hedging far enough around the subject to keep the geas from constricting and holding.

"Lord Croft, our guest has unintentionally taught me better endurance. Only let me take a few full breaths before you begin, if you please." Althea held her head up, despite the fear shining in her eyes.

"I see my first impression of you was woefully inaccurate," Peter admitted, a veiled apology hidden within it.

"Not at all, sir. Let us say I have been taught a few things since, that make me less, more," Althea shook her head, losing her words. She took three deep breaths, blowing them out fully each time. She swelled with the fourth, filling lungs and belly with air and nodded to Peter to begin.

He reached out to Althea with magic and the geas began to strangle her. He tried to pry the cords loose from her neck but couldn't grasp them long enough to make any progress. He pulled away and the geas relaxed.

"I can't do anything grand or she will sense what I am doing, just as I could feel all the grand things she was doing." Peter couched his words deliberately vaguely to keep from tripping the spell.

Althea took deep breaths again, more certain of his meaning than she might have been before Lady Aldergrove's torturous education.

"Sir, if I may," Althea paused, not knowing how to dance with words so well as he did.

"Go on," Peter prompted. "We haven't much time."

"More of the same will not solve this problem as easily as other methods might." Her expression was pained, both from clumsy words and straying too close to the edges of the geas. She winced, taking sips of air, and sitting down on the floor with a thump to keep from passing out.

Peter approached her carefully, but she held up a hand and shook her head. The geas grew tighter as he approached. He stepped back and it relaxed.

"Mr. Hamlin," an idea for getting around the geas came to her suddenly. "Ask Mr. Hamlin about our first conversation."

"We haven't the time," Peter protested.

"Some knots take time to unravel, more than a single evening, Lord Croft." Althea pursed her lips and stood up. "First, lead me outside, then go to Mr. Hamlin. Bring him to me, and," the geas cinched her cruelly, making her double over. "And," gasp, "look," she fought the geas, clenching her muscles to push it out just a little farther, "down". She panted with the effort and then pointed to the door.

Peter led her down the back stairs to the servants entrance. Despite the time of year, the past few days had been unseasonably warm, leaving the ground near the door soft and mucky. Althea pulled off her shoes and stockings, shocking Peter soundly, and stepped out into the freezing mud where she wished her footprints might stay. When she pulled her feet out, the mud collapsed around the impressions and stuck to her feet.

"Buckets," she mock-cursed and stepped into the snow that remained on the yard, there only due to perpetual shade, to clean her feet before trying again. But the snow did what the mud couldn't. It melted under her feet, forming to their shape and froze again as she stepped off, leaving two perfect, mud-laced impressions, a perfect cast of her feet.

When Hamlin and Peter returned, Althea was just slipping the second shoe onto her foot.

"There," she pointed behind her, to the small patch of snow, "is the key to a certain Lady's lock." Althea crumpled again under the geas as it struck her a blow to the stomach.

"There's no time left, Miss Chambers," Peter shook his head. "They seek you even now."

"Quickly then, show me the way," she demanded, hoping to hide any suspicion of the night's activities from her oppressors.

Hamlin remained behind, staring at her perfect footprints in the snow. He was still there when Peter returned.

"Perhaps she has gone mad after all," mourned George.

"Oh no, old boy, far from it," Peter patted his friend's shoulder. "She bid me ask you remember your first conversation."

George looked confused as he thought back. "She was not honoured by my attention," he began, and Peter laughed.

"How pompous you sound."

George grunted.

"She bid me to waste my time elsewhere. She claimed we were all trapped by the dance of manners. Called herself a penny, and said the world would rush to please me."

Such a bizarre conversation, thought Peter but held his tongue, not wanting to interrupt George's train of thought.

"Butterflies. Dance. Labyrinth." George's eyes grew wide then as the last piece came to him. "Shoes!" he blurted.

"That's it? Shoes?" Peter said doubtfully. "She did all this for shoes? Lord, the lengths women will go to." He rolled his eyes.

"No, Peter, you misunderstand. When we spoke of people trapped in the social dance, lost in a labyrinth, she said something about if she had a pair of well-fitted shoes, she would make her way in the world."

"That is the key to her spell?" Peter asked in disbelief.

"It must be. Why else would she give us two perfect footprints?" George looked down at foot-shaped splotches of mud in the snow.

Althea remained in either Mr. Wentworth's or Lady Aldergrove's line of sight for the remainder of the evening, fobbing off her absence with a story of spilling punch on her gown and needing to rinse the spill to keep it from staining. A quick splash from the kitchen sink as she hustled to the ballroom gave evidence of her tale, and their suspicions fled.

Althea settled herself in a corner of the room to watch the dancers, as she had in gatherings past, making sure to keep her face impassive, neither fearful nor playful, to keep all observers at bay. At one point John and Elizabeth Durston passed by her as they made their circuit of the room, pausing beside her to watch the dancers for a moment. They did not look at her, but pitched their voices for her to hear them.

"We received your key. You must bear up some time longer."

The spell cudgeled Althea again. She managed not to wince, though a small grunt escaped her.

The Durstons moved on.

Part 2

"How shall we get a shoemaker to make a pair of shoes for her?" George lamented once all the guests had left, and the house belonged to the guild once again.

Peter made a face. "Normally, he would measure her feet and then go away to cobble them together. Bit difficult to explain magically preserved footprints."

"Or making shoes for someone in secret," John added.

Elizabeth laughed as she entered the room with a tea service. "You men can be quite obtuse when you so choose," she sallied as Edna followed her and they all settled around the fireplace once again.

"Indeed, Mrs. Durston, you have a plan, then?" Peter's tone lofty and condescending.

Elizabeth rolled her eyes. "Leave it to me, gentlemen. I will have them made." She sat back in her chair, wrapping her hands around the mug of tea. "The only question is what kind of shoes she should have."

"For my part," Edna suggested, "I'd like them to be magnificent, something to make the Wentworths' eyes roll out of their heads," no small measure of fire in her voice.

"You've taken quite a shine to the lady," Mark noticed.

"If you'd heard her play, you would have too, my dear." She took a sip of tea. "She could make an elemental weep. And those 'relations' of hers, spending all their time maligning her in the most polite way possible. It would do them all some good to be humbled."

Elizabeth looked to George expectantly.

"I haven't the first idea about ladies footwear, Madam. If left to me, she'd have a warm and sturdy pair of boots she could run in." He shrugged.

"That is no bad idea. Magnificent, warm, sturdy, and one thing more," she glanced about the room. "Comfortable. That poor child is in great need of comfort. I'd like to see she gets it."

Lady Elizabeth Durston took a trip to a town well away from Briardowns to avoid word getting back to Wentworth. She had not yet been seen in the village, her very appearance would set tongues wagging, and her great commission would be on every lip before the day was out.

She reached her favourite shoemaker at the end of the third day of travel.

"Mrs. Durston, what a great pleasure to see you again," he greeted her as she came in. He paused his work, a delicate confection sitting upside down in his lap, as he soled it.

"Oh Devon, that is lovely," she praised him, her eyes on the slope of the arch and the sheen of the satin wrapped around the toe.

"Gracious as always, Mrs. Durston. I could easily make something their better for you."

Elizabeth sighed. "Not today, I'm afraid, Devon. But I may come back again and take you up on it another time."

"I should be delighted, Madam. Is there something else I can do for you?"

"Indeed you can." Elizabeth pulled the tracings she'd made of Althea's feet from her bag. She unfolded them, spreading them out on the table before the shoemaker. "You are an absolute magician and I am counting on your considerable talent to help me with a gift for a friend of mine."

Devon looked at the tracings dubiously. "It would be better if I could measure the lady's foot, Mrs. Durston. The curve of her arch, and so forth."

Elizabeth bit her lip.

"Then again," Devon changed tactics, "it might depend on what precisely you want."

Elizabeth gave him the criteria.

Devon nodded. "Are you opposed to a soft sole, Mrs. Durston?"

"Not at all. That might be best, actually."

"Then I may have just the thing. Please wait here a moment." He stood and left to rummage about his workroom behind the shop. He came out again a few moments later, holding a length of sheepskin. The one side was treated leather, water proof, the other lined thickly with wool. He held it out to Elizabeth to touch and examine.

Elizabeth ran her hand over one side then the other. "Oh, Devon, what a treasure."

"Indeed, my lady. More than one game keeper has kept his toes thanks to this."

"It's perfect. How soon can you have them made?"

Devon squinted his eyes. "Bit of a rush on these, Mrs. Durston?"

Elizabeth nodded.

"Two days," Devon said after a long pause.

Elizabeth breathed a sigh relief. "And a week's wages for your trouble," she decided.

"Mrs. Durston, your generosity is always appreciated."

Elizabeth nodded. "Until then, Devon. Thank you."

George and Peter were sharing a rare round of billiards as they awaited Lady Durston's return.

After the third miss in a row, Peter locked gazes with George.

"It seems we are both off our game, old boy."

George grunted and put up his cue.

"I hope you have a piano forte at the house, George, if you mean to offer her refuge."

George began pacing.

"George? You mean to tell me she's going to escape with nowhere to go to?"

"It wouldn't be proper, and Mater wouldn't have it. You all say she is very strong in magic but untrained. She would wreak havoc." George looked desperate.

"Well she certainly can't stay with me." Peter said defensively. "Just as improper, and though my staff is perfectly inured to magic, we have opposing elements. No," Peter shook his head. "It won't do."

They voiced their concerns at dinner with the rest of the guild.

John looked up, confused. "I rather assumed she'd stay with Elizabeth and I. I am the only Earth among us, and the girl will need training."

"What of Lady Aldergrove?" Asked Edna.

"No, we shan't take her in," John quipped.

All of them smiled at that.

"I've sent sylphs to every Air I know," Peter announced. "There is a Master in Ashington who is prepared to rally them and put her down."

John and the Weatherbys paled.

George looked from face to face in confusion. "You are going to insult her?"

"No, George," murmured Mark. "They mean to strip her of her powers. She would be no more magical than a stone."

"Rather less," said John. "Even stones have power."

"Most people live without magic," George ventured, still not understanding.

"Old boy, after having magic, being stripped of it is rather like going blind and deaf at once, and losing both arms. More than a few people have gone utterly mad after being stripped of their power."

George nodded slowly. "It is no less than she deserves," he declared, effectively ending the discussion.

A week and a day had Elizabeth reunited with the guild, coveted boots in hand.

47

"Oh Elizabeth," Edna breathed, "those are wonderful." She eyed the boots with obvious envy. A long tongue ran up the shin, two wide flaps would wrap around the leg, overlapping, and long heavy laces attached at the heel would wind around it all like a roman sandal, all the way up to the knee, keeping out cold and snow, and fitting like a glove once tied off.

Elizabeth opened one boot allowing Edna to see the sole. "Look, double lined for both warmth and extended wear." Edna pushed her hand inside the toe, her eyes rolling in pleasure.

"I think the good shoemaker may see two more orders for their like very soon," quipped Peter, looking at both husbands with amusement.

"Oh hush, you've no idea the foolishness we women put up with on account of fashionable footwear," Edna sniped. She returned her gaze to the boots with both longing and sadness. "But they are very plain."

Elizabeth nodded. "Any kind of decorative work would have taken longer to add. Miss Chambers has endured an additional week of waiting as it is." She looked slyly at her husband then. "Besides, I imagine only another Earth could divine what design she would best like."

John wagged his finger at his wife as he smiled. "I suppose you'd like it put there with magic, too?"

Elizabeth batted her eyelashes at him. "You suppose correctly, My lord," she simpered. "Your way is so much quicker, and your designs more beautiful than a poor shoemaker could hope to produce."

John laughed. "Leave off your flattery, woman. Bring them here." He held the brown leather in his hands, turning it over and over as he stared at it. "Ivy, I think, in a slightly lighter shade of brown than the leather." As he spoke, a wreath appeared around the ankle, and the ivy wound up and around as though growing there. When it neared the top, it wreathed again, as if trained on a trellis. "There, that should do it. What say you, Mrs. Weatherby, do they meet with your approval?" He held the boots out to her to inspect.

"Magnificent," she breathed.

"Well done, you old garden gnome," Peter clapped him on the back. "Just the word she used before your wife went a-journeying."

John blushed and ducked his head.

They sent the gift by way of the servants, the boots wrapped in a burlap sack and tied with a magical knot that only the touch of an Earth could unravel. Edna grimaced at the packaging, claiming the boots deserved so much better. Despite her dismay, even she had to concede that a beautiful package would arouse suspicion.

George left the party then, journeying home to reconcile his affairs and lay the groundwork with his family about his upcoming courtship. John and Elizabeth sent word ahead of them to their estate, advising the staff they would be home soon, and with a house guest. Peter co-ordinated with the Air Masters, all of them already arrived and taking lodgings wherever there was room to hold them.

Not a soul practiced even the tiniest of magics, to keep Aldergrove from suspecting. Mark and Edna tied up all the loose ends that come with taking a house and then leaving it again.

"Deuced rude to bring them all out for Michaelmas," Peter grimaced.

"Peter, you said so yourself. They let her regain her strength for mass tomorrow. It couldn't be a better time for her to run." Mark pointed out, Peter's reports confirmed by the servants.

Peter only sighed. "I shall owe more than a few bottles of our best before this is through," he mourned.

Edna laughed. "There is no reason you can't enjoy it with them, Lord Croft. Keeping company with more of your element might appeal to you, after all."

Peter looked thoughtful.

Mark entered the room and clapped his hands together. "Right then, we all know our parts?" He looked about the room at each person in turn.

Peter nodded. "I'm to give the signal when the spell breaks, then join the others surrounding Wentworth's estates.

Elizabeth stood, bag in hand and stepped up beside John. "We will make haste home to Longview, and wait for you and Miss Chambers there."

"And we," Edna clasped Mark's hands, knotting their fingers, shall wait at the post to take Miss Chambers away."

"What of George?" Mark asked.

Peter laughed. "Best have one more room made up, I doubt he will be far behind you.

Mark and Elizabeth shared a knowing look.

Althea endured Lady Aldergrove's attentions as best she could, unable to decide which was worse, her, or Mr. Wentworth.

I shall never feel clean again, she tasted bile as she gasped for air yet again while Lady Aldergrove spoke of magic during their walk.

Driven to her knees as the world grayed around her, Althea fought for every breath.

"Not so content now, are we, my dear?" Lady Aldergrove crooned, her face looming in front of Althea's.

Althea shook her head. Her fear and her hate warred within her.

"Save your moon eyes for another, mongrel. They shan't work on me," Lady Aldergrove cinched the geas around Althea's waist violently, making Althea double over in pain. She couldn't even scream. She could barely whimper, and dared not waste the air.

"Enough for this morning, I think. Consider it a Michaelmas gift that you should get off so lightly." Lady Aldergrove turned and began walking away. "Come," she ordered as though Althea were a dog.

Like a dog, Althea obeyed.

It had become habit for Althea to seek out the kitchen after her morning trials with Lady Aldergrove, the staff treating her tenderly, and Althea unable to resist what small comfort they offered. Lady Aldergrove allowed it, so the Wentworths didn't interfere, leaving Althea a small oasis in each day, where she was free from all of them.

Cook barely contained his excitement as Althea stumbled into the kitchen. Her tea was waiting for her, steaming on the table. Cook's helpers were at every door and window, keeping lookout for the family and "herself" as they'd taken to calling Catherine Aldergrove. At a nod from the others, Cook pulled the ratty sack from a cold oven and presented it to Althea.

Althea looked from it to him and back again. "I'm afraid you've got it backwards, Cook. I should be gifting you, and that not till the morrow."

Cook held his first finger to his lips and shook his head, then handed Althea a small card, little more than stiff paper folded in half. Althea unfolded it and read. "To make your way in the world. A good place to start would be the Post. Ask for the Weatherbys."

Althea looked again at the bag and touched it gingerly, afraid of what it might contain. The knot unravelled at her touch and the bag fell open like a flower blooming and Althea had to cover her mouth to stifle her surprise and shock.

"You have to hurry, Miss," Cook whispered. "No telling what might happen." He dropped to a knee and pulled off Mary's well-worn, thin slippers from Althea's foot while two of his helpers grabbed a boot each to wrap and tie them around her legs as she sat stunned.

She took a deep breath, the first full-bellied breath she'd had since Lady Aldergrove arrived, then tested the wards farther.

"Magic," she whispered. No answering blow came. She tried one thing more. "I've been bespelled," she whispered to Cook.

"An' don't we know it," he answered softly.

A shriek came hurtling down the stairs from above.

"An' herself to follow. Run, girl, don't look back!" He hissed and pushed Althea out the servants door and into the snow.

Althea ran, not looking where she was going, except to know she was headed for town, and nearly bowled over a stranger running headlong towards the house.

"Oh no, sir, you mustn't. She's a terrible witch," Althea tried to save him.

"Indeed she is, Miss. Get you hence, we will handle the Missus." He swatted her rump to get her going and then continued towards the house.

Althea ran, indignant at the man's presumption, but more fearful of what Lady Aldergrove would do to her next, if she were caught. Her heart pounded, and for the first time, Althea took great wheezing breaths to keep going. *I sound like a bellows,* she laughed as she ran, sounding quite mad, and fighting off hysteria only by pushing herself to run harder. She hiked up her skirts and ran to the Post as though the hounds of hell were after her.

When she finally got there she gasped in air, unable to speak, making the groom impatient waiting for her to catch her breath.

She pulled the card from her pocket and pointed at the word 'Weatherbys' while she struggled with, and revelled in, catching her breath. In a blink, Edna and Mark Weatherby appeared on either side of her and guided her into a carriage. In moments it lurched away from the Post and hurtled down the lane, the driver shouting warnings to all to make way.

Once Althea's heart slowed and her breathing came easier, she blinked slowly and looked around her, as though seeing the carriage for the first time and wondering how she'd got there. The blood drained from her face and she felt a well open up inside her, a great many wails climbing up from the pit of it on their long journey to get out. As she opened her mouth, Mark Weatherby handed her a hip flask.

"Oh no you don't, young Lady. Drink this. Take a good gulp and then three long breaths."

Althea was already obeying as Edna turned fiery eyes on her husband. "This is your first act as Guardian? Giving her alcohol?"

"You forget, my dear, I came to you only after the war. I've seen men come away from battle, or returned to us from god forsaken prisons of the enemy." He tilted his head towards Althea without looking at her. "She's no different. The shock and horror she's about to unleash is the same. The whiskey only takes the edge off it, for a time."

Mute, Althea held the flask out to him.

"One more big swallow, Lass. It will help," he commanded.

Althea obeyed, and handed it back.

"Good Lass. Smart enough to see sense when it is plain before you. Now you rest. You're safe." He tossed a cushion into the corner of the bench she sat on. "Curl up. We'll watch over you."

Althea's eyelids grew heavy, and she had barely got her feet up before sleep pulled her down into the dark.

She awoke twice, after a particularly violent lurch of the carriage, only to find the Weatherbys there with a quiet word of reassurance and an urging to sleep. The third time she woke there was no nodding back off again, for they were nearing their destination.

Althea could not have slept even a minute more anyway. Already she was sore from too long lying about, and a trickle of excitement was quickly overtaking her fears. She sat up and rubbed her face and then turned bright eyes on her rescuers.

"No words could be thanks enough for what you have done," she began.

"Hush, Lass. No thanks are owed." Mark patted her knee.

Althea looked down at her divine boots. "I'll work off the value of these. I haven't a penny to pay you with, but I can mend and clean."

Mark smiled at her as he would his own child. "We hear you have many a skill, but that won't be necessary, I assure you."

Althea withdrew and tilted her head, suddenly wary.

Edna read the look easily and paled. "Oh my dear child, not that too?"

Althea looked more like a cornered animal than a noble's ward.

"Mark, love, we'd best tell her all of it before we arrive. The poor girl's been tampered with and fears the worst."

"How?" Althea asked. "How could you possibly know?"

"I've seen it too often not to recognize. Fear not, there will be none of that where we are going."

"Where are we going?"

"To the Durstons at Longview. They are expecting us."

Edna told Althea what they had done, and where they were going and why as quickly as possible. The explanation helped her keep her temper, allowing her to focus on what was to be done, rather than what had been done. It salved her conscience some, hearing her own voice outline the measures they'd taken to free Althea, though a small voice still reproached 'not soon enough'.

Althea seemed to accept her words at face value.

"Then I say again, no words would be enough, and I will do all I can to honour my debts."

∿•∿

The first few days at Longview were a frustrating confusion for Althea. She kept company with the exalted guild members, knowing herself to be vastly inferior, yet they attended her as though she were an honoured guest. They insisted she rest and take her ease however best suited her. Elizabeth Durston was solicitous at first, giving Althea leave to explore, to play as often as she like in the music room, giving her a full tour of the house and grounds, so Althea would not fear getting turned around, and providing a full wardrobe of gowns, and the strange loose-fitting flowing tunics and trews they all wore after dinner. Then Mrs. Durston retreated, giving Althea time and space to heal and find her feet.

The servants were enchanted. Just as in the Wentworth's house, and in the house the Weatherbys had rented, they delighted in her consideration, and the way she asked after them, their health and families. Where she was shy and confused by the nobles, she could not have avoided the servants, and did not wish to, feeling far more comfortable among them than in the company of her rescuers.

Shameful of me, Althea accused, realising they may easily interpret her behaviour as ungrateful.

She needn't have worried. Just as before, the servants reported to their betters, to John specifically, since this was his house, and the others respected Althea's need for something familiar.

As before, Althea was drawn to the music room, and any in the house in earshot gathered to listen. The Durstons and Weatherbys joined them, almost giving everyone away as the servants shot up to resume their duties before being waved down by Elizabeth. Althea's fingers faltered.

"Is someone there?"

Alan, the butler, was quick to respond, stepping into the music room. "Sorry miss, just me, on my way to the kitchen. Didn't mean to disturb you." He bowed himself out again and resumed his post at the foot of the stairs.

John beamed at him and nodded. Althea's music resumed.

That night in bed, John commented on it. "There's no small measure of magic in her playing."

"I suspected as much," nodded Elizabeth. "You know how hard it is for me to detect magic of another element, I couldn't be sure."

"It is a good thing for all of us that she's found a way to channel it. Now that the spell is broken, the amount of power available to her is immense. She's a Master else I am a toad."

Elizabeth smiled and kissed him then. "Since you haven't transformed at all, I must assume you are a prince already, not a toad, and therefore, she is a Master."

John shuddered. "I haven't even a fraction of her power. How ever will I train her?"

Althea corrected her manners on the third day, attending breakfast with the others, rather than begging for scraps in the kitchen before the household awoke. She'd bathed in cold water from a pump, and dressed herself carefully, without troubling the staff. Now she sat demurely at table and thanked her hosts once again, begging some way to repay their kindness and generosity.

John took the opening. "First of all, you must let me train you."

"Sir?"

"No, not 'sir' to you."

Edna got Althea's attention then. "We are very pleased to inform you, Miss Chambers, that you come from a very good family. The men all loyal servants of HRMs Navy, the ladies not short on nobility, including your dearly departed mother. Your blood is as blue as anyone's, and your uncle, Lieutenant Matthew Chambers, was delighted to discover you are alive and as well as could be expected. He and his wife are prepared to assume Guardianship of you whenever you are ready."

"Which you are not, yet." John concluded. "You've far too much to learn about magic before you are safe to leave."

Althea blinked. "I am still in danger then?"

"More accurate to say you are a danger to others. Have you any idea how much power you command, Miss Chambers?"

Althea shook her head.

"A tremendous amount, and you must learn how to use it and bank it, before we can unleash you upon the world."

"Oh dear," she bit her lip. "Have I-?"

"Done anything yet? No. But I suspect that is only because you have been so unused to being able to touch it or even think about it until now."

"I am a troublesome houseguest, aren't I?"

Elizabeth smiled. "Just the opposite, Miss Chambers, I assure you." She winked.

Althea turned back to John. "Very well, I accept, though it only makes my debt to you greater."

"If you can learn what I have to teach, and begin to use it, then there is no debt between us."

Althea nodded, rather than openly disagree with him. Between her freedom and his tutelage, she knew the debt remained, but pushed it aside for now, trusting an opportunity would present itself.

After breakfast, John invited Althea out to the greenhouse to begin her training. She'd changed into the strange yet comfortable tunic and trews they favoured at his suggestion, and appeared promptly, immediately feeling at ease among the thriving plants that grew everywhere, most overreaching their pots and plots.

"What a wonderful place, Mr. Durston," Althea breathed, bending low to sniff a blossom.

"I am glad you think so, Miss Chambers, for we will be spending much of our winter here."

Althea let her eyes drink in the leaves and stems around her, stopping along the cultivated path that wound round the hothouse. When she reached the roses growing along the wall opposite the entrance she paused to admire them.

A pair of eyes looked back at her from between the branches. Althea blinked, certain her eyes were playing tricks on her. The pair of eyes blinked in response. Althea looked over her shoulder for Mr. Durston. The concealed eyes followed her gaze.

"Ah, yes. The elementals. I hoped to introduce you today. Truthfully, it has been all I could do to get them to wait, for they are all very eager to meet you." John stared past her to the rosebushes. "It's all right, come on out and say hello, only be slow, we don't want to frighten our guest."

Althea turned back to the roses to see a squat little man hobble out from among the thorns. He took off his little blue cap and bowed deeply before her. Althea beamed and dropped him an equally formal curtsy.

"Master," the little man acknowledged Althea as she stood straight, his voice unnaturally large for such a tiny body.

"I think you mean 'mistress', sir, or else you mean Mr. Durston here."

The gnome laughed silently.

John came to stand beside Althea. "No, Miss Chambers, he meant precisely what he said. You are an Elemental Master, or will be once you are trained. No doubt of it. The amount of power that seeks you out is too great for you to be anything less."

Althea looked from John to the elemental, who remained bowed, and decided. She knelt on the path, so that she no longer loomed over the gnome, and could look him in the face.

"Please stand up, you will grow awfully sore remaining stooped so."

The gnome straightened with surprise written in all his features.

"I doubt very much that I would make a very good Master to anyone, sir," she addressed the gnome. "But I could very much use a friend, if you were willing."

The gnome danced in place and laughed his silent laugh, delighted.

"Oh, she will be a wonderful Master!" He chuckled at Mr. Durston. "Wonderful, wonderful, I must tell the others. Thank you Durston for bringing her to us at last." Then the little gnome dove into the dirt as Althea might dive into a lake, and vanished.

Althea was so enchanted by the one little gnome that she hadn't noticed the dozens of elementals that crept from their hiding places to stand around her, at the edges of every boundary in the garden. When she turned her head to ask Mr. Durston about the exchange her eyes grew wide, and she sat down with her back pressed against the box holding the roses.

"Mr. Durston?" she asked, slightly alarmed.

"I told you they were eager to meet you, Miss Chambers."

Thinking it rude to talk about them as though they were not there, she directed the next sentence to the elementals.

"But there are so many of you," she looked at each of them, seeing different kinds of creatures everywhere. Some looked like the first, squat, but very human-like, others looked like exaggerated garden animals, toads and squirrels and the like, still others were like pictures out of children's books, wholly fantastic with too many arms and legs, or eyes at the ends of antennae, or gaping mouths and long tails.

A bird-like creature flew slowly towards her. Althea held up her hand for the elemental to land on.

"Hello," she smiled.

"Hello mast-t-t-err," the creature chirped the t's and trilled the r. "We are verrry happy to meet-t-t you."

"I am very happy to meet you, too. Do you speak for everyone here?"

The little bird bobbed his head once.

"Then, just to be clear, I shall tell you the same as I told my friend a moment ago. I am no Master, but I can be a good friend, if you'll let me."

The bird-like elemental bobbed his head again, then launched from her hand to fly a circle around her. He landed lightly on her shoulder and nuzzled her cheek with his head.

"Yes, we would like that-t-t verrry much."

John looked on, bemused. "Do you know, I had to beg and tempt and bribe before an elemental would come to me?" he told Althea as she stroked the bird with her first finger. She looked up at him from her sitting position on the floor where all the elementals were slowly coming closer.

"Oh dear, I hope I haven't offended you, Mr. Durston."

He smiled, shaking his head. "Not at all, Miss Chambers, though I think you may have broken every rule I've ever been taught about dealing with magical creatures. I suppose, with power as great as yours, the rules need not apply."

Not understanding at all what he meant, Althea returned her attention to all the creatures that surrounded her. She pulled her legs up, to make more lap and sit more comfortably, then smoothed her tunic and trews, that no wrinkles would make treacherous folds where a tiny hand, paw, tail, or wing might get caught.

"Don't be afraid, little ones. Come, take your fill of me. I can see how curious you are."

They needed no further invitation, and practically swarmed her, crawling up into her lap, some up her arms, others into her hair, unpinning it and wrapping themselves in her curls. She laughed, her heart full, as though playing with a litter of puppies.

The bird who had claimed her shoulder preened her gently then whispered in her ear, "a verrry good mast-t-t-err you will be. We shall all come with you wherrreverrr you go."

"You mustn't leave Mr. Durston. He has made you such a beautiful place to stay in winter, surely, you must want to be here above any other place."

John's eyes danced with light. "Fear not, Miss Chambers. I know well that elementals are as drawn to power as power is drawn to you. I shall not suffer any harm. In fact, these have only arrived since you did."

"But how is it that I have never seen any before?"

John turned to a human-like lady who straggled behind the others. She was maybe a hand's length tall, and seemed somehow older than the others. John stooped and placed his hand palm up before her. She accepted his offer and climbed up. He brought her to Althea who held up both palms to receive the elemental.

"We couldn't get near you without hurting you, Master. When you were a wee babe, before the curse, we played all around you, making you laugh, whenever your mother could not attend you. But then she died and the curse came, and whenever we got too close you'd cry and cry. It wasn't until you were a bit older we figured out why. Then we stayed far enough away to keep from triggering the curse. We're sorry we hurt you, Master." The lady bowed her head.

Althea lifted the elemental up higher so she could look into those downcast eyes.

"Please don't bow to me. I was too young then to remember the pain now. You couldn't have known, and I couldn't have told you."

"You've a gracious heart, Master," the elemental appeared as though washed clean by Althea's words, her forgiveness bathing their spirits free of a burden long carried.

John chuckled, choosing to break the sombre mood, as all the elementals had stilled when the old one began to speak. "I have never seen a magician cuddled up with dozens of elementals in all my life. You are extraordinary, Miss Chambers."

Althea blushed and looked at all her new friends with hope.

"I'm sorry to say this, but we should retreat to the work room for a time," he finished.

All eyes turned up to Althea then, their expressions, young and old, like those of children.

"I will come back as soon as I can. I promise. But first I must go learn as much as I can, so I don't hurt anyone, or any of you, in my ignorance."

To a one they gave her some gesture of affection as they climbed off of her and returned to the earth and leaves in the garden. Althea sat still, careful not to bump or jar any of them as they climbed and tumbled off and away. When she was certain they were all safe, she stood, brushing off her seat.

"Lead on, Mr. Durston, I should very much like to see what constitutes a magician's work room."

When the time came to prepare for dinner, Althea felt her head was ready to split open. Mr. Durston had attempted to condense weeks of teaching into a single day, and Althea strove to keep up, feeling guilty for every extra minute it took her to understand.

Despite her protestations that the servants not fuss over her, she had a lady's maid insist on helping her into a gown that was pure confection, and pile her hair, all undone by the elementals, into a whimsy of curls that hung fetchingly about her face and neck.

The guild gathered early, wanting to meet before Althea joined them for dinner.

"You wouldn't have believed it," John told them of Althea's introduction to the elementals. "My teacher was exasperated by my inability to get an elemental's attention. She had them captivated in her first words. All the wards and boundaries I'd been taught to make when calling an elemental simply didn't apply to her."

Edna grew concerned. "Those boundaries are there to keep the magician safe from the spirits. How could you let her among them unprotected?"

"You didn't see them when she first arrived. They were like children whose favourite aunt has come to visit. Besides, they adore her, and not a one would hurt her." John assured them, seeing their concern.

"I don't know, my love," even Elizabeth was worried. "What if she should meet an elemental who is not bewitched by her charm?"

"The others would protect her, I am certain of it."

"It won't do any harm to teach her, John," Mark said quietly. "Unless she isn't bright enough to learn?" He raised his eyebrows, inquiring.

"Oh, she's bright enough. I think she will outstrip all I can teach her in a matter of weeks, not months, as I originally thought." John looked around the room to find all of them sitting back in their chairs, stunned speechless.

It was then that Althea appeared in the doorway. All eyes turned to her, and again they were silenced. The work of the maid coupled with Elizabeth's fine taste in gowns combined to transform Althea from merely pretty to breath-taking.

She stood there, uncertain. "I hope I haven't interrupted, or kept you waiting."

Edna was the first to recover, and stood, reminding the gentlemen to stand as well. "Not at all, Miss Chambers, do sit down," she indicated the chair beside her. "You look lovely."

Althea blushed, and thanked her. "Mrs. Durston was generous in her choice of loaned garments." Althea deflected the praise to Elizabeth as she sat down.

"John tells us you are an excellent student, and a charmer of elementals, besides," Mark opened.

"I hope very much to prove worthy of Mr. Durston's generosity as well."

"John," Mr. Durston said. "You are among friends, Miss Chambers. I am John to my friends."

The rest nodded and offered their given names.

"Then you must all call me Althea."

They were in the worst of February when John professed Althea's studies complete. She'd managed to learn wards and protections, and the basics of enchantment, though she adamantly refused to learn any offensive magics. Where she excelled was with those things unique to Earth magic. Making things grow, nurturing the energy and life within even the most dormant, reading and following the veins of power that flowed underground, even in areas hidden.

John had no doubt that if necessary, Althea could even find power in a desert, or rather, it would find her.

Most promising, as far as John was concerned, was Althea's insistence on purifying the lands around Longview. He'd sensed some whiff of taint, but couldn't find the source, nor could he heal the areas affected by blight. But Althea had found them, and could not abide them, so she followed them to their source and asked her elementals if they could help her cleanse it.

They were so remorseful when they had to admit they couldn't. When it finally came to light that they too would be poisoned by the effort, it was Althea's turn for remorse.

"If I'd any idea what I was asking, I wouldn't have asked," she recounted the conversation to John and he only shook his head.

"Any other magician asking that of them would have been attacked, swarmed by every elemental in the area no matter whether he knew the consequences to the creatures or not." He looked at Althea thoughtfully then. "No doubt about it, Althea. Your elementals don't just obey you, they love you."

"They certainly do not 'obey', John, for I don't command them. Not ever."

"Most magicians would call you foolhardy for that. They'd advise you to rule, wisely if you could, with an iron fist if you couldn't." John admonished.

Althea shrugged. "I am no ruler, and I know all too well what it is like to be forced into obedience by magic. I won't do that. Not to them. Not to anyone."

It wasn't until the roads and weather cleared that Peter made an appearance at Longview. The guild had sent letters, of course, but only received the briefest of replies in return. He arrived one evening shortly before supper, and was chatting amiably with Mark when Althea made her entrance.

The guild had become inured to her splendour, so Mark was amused by the shock on Peter's face as she arrived.

"Mr. Croft, what an unexpected pleasure," she greeted him. "I am so glad to finally be able to thank you for your part in my deliverance." She curtsied low before him. "I don't know how I shall ever be able to repay you."

Peter stood there, his mouth hanging open as he stared at her. Mark elbowed him lightly in the ribs.

"Uh," Peter blinked himself awake. "There is no debt, Miss Chambers. Aldergrove would have had to have been put down eventually. She was quite mad, even before. You only gave us cause to do what should have been done sooner." His face grew gray as he spoke, remembering. "Grim business it was." Then he swallowed and brightened. "But more than small good came of it, at least as far as you're concerned, Miss Chambers."

Peter glanced at Mark before turning back to Althea. "But perhaps that is better spoken of privately."

Mark stood, graciously excusing himself.

Peter waved her to a chair then sat across from her, still a bit stunned by her appearance.

Althea bit her tongue. While she wanted to call Mr. Croft on his poor manners, staring as he did, she did not want a replay of their first meeting.

"I'm sorry, Miss Chambers, I simply cannot get over your transformation."

Althea smiled, "Elizabeth's lavish generosity, and a maid who always wished for a doll with long hair to play with as a child." She became as she had been all those times George Hamlin had watched her. A fine lady, with amusement dancing just beneath the skin, just waiting for a chance to peek out. It was then that Peter saw the Miss Chambers George had waxed eloquent about. Again he was stunned.

"How thoughtless of me," Althea said, turning the conversation abruptly. "Here you've travelled who knows how far or in what conditions today. You must be famished and exhausted." She rose from her seat, causing Peter to do the same. "Come, let us to dinner. Whatever news you have can surely wait until morning."

Peter remained speechless and mutely followed her to the dining room.

Dinner passed with the usual conversation among the guild, while Peter remained quiet throughout, watching Althea, captivated by the changes in her, and suddenly not the least bit put off by her opposing element, though she fairly glowed with it.

As the plates were cleared Althea looked to John.

"With your permission, I think I'd like to make the rounds of the estate."

John cocked his head. "You sense something?"

"I am sure it is nothing but I will feel better for having checked."

John nodded. "By all means, Althea, with my thanks."

Althea curtsied her way out the door and to her rooms to change. While she was not immune to the delight and greed Elizabeth's fine gowns inspired, she found she preferred the strange yet comfortable post-dinner attire the guild seemed so fond of. A few moments of fighting with laces and tiny buttons, and she was comfortably wrapped in silk-lined wool, with her magnificent boots besides.

She stepped out into the winter air, and breathed in the evening. All the world slept and Althea took a moment of peace.

"Master?" A gnome appeared at her feet.

"Hello, my friend. How are you this evening?"

The gnomes always preened when she asked after them, and she loved to see the tiny people puff themselves up to their full six-inch height.

"Very well, Master, thank you. But, why are you out here, at this time of night?"

Althea smiled as she knelt down in the snow to make herself less of a looming giant. "Would you believe me if I said it was because it felt right?"

The gnome's face split into a huge grin, with large teeth poking out. "Such is the way of the Master, Master."

Althea nodded. "Well and good. Were you on your way somewhere that I interrupted?"

"No, Master."

"Then would you like to keep me company while I walk the grounds?"

"Yes, Master."

Althea held out her hand for the gnome to hop into, then placed him on her shoulder, inside her cloak so he could see out and stay warm at once. The gnome nestled himself in, wrapping himself in her hair and tucking close to her neck.

"I never would have imagined this," Althea mused as she checked the nearest wards, finding nothing amiss.

"What, Master?"

"Living fine, elementals, you, all so affectionate. If you had told me that one person could be so well tended, I'd scarce have believed you." She gave a gentle squeeze of her shoulder.

"You are a Master, a good one, why shouldn't we prefer you above others?"

Althea raised an eyebrow. "I'm sure it doesn't hurt that I am local, at least for the time being."

The gnome snorted. "Distance is of no consequence to us. When we choose, we have physical bodies. When we don't, we are energy, light, no heavier nor slower than a thought."

Althea checked the next set of wards carefully, satisfied that they had not been disturbed either.

"You might try the west wall, Master," the gnome's voice was rich with amusement and heavy with knowing something she did not.

"So there is something," she accused lightly. "You might have told me."

"And you might have asked, Master."

Althea laughed at his nerve.

"Very well, can you tell me what I shall find on the west wall?"

"No, Master."

"Do you know if it is something bad? Should I call the others to come out and help?"

"No, Master. The others will not be needed."

"Should I be afraid?"

"With an army of elementals no more than a wish away? Not hardly, Master."

Althea nodded and headed west, away from the house. As she approached she could feel a growing sense of wrongness. Something was damaged, tainted, something great brought low and diminished. Althea stepped carefully, making little sound as she homed in on where the feeling was strongest. As she cleared a bend in the path, the moonlight bathed the place, as though a single ray shone down on this spot deliberately.

There, in the centre of the pool of light lay a wolf, wounded, still, in the snow. Neither foolish nor fearful, Althea approached slowly, staying in the wolf's sight line. She murmured softly to him, while trickling a thread of magic into him. Some gaping wound opened his ribs, while his hind leg was little better than hamburger from being caught in a trap. The bone gleamed in the light, exposed.

Althea knelt beside the wolf who was mostly unaware of the world, his remaining breaths countable on two hands. Althea stifled her anger and outrage, for those were man-made wounds, and cruelly done. If they'd had sense, or decency, they would have put the poor creature out of his misery. Instead, they let him loose to suffer until he died. Althea laid hands on the wolf. He didn't even stir.

She pulled the magic into his body, giving it strength to fight for life. She reminded bone and muscle what it was like to be whole and tugged gently at the wounds to close them, working from the deepest injuries and slowly coming towards the skin, leaving neatly knit tissue in her wake.

The wolf began to grow restless and Althea carefully took her hands away, shuffled backwards, then stood slowly, all the while continuing to use her magic to heal him.

He stood, stronger than he had any right to be, considering his state only moments before. He looked at her a long moment, as though deciding. Althea pulled more power to feed his recovery. Hesitantly, the wolf stepped one step towards her. He wasn't hunched, the mane of hair around his neck had not puffed out, both sure signs of a hunter about to attack.

Althea held her ground, not moving, still trickling healing into the wolf, though hardly any was needed now, for his injuries were closed, little more than scars that would fade in time.

The wolf took another step.

The one thing he will be is hungry, Althea realised too late. *Nothing I could do about that. It is not as though I walk about with a brace of rabbits over my shoulder.*

The wolf stepped forward again. Two more steps and his muzzle would be in range of her hands, grown cold, exposed to the winter evening.

Althea dared not speak to the gnome on her shoulder. Her voice might spook the wolf into attacking her. No matter what he'd said about being a wish away, while Althea didn't relish being wolf supper, she also couldn't ask them to hurt this massive, noble creature she'd just fought to save.

Althea waited.

The wolf closed the distance between them and brought his nose to her hand. Treating him as she would a known and friendly dog, she held her hand open, letting him sniff her. Finally he licked her fingers and pushed his head into her hand, obviously wanting a scratch.

Althea breathed a sigh of relief as she rubbed his ears and his tail began to wag.

"Nicely done, Master," the gnome whispered in her ear.

"Hmm," Althea kept her voice soft to keep from startling the wolf.

"We had faith in you, Master, but we had to be certain."

Althea's voice remained low and even, but the bulge of her cheek pressed against the gnome to tell him she was smiling. "A test, was it?"

"Yes, Master. One you passed beyond our hopes."

"You didn't harm this glorious creature just to test me," Althea was concerned, but kept calm, attentive to the wolf who continued to ask for and receive affection.

"We only took advantage of opportunity. Someone else did this, Master," the gnome assured her.

Just then the wolf took to hijinks, cavorting away from them a few feet, into the snow. He danced and dodged rather like a puppy hoping for a ball to be thrown for him to chase.

Althea chuckled. "I dare say we are both of us, all of us, safe enough now." She turned back to the path that led her here, satisfied that the wolf was well. A spray of snow flew beside her as the wolf plunged towards her. His head was as tall as her waist and he looked up at her with bright eyes and his tongue hanging out. Althea's heart pounded suddenly in her ears, shot with adrenaline, as she feared he'd turned on her and was set to attack, but the goofy look on his face shook the fear from her and made her laugh.

"It seems you have a new pet, Master."

"Oh no. Wolves, no matter how magnificent," she patted the wolf's head, "are not pets."

He accompanied them as far as the barn, where the horses caught his scent and grew restless, afraid.

Althea pointed back the way they came. "Off with you, go."

The wolf rolled over, exposing his belly, hopefully.

Althea kneeled and rubbed it affectionately then stood and pointed once again. "Thank you for the escort, you've had your extra measure of love, now go."

The wolf stood, licked her hand, and loped away, tail high.

"Well, my friend, that was certainly an evening to remember. I thank you for your company and your council."

"Always my pleasure, Master," the gnome spoke softly in her ear then vanished in a breath of wind leaving the head of her cloak.

Althea stepped back into the house and headed to her rooms in search of her bed.

∽∾⤫

When morning came, Althea found herself unusually tired and loathe to rise. Her lethargy showed at breakfast, and John grew concerned.

"By the look of you, you did find something last night. When you didn't seek anyone out, I assumed all was well. Perhaps I shouldn't have."

Althea mustered a wan smile. "No need to worry, John. Just an injured animal in need of a little magic to heal."

Peter watched her, but said nothing, afraid to be too solicitous.

"Ah," John nodded, remembering now that his teacher, a Master, had told him the story of being tested by the elementals with something similar. The choice whether to put a dying creature out of its misery or to try to bring it back to health, in the eyes of the elementals, was a defining one.

Elizabeth, coming late to breakfast, took one look at Althea and exclaimed, "good gracious! What happened to you?"

Peter sat shocked by their familiarity, but kept his mouth shut.

"Earth Master's test," John summed up for her.

Elizabeth looked at Althea again. "Heavens, what did they ask you to heal, a woolly mammoth?"

Althea chuckled and shook her head. "Wolf," she held her hand up, "this high at his head."

Elizabeth's eyes grew large. "Right then, change in the dinner menu. Excuse me." She whisked out of the room.

"What was that about?"

Mark answered, "great magic drains your body of minerals and vitamins. Which ones depend on your element. After a great working it is important to replenish them quickly to keep from getting ill." He tilted his head towards John. "Living with an Earth herself, Elizabeth knows just what you need, and will make sure you get plenty of it at dinner."

"Don't exaggerate, Mark," John said, tucking into his food, "I could no more work a great magic than huff and puff and blow your house down. Elizabeth has no need to know what a great magic will cost an Earth." John smiled self-deprecatingly at Althea across the table as he chewed.

"Still, she seems to have an idea," Mark said to his plate, not wishing to argue.

"Miss Chambers," Peter finally spoke up. "Perhaps we could resume our discussion of yesterday? In the parlour?"

"We shall be forever at odds, Mr. Croft. When you are well, I am poorly and vice versa. Were I especially good, I might always wish myself ill that you might benefit." She gave a tiny shrug and offered a wan smile. "Alas, I am not so good as that." She rose from her chair. "If you'll excuse us?" She offered to the table.

Edna watched their departure with a shrewd eye. "Mark?" She gave him a significant look.

"Aye," he nodded and turned his attention back to his plate.

In the parlour, they resumed their seats from the eve before.

"Miss Chambers."

"Althea, please. It seems odd to be 'Althea' to everyone else and 'Miss Chambers' to you," she interrupted him.

Peter nodded. "Very well, Althea," her name sounded different in his mouth, as though laden with weight. "When we went through Lady Aldergroves possessions, we found your father's last wishes. We pressed Henry Wentworth for information, and discovered a rather sordid story."

Althea grimaced. "The kind one might find in a novel, I suppose?"

"I'm afraid so." Peter paused, trying to find words that would cause her less grief, at least no more grief than necessary. His struggle showed on his face.

"Mr. Croft."

"Peter," he looked at her pointedly.

Althea conceded with a nod. "Peter, do not fear for how I shall receive the news. I find the best way is to simply begin from the beginning and let the story tell itself." She sat still and quiet then, receptive to whatever tale he would tell.

"Very well," he took a breath. "The Aldergroves and Chambers had an understanding. When your father, Captain Edward Chambers was commissioned a rated ship, he and Miss Catherine Aldergrove would wed. While he was Captain, his ship, HRMs Reliant, was damaged, and they put in at Falmouth for repairs. There, your father met, fell in love with, and married Miss Angelina Fairchild. You followed soon after, though your father had gone home, shared his news, and was back at sea by that time. Angelina fell suddenly ill, and the people whispered of dark magic at work. Nothing could be proven, of course. When a sudden and uncanny storm swallowed Edward's ship, it struck with enough warning for him to get everyone else to safety, while he went down with his ship." Peter paused and looked to Althea.

She nodded, encouraging him to continue.

"He'd drawn up papers, to make sure you and your mother were provided for, and gave them to a then Corporal Henry Wentworth. Corporal Wentworth had long admired Catherine Aldergrove, but she was body and soul for Edward.

When Edward returned with news of Angelina, Catherine was heartbroken, and vowed revenge. Wentworth, outraged on her behalf, shared her desire to see Edward destroyed. So when your father's final wishes fell into his hands, he took them to Catherine. They concealed the papers and Henry assumed custody. The rest of your tale, you know. What you don't know is this."

Peter reached into a pocket and produced a stack of papers.

"Captain Chambers settled his entire estate upon you, including title, rank, and lands, and named his brother, your uncle, Lieutenant Matthew Chambers your Guardian. Angelina brought more nobility with her than Edward realised, being the second daughter of Duke Fairchild. Angelina's sister, Sarah, passed away a few years ago, childless, making you the last descendent of the Fairchild line."

Althea sat still for a long moment, letting the news sink in. "I am the last," she mourned.

Peter nodded. "Indeed you are. Duchess. Your grace." He handed her the papers.

Althea read them carefully, mindful of how tired she was, and so took no small amount of time. Once she read the last, she blinked slowly.

"If you'll excuse me, Peter, I believe I have some correspondence to take care of."

"Yes, your grace."

"Oh, leave off of that, and not a word to anyone. This," she waved the papers, "is by no means certain."

Peter's expression was unfathomable.

George arrived midday the same day as Althea received her news from Peter. He came unannounced but not unexpected, as all the guild had been on the lookout for him for weeks. But despite their vigilance, he came upon them unawares as they gathered like spectres around the music room to hear Althea play.

Elizabeth had left standing orders that any and all might sit and listen, while she played, provided Althea was never disturbed. This was how George came upon them, himself moved to silence by the notes thundering, rising, and crashing down like a heaven-sent storm, Althea's power laced through the music, in the spaces between the notes.

He sat down hard at the outer edge of the group, between Althea's maid and the butler. The butler nodded to him before turning back to the music, which wound and wailed like an angry wind, the creak of a ship tossed at sea in the creak of the bench as Althea's weight shifted. One of the staff, a former seafarer himself, unconsciously planted his feet farther apart, bracing for the buck of the imaginary ship beneath him.

The storm raged, the ship was lost, and all the sea grown calm, as the notes decrescendoed. Then the loss began. The quiet weeping as sobs tripped haltingly down the keys. The longing, for comrades lost, for land, for family. The great unfairness, that some should live, while others perish, that all the world should be smashed, like a child's toy, and the universe indifferent to the pain of men. Althea's music told the story, her father's story, her story, a metaphorical story, shared by too many.

The right hand trilled. Land. Hope. The left hand pulsed in time with perpetual waves, pushing her ever closer to shore, until, on land, she rested, languorously making angels in the sand, warm sun on the skin. She wound down, ending on a major chord, a promise, of something simple, something better. She let the chord hang in the air and waited.

Silently, the staff crept away, with bows and curtsies to Lady Elizabeth, who nodded and pressed a finger to her lips. Then she turned to find George standing in the hallway and almost gave them away in her surprise. She pressed both hands to her mouth, then shooed him away in front of her.

The guild gathered in the parlour, far away from the music room, where George was greeted warmly.

"When did you hire such a musician?" He asked once all the pleasantries had passed.

Elizabeth smiled. "That is no hireling, George. That is Miss Althea Chambers."

George sat stunned.

"Didn't know her so well as you thought, eh, old boy?" Peter ribbed him, only half joking.

Edna looked sharply at Mark who only nodded.

George was so stupefied by Althea's sudden talent that he missed the bark in Peter's words.

Elizabeth, ever the Water mage, sought to smooth things over. "We've only a few more minutes before she makes an appearance. She recovers quickly from her performances. I suggest you prepare yourself as best you can, George, for you may find her changed since last you saw her."

George assumed the worst, not knowing how her battle for freedom had left her, nor her journey here, nor her teaching. Only a few lines of 'she arrived safe as could be expected', and 'her magical studies frustrate poor John daily', left George woefully unprepared for Althea's entrance.

Her hair was piled in curls atop her head, her face was flushed from her musical and magical exertion, her gown, another gift from Elizabeth, was simple, with elegant lines flowing around her figure and down to the floor. Her eyes lit with the smile that conquered her whole face when she saw George sitting, soon standing, along with the other men in the parlour.

"Mr. Hamlin, what a delight. I owe you more than I can ever repay for bringing me to the attention of your friends." She crossed the room, clasped his hands, and squeezed them before taking a seat near Edna. The men sat, and George remained speechless.

Again Elizabeth smoothed the silence by catching Althea up on George's travels to get here. "Will you be staying, George?" Elizabeth concluded.

"If it's not too much trouble," George stumbled through the dance steps.

"Not at all. We've rooms ready to receive you, which I hope you will find comfortable."

"I am certain there is not an uncomfortable room in your home, Lady Durston," George replied more easily, if more formally, now distracted from Althea.

"Perhaps you'd best see for yourself before you declare your satisfaction with the rooms. After such a journey, surely you'll need a rest." Lady Elizabeth rose, as did the men, and she led George out of the room.

Althea watched him leave, that same amusement lurking beneath her expression.

"Well, Althea," began John, "you look quite rejuvenated since this morning. Shall we visit the hothouse?"

Althea nodded, glad to visit with her elementals and do the Durstons any service as part of her repayment of their generosity. They left the Weatherbys and Peter in the parlour. As soon as Althea and John were out of earshot, Edna fairly pounced on Peter.

"Now you listen to me, Peter Adam Croft," she began, all Fire.

"Mrs. Weatherby," Mark warned.

"Don't you 'Mrs. Weatherby' me, you've seen what I've seen, and it needs sorting."

"Sorting, my love, not scorching."

Edna sighed. "Very well." She turned to face Peter. "You've an interest in her now, Peter."

Peter opened his mouth and then closed it again.

"While George had an interest in her then," Mark continued.

Edna shot him a seething glance. "Never mind her say in any of it, where her interest lies." She looked again at Peter. "There is no need to make trouble between you and your oldest friend. There are women enough in the world to go around. Women who would burst with joy at having you."

"But no women like that," Peter mourned already.

Edna snorted. "Don't be a romantic, Peter. It serves no one."

Mark slid his hand in hers and squeezed, silently calling her on her lie. She squeezed back, conceding the win. "At the very least, let her make her feelings known before you pursue her."

Peter nodded.

"Hello, my friends, what have we today?" Althea greeted the elementals as she and John entered the sun room. As usual, they flocked around her, flying to land on her shoulders and in her hair, or crowding around her skirts.

John stood back to watch and marvel.

Her favourite gnome appeared and climbed up her skirts to sit upon her right shoulder.

"Your wolf stays close, Master."

"Does he indeed? He's not upsetting the horses, I hope."

"No, Master."

"Nor poaching chickens?"

"No, Master."

"Children?"

"No, Master. He's being a gentleman in every way we could want."

"Good enough then." She turned to John. "I am not sure, but he may leave with me when I have exhausted your hospitality."

"Oh, aye. You have yourself a Guardian now, Althea. It was the same for the Master who taught me, and many others besides." John shrugged. "We are the slowest of the Elements. We don't dodge enemy attacks as well as the others, which may be why we tend to acquire Guardians more often than they do."

"He's right, Master," agreed the gnome.

"Well, so long as he behaves, he is welcome," Althea settled it. "So, John, what magic are we working today? A treat for the dinner table? Some pre-spring maintenance?"

John smiled. "Nothing today. You may be feeling better than you were at breakfast, but it is a false boost, and if you work any magic today you will surely do yourself damage." He shook his head. "Today is when you learn to take back what you gave. Today we just sit and rest and enjoy the fruits of our labours." He settled himself on a long chair and closed his eyes. "And there is no better place than here to bask in the glory of the Earth."

The gnome body-checked her cheek. "He is wise, Master. You should listen to him."

Althea chuckled. "I should, should I?"

"Yes, Master. You gave much of yourself to your Guardian. Now is a time to rest."

"Far be it from me to disagree with my friends and teachers," she quipped, and collected her Elementals to fall around her like puppies in a pile as she settled into a bench. She eased back into the armrest, surprisingly comfortable, and closed her eyes. She took a deep breath, and all the Elementals sighed with her, making her smile.

"You're right, John. This is just the place for an Earth to find peace."

"I know."

❧•❧

She received a reply from the lawyer sooner than from her uncle, which surprised her. According to the letter, the steward had been named heir to the Duke until a descendant could be found, and if Althea could prove her lineage, then the duchy would be hers. Althea paced in her rooms. She might leave the matter at that, her identity unproven, and make her way in the world, as she'd dreamed of. She might implore Mr. Hamlin's friends to help her prove her identity, but that would mean a greater debt, and she'd have to tell them why. Then there was the matter of what to do with all that wealth and responsibility once she had it. She might very well settle it upon her Uncle Matthew, or his offspring, if he had any, if only she knew their wishes.

Althea continued her pacing, playing a table tennis match in her mind over the choices, until a hesitant tap on her door jarred her from her consternation.

"Miss Chambers?"

Only one voice in the house still called her that. She opened the door to find Mr. Hamlin standing in the hall.

"I am sorry to disturb you."

"It does not follow that the interruption is unwelcome, Mr. Hamlin."

His eyes narrowed at that, suspecting Althea of flattery.

Althea took pity on him, and invited him downstairs for some tea. Once they were settled, Althea looked at him expectantly.

"I wonder if you'd given much thought to what you might do next?" Hamlin began, haltingly.

Amusement danced just beneath Althea's countenance. "As a matter of fact, I was doing just that when you knocked."

"Did you come to any conclusions?" Hamlin asked, fishing.

Althea sighed. "None. It is not wise to make decisions on little to no information, and I have rather less than that."

"Perhaps you could use some assistance?"

"I am indebted beyond what I can repay as it is. Besides, it is complicated," Althea frowned unwilling to speak her secret aloud.

Hamlin misinterpreted her meaning, and feared she had developed feelings for Peter, and was fearful of hurting him. "It always is where the heart is involved." He rose to leave, startling Althea.

"Mr. Hamlin, wait," she said to his back.

He stopped and turned to face her.

"Would you be so kind as to accompany me to the greenhouse?"

Despite the non sequitor, Hamlin's graces saved him, and he obliged her. Althea knew that John was in the work room today, and so they would not be disturbing him. They entered, and the elementals remained hidden, shy of the stranger in their midst.

Hamlin looked around him in shock, seeing plants in full bloom that should be barely budding this season. "What a wonder," he breathed.

"The hands of God and man together, encouraging life, Mr. Hamlin."

"I wouldn't think you would believe in God with what you've been through and learned."

"Not the hoary face of equal measures benevolence and wrath, no. But one cannot altogether dismiss the idea of 'something greater'."

"You refer to the calling you share with my friends."

"I do. That and more."

"You did not bring me here to discuss theology, Miss Chambers." Hamlin grew impatient.

Althea smothered a grin. "No, sir, I did not." She turned to the nearest growth of long grasses and placed a hand, palm up, in the dirt. "Do come out, my friends, if you've a mind to. I should like for you to meet someone."

Her favourite gnome appeared and climbed awkwardly onto her palm. She brought him up to face level. "Am I disturbing you?" she asked him.

"No, Master. We were none of us certain of your company, is all." He jerked his head towards Hamlin.

"Ah, my prudent friends. I have not seen this side of you before. I apologize if I've alarmed you. Do not be afraid. He is a friend." She helped the gnome onto her shoulder and turned to Hamlin, as others came out from their hiding places to be near her.

Hamlin stared in awe at all the little creatures that flocked to her.

"I brought you here, Mr. Hamlin, to show you where my heart is involved, as you put it." She looked at him pointedly, then crouched down to touch and embrace her army of elementals, her care and affection plain on her face and in her dancing eyes.

George was relieved, elated, and confused at once, watching her.

"Then you and Mr. Croft haven't, I mean, you don't have an," he paused, unable to say the rest.

Althea looked up then. "An understanding? With Peter? Heavens no."

"Peter?" Hamlin was stunned hearing Peter's Christian name in her mouth.

"Yes, Mr. Hamlin. Peter. Just as I am on a first name basis with everyone else here, save you, as you insist on calling me 'Miss Chambers', when my name is Althea."

"Althea."

She nodded.

"Then you must call me George."

"I should be delighted."

"Your thrice cursed 'should' again?"

Althea sighed. Her gnome nuzzled her cheek then, startling a laugh out of her.

"Too serious, you are, Master."

She mock-scowled.

"I assure you, George," she placed emphasis on his name. "The complications of my choices have very little to do with Peter, or anyone else, for that matter." She refrained from saying 'except my family' thinking of her uncle, only because she was not yet ready to share, nor did she want George to think it a veiled insult. He read far more into her words than she intended him to infer as it was.

"I see. I shall leave you to your, your..."

"Friends, George. They, like you, are my friends."

George nodded awkwardly, bowed, then fled the greenhouse with a stilted walk.

When he was gone, she sighed again.

"Master?" Her shoulder gnome inquired.

"Yes, friend?" She nuzzled him gently with her cheek.

"There may not be room for all of us in your affections, Master."

"Love is not a finite thing, my friend. It is not a locked room that can only hold so many, leaving others out in the cold. It is not a pie that can only allow one to have more if another has less." Althea arranged her skirts as she sat down to be closer to her elementals. "How is our Guardian today?"

"He is well, and well-behaved, Master, but surely wishes your company as we do."

"Then we should go out to see him this evening." Althea paused. "Well, I should. If you've other things to attend to, I won't pull you away from them."

"What of your other friend, Master? He who just left?"

"Mr. George?" she corrected herself.

"Yes, Master. Love may not be finite, but in the context of a human life, even a magician's life, time is."

Althea sat quietly then, enjoying her elementals, and ruminating over the gnome's words.

George sat in his rooms. The reality of magic now plain before him. If Althea came home as his wife, she would no more be able to hide the magic and magical creatures who adored her than he could stop breathing. His family already thought him mad for pursuing her. She was no more than a ward, after all, and their sense of nobility did not include marrying well beneath his rank. Worse, they would disdain her as they did his aberrant friends, as they called the guild. All of that might be tolerated, but the first time one of Althea's creatures made an appearance, Mater Hamlin would make a scene, and end their association.

No point in asking Althea to hide them, or better (worse?) give them up altogether. Both sides made it clear that their affection was wide and deep. One might agree to give up the others, but the others were unlikely to give up the one.

Yet she had nowhere else to go. If he didn't offer her a place, when her welcome wore thin with the guild, she would be on her own, penniless, and prey to all too many.

Peter spent no less time pondering Althea's fate. Her inimical element no longer affected him, and magic was natural among his people. But what would a duchess want with him, when his lands were far less than her duchy would be? Worse, it was George's obvious affection for her that started this misadventure to begin with. How could he, Lord Croft, vie for the same woman? Was he so morally bankrupt as to believe his own wants above another's? And his oldest friend at that?

Peter berated himself for every kind of fool and took his ill temper outside, that he might spare the household, and himself, any more discomfort.

Aunt Hannah's letter arrived only a few days later, giving Althea an excuse to escape the company that had become so awkward since George's arrival. The one was wounded, the other besotted, and both looked to her for salvation. She daren't nod at one without fearing the other would be hurt or start a scene. Peter's private barbs of 'your grace' didn't help matters.

So when Althea fair flew to her rooms, no one, save the suitors, was surprised. Edna pulled Elizabeth aside.

"No wonder she'd rather keep her own company, with those two badgering her every minute your John doesn't call her away for practice."

"She doesn't need the practice. He calls her away that she might have a moment of joy with her elementals," Elizabeth agreed.

"If you could have seen her when she made the carriage, leaving Briardowns, you'd be as like as I to crack their heads together. After all she's endured, now this," Edna fumed.

"Odds are we shall enjoy more music before this is settled," Elizabeth looked in the direction of the music room.

Edna snorted.

"You don't enjoy her playing?" Elizabeth looked surprised.

"With two tom cats prowling, both affected by her humour, her talent, and her magic?" Edna shook her head. "I much preferred it before either arrived."

Elizabeth patted her friend's hand. "It will pass, soon enough."

❧

My Darling Niece, how wonderful to finally hear from you. We'd only heard word of you, and that in the autumn. Your Uncle Matthew and I, you might imagine, were more than a little surprised to find out his brother had been blessed by a child so soon into his marriage, and no word of you these twenty some years. We long to establish our connection as soon as possible, for you are only too welcome in our home. Your uncle shall be home on leave in a few weeks' time and I am certain he would be overjoyed to find you with us already when he arrives.

The letter went on in that vein for some time before her aunt implored her to send word of her arrival at her earliest convenience, and closed the letter.

They, who would be more put out were also more ready to accept that she was who she claimed, than the lawyer representing the duchy. What was it to him if she were a fraud? Surely less than these people, whom she'd never met, who were nonetheless eager to open their doors to her and take responsibility for her for an indefinite time. Althea shook her head at the disparity and decided to visit her elementals before fixing the date of her departure.

As usual, they near swarmed her, only too eager to listen to her unburden, eager to bring a smile to her face with their antics, or any service she might ask of them.

"What think you of a journey, my friends?"

Her gnome laughed his silent laugh. "Distance means nothing to us, Master."

"Very well. But what if my destination has fouled ground, or people wary of you?"

"We cannot abide tainted earth, but rarely is a place wholly poisoned," he assured her.

"As for people, Master," the elderly lady approached in her languorous way, time of no consequence to one who has seen so much of it. "We hid from you, and others, still do from many. Don't fret there, Master. We shall be near enough, and no trouble to humans."

"What you *should* worry about," her gnome interjected, "is your Guardian, Master. He *will* follow you, and he may not be welcome where you are going."

"Oh dear," Althea bit her lip. There was no doubt of the reception he'd get, no matter where they went. The thought of feeding him if there weren't game around, or protecting him if there were wardens, made Althea's head begin to ache.

Again the gnome laughed his silent laugh. "He is no ordinary wolf, Master."

"Of that I am certain."

"He knows you are safe here, which is why he abides the distance between you. In a foreign place, he will not be so complacent. He will be by your side whether you will it or no. Best make up some tale to get him past anyone who might want him banned."

"Which will be everyone," Althea sighed.

Sensing the dip in her spirits, the elementals began again to cheer her, playing among the plants as much as in her hair, diving into the dirt as though it were water, to bob up again somewhere different. Soon they had her laughing again.

Her maid fretted over the state of her hair as she dressed for dinner, as Althea fussed over announcing her departure to her friends. What excuse could she give them? How could she repay their courage, charity, and generosity? How could she tell them her reasons? How could she not? Alas, the maid had set her curls long before Althea settled her mind.

She went down to the dining room still unresolved.

As the meal commenced, it was Edna who sparked the topic Althea wrestled with.

"So, Althea, you've a letter from your family at last. You must be eager to see them," Edna took a delicate bite, looking to Althea.

"I, yes, I am."

"You will write, once you've gone to them, won't you?" Elizabeth implored. "You've become rather like a sister, and we shall miss you terribly."

John leaned forward. "Now, Elizabeth, you'll make her loathe to leave us."

"Oh, but I am," insisted Althea. "You've all been so gracious, and generous, I shan't ever find your like again, I am sure," Althea rushed to reassure them.

Then she turned to Elizabeth. "Since you are so kind to ask, I will be sure to write as often as I can."

"There now," winked John. "Be at ease, my love, you shall have your letters."

"And I?" Asked Edna.

"I shall be delighted," Althea answered, glad that her friends were making her announcement nothing of the sort.

"The staff will mourn you," Mark noted, watching as both wives put Althea at ease.

"Only to appreciate her more when she visits and fills the halls with music once again," Elizabeth agreed. "I haven't your passion, Althea, much as I enjoy playing."

"You'll need an escort," Peter blurted, unable to contain himself any longer. George shot him a look of confusion.

"I rather thought I would accompany Althea."

"Croft lands are on the way. Your estates are clear the other way, old boy," Peter reasoned smoothly, prepared for this encounter.

John cleared his throat, and both men stopped, turning to look at him.

"I believe the Weatherbys intended to accompany Althea, as they are on their way to London."

Mark nodded. "We were only waiting to see if Lt. Chambers and his wife would welcome her."

Both suitors sat back, defeated, as Althea breathed a silent sigh of relief and shot a look of gratitude to Edna, who nodded with a wry smile.

Part 3

Althea was only too glad when dinner was over and she could plead Earth duties to escape the company of both men. She changed clothes in a trice and fled to the grounds to keep her Guardian company while she decided what to do with him.

For the first time since her introduction, her elementals were nowhere to be found. She'd half-expected a gnome, at least, waiting for her to leave the house. She wondered at it, but shrugged. She'd meant this evening for her Guardian, and it appeared the elementals were respecting her wishes.

She had barely cleared the barn when he appeared, loping strides bringing him to her side more quickly than she had expected. She'd rather thought she'd have to search for him. His lupine grace was beautiful to behold, and threatened to mesmerise her. Althea forced herself to assess him with a healer's eye. His wounds were fully healed with no residual stiffness or tenderness. He did not favour the leg that had been caught in the trap, nor guard any sort of hurt anywhere.

Althea smiled as she sank to her knees to embrace her mastiff of a Guardian. "Well hello, Guardian, I am glad to see you looking so well." She scratched his ruff and almost fell over as he leaned into her. He looked over her shoulder, in the direction of the house and growled softly.

Althea followed his gaze. "There is nought there to fret over. Just some confusion that will likely sort itself out in my absence."

Again the wolf growled softly, this time looking at Althea.

"You're quite right. Our absence."

The wolf wagged and then leaped away from her, towards the woods.

"There is something comforting, knowing you are not really a wolf, or, more than a wolf." She called as she got to her feet. "It makes me braver than I might have been with one of your less gifted cousins." She chased after him, as he'd clearly hoped she would, and they made a game of it. He would stay just outside her ability to catch him, then rush ahead, and let her catch up. As she got within touching distance, he'd leap away in a burst of energy.

Before long, they were in an overgrown area of the grounds. Althea picked her way through the spindly bushes and scrub, grateful not to be wearing a gown. She smiled at the practicality of the guild while enjoying the comfort of their unofficial uniform. The bracken cleared, and an open space appeared before her, where her wolf waited patiently.

In the center of the grove was a large tree stump, ideal for sitting on. As Althea arranged herself, her Guardian settled beside her, in easy reach of scratching and pets. The position was not lost on Althea who immediately began running her fingers through his luxurious coat.

"We must divine how I shall get you safely into and out of London. It's all fine and good that we are out here, and you have ample lands to hunt in. Thank you, for being such a gentleman in the regard, by the way. I don't know what I would have done if we'd managed to burden the Durstons hospitality any further. I am far too indebted to them as it is."

The wolf rested his head in Althea's lap, looking up at her with his large yellow eyes. They seemed to glow in the moonlight that bathed the clearing.

She stared into his eyes as though some invisible tether pulled her gaze. Deeper she fell into the gold flecks of his irises until they were all she could see. Magic thrummed around her, steady as a slow heartbeat, building with each pulse, until it climaxed and released her and she was able to pull herself back out of the golden depths, and could see the face surrounding those lupine eyes.

It was no longer a wolf before her, but a man. His long cloak was a similar colouring to the wolf's coat, and the eyes were still shining gold, but there the resemblance ended. The man seated in front of her was large, with a face that was both strong and gentle at once. The rest of him was mostly concealed by his cloak.

"Master," he breathed, his voice barely audible.

Althea sat frozen in shock, belatedly realising that her hand was still on the back of her Guardian's neck. She lifted it slowly, pulling it back into her lap, more wary of him now than when he was in wolf form.

"I displease you, Master?"

"I," Althea stammered. "Not at all." Words failed her and she fell silent.

"No one taught you about Guardians, Master?" He tilted his head, confused.

Althea blinked slowly, her mind trying to grasp what had happened. She shook her head to clear it. "No, not yet anyway. But before we continue, you must understand that I am not your Master, nor anyone's. I will answer to it, as the elementals have taught me to, but I will not command you, or try to coerce you into doing anything. I am no one's Master, but I can be a fair friend, if you'll let me."

"Then you will be a very good Master," he rumbled.

Althea pondered his face, trying to read his expression, and reconcile golden eyes in a striking and otherwise human visage.

"I suppose this is your answer to my initial concern of how to smuggle you into and out of London?"

"Yes, Master,"

"I see," she bit her lip. "Well, I think this is a fine solution, but you cannot continue to call me 'Master' when we are in company. Civilized society rather frowns on slavery."

A slow smile crept across his face. "What shall I call you, Master?"

"I suppose 'Miss Chambers' in company outside of the guild, 'Althea' among them," she paused. "What shall I call you?"

"You may call me as you will, Master."

"Surely you have a name."

"Faorel, Master."

"Faorel," Althea tasted his name on her tongue.

He jerked his head up at the sound of it.

"I do hope you don't snap to attention every time I say your name, Faorel. People will notice," a hint of her former lurking amusement twisting her lips.

"No, Master, I will not," he cast his eyes down.

Althea reached out, gently raising his chin with just the tips of her fingers.

"Faorel, I am your friend, or at least, I should like to be. If you are my Guardian, you must understand that while you may help protect me from enemies, you may also have to protect me from myself. You cannot do either with downcast eyes or fear of my displeasure." She spoke gently, hoping to reassure him of her nature and intent. "I am not cruel, Faorel, and I can appeal to the testimony of the elementals and to that of much of the guild for confirmation."

Hope shone in his eyes.

"Do not be at war with yourself. I haven't the first idea of what to expect of a Guardian beyond what the name implies. I will rely on you to show me."

Faorel sat up straighter.

"Much better," Althea nodded.

"You will be a very good Master," Faorel decided.

"A good friend, I hope," Althea corrected. "Now, you must be freezing, still sitting in the snow as you are. Shall we walk the grounds and check the wards together?"

Faorel stood in one fluid motion, reminiscent of his lupine grace. He offered a hand up as he looked over her head, past her, assessing the danger of the path ahead. He let her take the lead as they did their rounds, watching for anything that might threaten her. They were mostly silent as they walked the circuit. Althea's mind divided between the task at hand and her Guardian, Faorel concentrating on guarding and learning the way the grounds looked and sounded with human senses.

"All is well," Althea announced as they closed the circuit.

"Yes, Master, it is," Faorel confirmed, though meaning something other than tripped wards.

"So," Althea stepped beside him and slid her arm in his. "It is a mild night, and I am in no hurry to go back to the house. Will you take a stroll with me?" She looked up into his face with a hopeful smile.

A shadow crossed Faorel's face, his eyes flashing and fierce. "They," he jerked his head towards the house, "will not harm you." He growled, knowing of both Peter and George via the elementals.

Althea chuckled. "No, they will not. They haven't any intent to, so you need not challenge them."

Faorel grunted.

"Master?" A voice spoke at her feet.

Althea looked down to see her favourite gnome. "Hello, friend. Have we disturbed you?"

"No, Master."

"To what do I owe the pleasure, then? I'd thought you all abandoned me this evening?"

"Never, Master. But the waking of a Guardian is a private affair."

"Is it indeed?" She looked up at Faorel, one eyebrow raised.

Faorel nodded once.

Althea stooped to gather up the gnome and tuck him into her hood.

"You seem solemn, my friend. What troubles you?" She asked the gnome as she reclaimed Faorel's arm and resumed walking. Faorel sighed, a measure of tension leaving him.

"You do not understand your Guardian, Master. Nor he, you. It will cause you both harm."

"Then by all means, if you can help me, and are so minded, I would welcome the guidance."

"He is wolf, and man, and more, Master. He is bound to you, and you to him by the magic you shared. He cannot leave you, even if he should want to, no matter how you treat him."

"Do you fear I will mistreat him?" Althea asked, concerned.

"No, Master. It has been long since we met such a fine Master as you. But you must understand your Guardian if you are going to avoid friction. We elementals can love you, or not, abandon you if we disagree with you, as we wish. He cannot."

Althea looked up at Faorel then. "Is this true? Am I your Master in more than just name?"

"Yes."

"If you disagree, you must reconcile. He cannot abandon you in anger or for any other reason, Master," the gnome continued. "Nor can you order him to leave you. He is bound to your will, and the conflict would be cruel."

The weight of the gnome's words, of the responsibility she now carried, however unwillingly, almost brought Althea to her knees.

"I had no idea," she said mostly to herself, then turned to Faorel. "Had I known what I was sentencing you to, I might have, I wouldn't have," she grappled for words. "Faorel, I am so very sorry."

Faorel smiled into her horrified face. "You made a choice to help a creature in need, Master. Heedless of the cost to you, you saved me. That choice proved you a worthy person to hinge my life to. I am a Guardian. All Guardians wish for someone good, kind, generous, to serve. It is no bad thing you did."

"I have much to live up to, and will strive to," she vowed.

"You see now, Master," the gnome was satisfied.

"I do, thank you. Is there more?"

"All else will keep, Master. For now, it is only important that you get to know your Guardian."

"Thank you, friend."

A tiny puff of air brushed her cheek and the elemental was gone.

"Tell me more, Faorel. Tell me of Guardians. Tell me of you." She looked up into his face to find him still smiling.

"With pleasure, Master."

They didn't return to the house until well past the time all should be asleep in bed. Althea could not explain the stranger she was returning with to the entire guild. They crept up to her rooms silently and whispered once they were safely shut in.

"Master, I can be either man or wolf, as you prefer. A pet might be easier for them to accept if they didn't know enough about Guardians to teach you."

"You'll frighten the staff out of their wits."

Faorel's face was cast in the flickering candle light. "I can appear harmless. I disarmed you, didn't I?" He looked playful.

"Indeed you did. We shall try. But we must share this with John directly after breakfast. I cannot deceive him in this."

Faorel shrugged. "As you see fit, Master. Though," he paused.

"Yes?"

"Are you not deceiving them all in some way?"

Althea sighed. "Too true, and I don't like that any better. But unless you tell me otherwise, I don't see why we should conceal this from John."

"Perhaps a wolf Guardian would be easier for them to accept for now. Once we are away, or when we return, we can explain. Would they be entirely comfortable with a man sharing your rooms, for instance?" He reached for her cloak to help her disrobe.

Althea looked over her shoulder at him, amusement lurking just beneath the skin. "A good point. It seems rude to ask it of you, though."

"It would be rude to put me in a kennel, Master," he grinned.

Althea's jaw dropped. He brought the tip of his finger under her chin and gently tipped it shut, his eyes dancing with silent laughter.

She left him standing with her cloak in his hands as she changed into her nightdress behind a screen. When she emerged, he'd already assumed his lupine form and waited for her, curled up on one side of the bed.

She crawled under the covers and rested a hand on his paw. "I think we are off to a good start, Faorel. I am touched and honoured that you chose me. Sleep well, my Guardian."

Faorel licked her hand and they slept sound until morning.

∾∾

Faorel woke sooner than Althea would have liked, well before the servants came to rouse her for breakfast. His cold nose pressed to the tip of her nose, and his warm breath in her face meant she opened her eyes to a very large wolf's visage pressed close. Her eyes went wide as she gasped, only just managing to stifle a yell. As her heart raced, she laughed softly.

"*That* will take some getting used to, my Guardian. Perhaps tomorrow you might try a different technique. You nearly scared the life out of me." She ran her hands through his luxurious coat to make sure he knew she wasn't cross, then curled up with him, her head between his paws, one arm draped over his rib cage. She breathed deeply. "You smell of moonlight and snow." She nuzzled him.

Faorel rested his head on hers, returning her affection. There they stayed for the better part of an hour, dozing off and on, saying nothing. He heard feet on the stairs before Althea did and scrambled off the bed with a quick lick to her face as he flattened himself to the floor on the other side of the bed.

A quiet knock sounded at the door. "My lady?" the servant called softly.

"I am awake, thank you, and will dress myself this morning." Althea called, buying a few more minutes with her Guardian.

"Very good, my lady." Steps retreated.

Faorel's face popped up from the side of the bed, his eyes bright.

"Enjoyed that, did you?"

He shook his head.

"Not the hiding? The game playing?"

He shook his head again.

"Well, perhaps you'll tell me when we go walking later."

Again, Faorel shook his shaggy head.

Althea deliberately phrased it so it was not an order, so Faorel could share or not, as he chose. She smiled at his deciding to keep a secret from her.

"Very well, oh mysterious Guardian. Keep your secrets." She tossed a pillow at him that he caught in the air with a quick snap of his jaw. Althea could not help but imagine how quickly he could move were she in danger. With that sobering thought, she chose another guild uniform from the wardrobe and changed behind the screen in the corner. She pulled her curls into a loose braid and then reached out for Faorel. "Come, let us see you disarm the household with your gentlemanly and puppy-like behaviour."

Faorel bounded to her and pushed his head into her hand, wanting some affection before they braved the others.

"Oh, all right, a greedy puppy," she scratched his ears with enthusiasm.

Faorel popped up on his hind legs to lap her face then landed, nose pointed to the door.

Althea chuckled, shaking her head, and opened it.

They were the first to arrive at breakfast, much to Althea's relief, and by some small miracle, encountered no servants en route. Since breakfast was generally a sideboard affair, she was able to fill her plate and pour a coffee, and be completely settled in, Faorel lying beside her chair, before anyone arrived.

"Are you certain you can stand to wait for your breakfast, Faorel? It seems cruel that I should eat and you should be hungry."

Faorel looked up at her with a lupine grin.

"Very well, and thank you," she patted his head and he settled back down on the floor making himself as small as possible.

The Durstons were the next to arrive, Elizabeth stopping dead in the doorway as she stared at Faorel.

"Good heavens," she breathed, leaving John no choice but to peer over her shoulder to see what had alarmed her so.

"Althea?" he asked.

"It's all right. Come in. He is my Guardian and insisted on being by my side. I am sorry about the shock. But you know what they say. Where does a three-hundred-pound gorilla sit?"

"Wherever it wants," Peter finished, coming onto the room from a different entrance, unable to see Faorel and hearing only the last of what Althea said.

Faorel wagged just the tip of his tail, and looked up at Elizabeth with hopeful golden eyes. She took a hesitant step into the room.

Peter's brow wrinkled, unaware of Faorel. "What is the matter, Elizabeth? You look as though you've seen a ghost."

John chuckled, moving around Elizabeth to approach Faorel. "A rather large and shaggy ghost," he paused half way to where Althea sat and went down on one knee, his hands open before him. "May I?" He looked from Faorel to Althea, unsure whom to address.

"Well, my Guardian? May Mr. Durston introduce himself?" Althea asked, wary of her ignorance.

Faorel wagged his tail as he looked first up to Althea, in answer, and then to John.

John approached slowly and let Faorel sniff his hands. Faorel evidently liked what he smelled, for he nudged his nose under John's hands, clearly wanting a pet, which John was only too glad to oblige.

"Really, Althea, you make the most magnificent friends," he crooned, relishing the feel of Faorel's fur.

Elizabeth ventured only a little closer, and Peter, wanting to see what the fuss was about, stepped around the table to look at John and the wolf. He froze.

So did Faorel.

Please don't growl, Althea wished silently. She reached down and placed her hand gently on his back, projecting reassurance and calm, hoping he would understand her.

John saw it all and backed away slowly, giving Faorel space.

"I hate to say it, Althea. But this room is going to seem awfully crowded as we all impose ourselves on your Guardian. Perhaps you should take your breakfast in the greenhouse?"

Althea flashed eyes filled with gratitude at John.

"I think you may be right, John." She looked down at the wolf at her feet. "What say you, my Guardian? Will you accompany me?"

Faorel looked back to Althea and wagged once.

"Forgive me. I shouldn't have imposed so. Please, enjoy your breakfast in peace," she stood, taking her plate and coffee with her just as George and the Weatherby's entered.

When they'd gone beyond earshot, George found his tongue. "Was that a wolf?"

"That was Althea's new Guardian," John corrected, the only one not put off by seeing a wolf at the breakfast table.

"What does she mean by having a wolf at the table?"

"Her grace can do as she wishes," Peter scorned Althea, the wolf, and the company at large.

All eyes turned to him.

"Peter," Mark began, a warning tone in his voice. "Why would you call her 'her grace'?"

"She's a duchess on her mother's side. Didn't she tell you? Did you think she'd remain a nameless ward forever?" Peter's words burned like acid, his bitterness cemented by the silent exchange between he and the wolf.

"Peter!" Edna exclaimed, her fiery temper always close to the surface, now roused by Peter's bad manners and Elizabeth's tension, brought on by her fear of dogs.

The exchange might have escalated but for John, who, seeing his wife, the peace keeper, immobilized, stepped in to assuage tempers, his own virtually non-existent, and besides, he had nothing to be upset over. In a few words he had them each at table with a selection of their favourites in front of them, and turned the conversation away from anything the least bit volatile.

When he finally made an appearance in the hothouse, he looked haggard. Althea and Faorel had chosen to wait for him before heading outside for Faorel to hunt. He found them curled up together near the roses, Althea listening intently to the elementals as they attempted to teach her about her Guardian.

When he arrived, Faorel turned to look at him, his eyes sad, his ears down: an apology.

Althea felt him turn and followed his gaze as the elementals went silent.

"John, oh dear, you look as though you've run a mile through a storm." She stood with Faorel. "My friends," she turned back to the elementals, "might you join us, and offer John some comfort?" Again she couched her words carefully, and then came to sit at the benches, John collapsing into one, while she and Faorel settled into the other. Faorel leaned into her, offering and taking comfort at once. She wrapped an arm around him.

"Well, Althea," John began after dragging both hands down his face. "I am sorry to say that we are all unsettled by your guest."

Faorel's ears pinned back to his head as he whined.

"I am, that is to say," Althea squeezed Faorel gently, "we are both sorry, John."

"If it were just me, I'd be delighted to have a Guardian in the house."

"But it is not just you." ·

"No, it is not. Elizabeth was attacked by a dog in her youth and never quite got over the trauma of it. Your Guardian is a bit too much for her to be comfortable with."

Faorel shrunk down, understanding every word, and feeling worse by the moment.

"We had no idea, John. If we'd known,"

John held up a hand. "You couldn't have known. Fear not, Althea, she is not angry. Only afraid, and ashamed of her fear. As for the others," he paused, unsure of how much to say.

"The others?" Althea stilled, a dread weighing down her stomach.

"Peter told us about your family."

"My," Althea's mind blanked.

"Your grace."

"Oh," Althea drew out the word, letting out a long slow breath. Faorel pushed her gently. "Yes, you told me so. You are far too articulate, even within your wolfish limitations." She patted him. She looked back up to John to find him waiting for a better answer.

"Peter traced the Fairchilds as far as he was able. I contacted the lawyer who demanded I substantiate my claim to the duchy. I couldn't, not without an even greater debt to you, which I already cannot repay. So I didn't say anything, and intended to let the duchy go to the next eligible heir unless my aunt and uncle in London had some great claim or information on my lineage, which I deemed infinitely unlikely. There was no point in getting you all flustered over an unproven lineage. If something came of it, then I would have told you." Althea turned pleading eyes on John.

John took a slow breath, then another while Althea waited patiently, knowing she was in the wrong, that she'd hurt her friends, and that Peter hurt them when he blurted whatever parts of the information he saw fit.

"You understand, of course, that the others have only heard what Peter told them, and that was none of it flattering."

Faorel growled, alarming John.

Althea patted Faorel. "I know you and Peter may never be friends, my

Guardian, but please do not paint John with the same brush. Besides, I must own my portion of the wrong, whatever Peter has said."

Faorel subsided.

Althea looked to John who continued to look uncomfortable even though Faorel was quiet once more. Althea took pity on him, guessing at the reason for his discomfort.

"Fear not, John. I will not ask you to repeat his slander. I care more for you, for Elizabeth, for the Weatherbys, than I do for him. I will either win back your good opinion, or not. Time will show whether or not I can be a worthy friend, duchy or no. As for Peter," she shrugged. "I believe he and I are destined to be at odds with one another."

John shook his head, chuckling. "He thinks he loves you."

Faorel growled again. Althea patted him gently, a warning and comfort both.

"He will understand otherwise when he is among other single ladies again. I am only valuable to him and to George, because I am the only unattached female for no few miles." Faorel looked up at her, hurt in his eyes. "You are quite right, 'unattached' was a horrible word. Can you forgive me?"

Faorel pushed his head against her.

"Yes, we can talk later, my Guardian." To John she said, "I cannot tell you how sorry I am for all the trouble I've caused you and Elizabeth, and the Weatherbys. I owe you more than I can ever repay."

John smiled. "You owe us nothing save your continued friendship, and perhaps a piano recital or two."

Faorel's ears perked up at that and he looked to Althea with a quick jerk of his head.

"Yes, I play. But you shall have to wait for a more appropriate time to hear it," she said to Faorel. She turned back to John. "I'm sorry, John. Please believe me when I tell you I had no idea what trouble I would be. I think I had best take my Guardian out for breakfast and conversation. I will, we will, be back in an hour or so, and I would like to address all of you then, if it please you."

"A wise choice, Althea," John stretched out on his bench. "I think I will enjoy the fruits of our labours for a time, before venturing once more into the fray."

"Thank you, John, for everything." Althea led Faorel directly outside, without stopping at her rooms for a cloak. Fearing an encounter with any of the others, she took the door from the hothouse that faced the barn, and stepped out into a winter morning wearing only her thin lounging pants and tunic.

Faorel barked at her as she stepped away from the house.

"You are certainly more aggressive in wolf form than you are as a human," she noted.

Faorel barked again and sat down in front of her, barring her way.

"There's warm clothes in the barn if you'll let me past, Faorel."

He stepped aside.

"Thank you. I know you must stay close, but if there's anything you could do to stay downwind of the horses, I'd appreciate it," she called over her shoulder,

"I'd rather not scare them if we don't have to."

"There's more than one way to keep from spooking them," Faorel's voice murmured as he came up behind her, wrapping her in his cloak and startling her.

She would have jumped and yelped, but that he held her close and still, with one hand over her mouth. He whispered in her ear, "I am sorry, Master, for alarming you, but if you scream, the horses will be no less upset, if for different reason."

Althea wilted, the fight-flight instinct leaving her.

Faorel took his hand away. "I *am* sorry, Master."

Althea turned to look into his face, only to see amusement in his eyes. She fought a smirk.

"You are not sorry, Faorel. But if you continue to scare years off my life, ours will be a very short partnership," she whispered back, then turned to the barn for the heavy riding cloak she knew was there. Wrapping it about her, she turned back to Faorel who stood waiting, offering his arm.

She stepped into the opening he made for her and they made their way deeper into the woods.

"You must be starving," Althea said as they reached the clearing where they'd first met.

"I can wait, Master," Faorel said just before his stomach protested.

Althea smiled, catching him in a half truth. "I am sure you could, but there is no need. I am safe here. I wouldn't be surprised if an elemental came by to keep me company while you hunt."

"You'll stay here?" Faorel's tone was stern, more of a demand than a question.

Althea stepped back, daunted by his intensity. "Faorel?"

"I cannot leave you unless I am certain you are safe, Master."

"Another rule of Guardianship?"

"Yes, Master."

"Consequences should something happen to me?"

Faorel shuddered.

Althea took his hand in both of hers. "Then rest assured, my Guardian, I will remain here until you return, and I will wish for an elemental to stay with me. Perhaps he or she will be accompanied by an army to protect me. I will stay safe, I promise you," she pledged, looking into his golden eyes.

"Thank you, Master," Faorel raised her hands to his lips and kissed her knuckles. He loped out of sight and was gone.

"Nicely done, Master," an elemental peeked around a nearby tree, this one mostly squirrel-like, if a bit large.

"Thank you, friend," Althea smiled up at her. "Do you by chance have an army of friends willing to keep us company for a time?"

The elemental chittered. Althea's refusal to command or coerce them delighting every elemental she encountered.

"We are already here," her favourite gnome said at her feet, as others poured in from everywhere, surrounding her. "I told you we were no more than a wish away, Master," he said as she lifted him to her shoulder.

"Thank you, friends, for helping me keep a promise." She settled in, swarmed by every manner of creature, to wait for Faorel, and to learn from them, that she might not trespass in or neglect her duties as an Elemental Master with a Guardian.

"They are old, older than any elemental. 'Tis said that when an elemental dies, that he can come back as a Guardian. But to come back as a Guardian, one must wait, watch and wait, for a perfect storm of events. A creature of your element, near to a Master of your element, and the creature must be grievously wounded."

"Then you dive into the body, freeing the soul residing there, and wait for the Master to appear. While you lie in agony, you wait, wondering if the Master will find you in time, or if you will die again, and wait again. Even if your Master finds you, it is even odds whether she will heal you, or end your suffering."

"Some Masters cheat. They hire others to mortally wound such a creature near enough to the Master. They take our service, the gifts a Guardian brings, without regard for the Guardian. We cannot always foresee this. Then we are trapped, serving a cruel Master. Sometimes we do see, but think we can redeem the Master with faithful service. Not that we have a choice to be loyal," he said bitterly.

Silent tears coursed down Althea's cheeks as she listened.

"But to come back as a Guardian to a good Master," light filled his face as he closed his eyes in rapture. "The gifts the Master receives are great, no matter the soul of the Master, be he devil or angel. But the gifts the Guardian receives if the Master is good, are without equal. We find joy, we live in the world as part of it, not only limited to our one element, but able to touch all elements, without fear. We transcend to be greater than we are. All because of the love of a good Master."

Althea smiled through her watery eyes, understanding why an elemental would take the chance of being a slave to a bad Master.

A sparrow came, wiping Althea's tears away with the clever swipe of soft feathers.

"Do not mourn for us, Master. Do not fear hurting us. We are all of us glad to have found you," she twittered in her high, light voice.

"You are too kind," Althea shook her head.

"No, Master," resumed the gnome. "There is no such thing as too much kindness, for there is little enough comfort in this world."

Althea reached for all the elementals then, to hold them, just for a moment, in silent gratitude.

"Can you tell me, what would happen to a Guardian, if his Master were harmed in his absence?"

The gnome chucked her cheek.

"*Mortal* harm, in his presence or out of it would condemn him to start again. He would return as something rather less than an elemental, and have to earn his way back up to the chance to be a Guardian again. Anything less than mortal harm will only make him fear, but do no lasting damage to his chance at transcendence. But he *will* fear, he will make himself ill, wondering 'what if it had been worse?' We cannot always manage our fear well, Master."

"I should wish for a quiet and peaceful life," Althea concluded.

A chorus of elemental laughter surrounded her.

"You are an Elemental Master, Master. They rarely have quiet lives. That is why they need Guardians to protect them. To die saving your Master is as sure a way to the next gate as having your Master pass peacefully in her sleep of old age, and far more likely."

"I would be heartbroken and wracked with guilt if any of you, or he, died for me. I would never forgive myself," Althea felt sick at the thought.

"Then take care to only pick battles we can win, Master," her gnome said lightly.

"I shan't pick battles at all, thank you."

"Sometimes, they pick you."

Althea had no answer to that, her mood darkening with the weight of the responsibility she carried, despite all her protestations. Whether she willed it or no, these creatures were hers to care for, to protect, just as they claimed her, protected her.

The elementals sensed her mood and sought to distract her, to amuse her, gamboling about, telling elemental jokes which didn't always translate, but she appreciated their efforts no less for that.

Faorel found her that way, surrounded by her friends, smiling and laughing, and thanked the powers for his chance, for his time with her, no matter how it turned out. The elementals noticed him long before Althea did, but did not let on, determined to show the Guardian that he need not be jealous of them, determined to show him another facet of his Master.

He chuckled as he broke cover and got Althea's attention.

"You are true to your word, Master. I thank you. Though, you all don't look fierce enough to chase off a yearling rabbit," he waved a very human hand at all of them in general.

"Don't be fooled," Althea warned. "I have no doubt my friends would have helped me defend myself were I in trouble."

"Ah, but you *are* in trouble, Master," said the gnome. "You have a Guardian."

"Yes, I see your point, my friend. A fairly determined one at that," she winked at the gnome where Faorel could see.

He rushed her and scooped her up, one arm behind her back, the other under her knees and spun her around. "And what lies have they been telling you about me?"

Althea laughed as the sky and trees flashed crazily by. "I can't be certain, but I don't think an elemental *can* lie, can they?"

A large insect-like elemental landed on her chest as Faorel continued to spin.

"No, Master, but we can omit things, let people believe things that are not strictly true."

"Then just as I am careful when I speak to you, that I do not unintentionally order you about, so too must I be a careful listener. Thank you for the enlightenment."

The bug flew off, helped by the centrifugal force of Faorel's spinning.

Althea clung to Faorel's shoulder, laughing at his playfulness, delighted by his energy. About the time she got dizzy, he set her down carefully, light as falling snow.

"Master," he bowed.

"You are mercurial, my Guardian. I shall be forever on my toes with you," she tousled his hair, his previous mood infectious. "Thank you, my friends, for your company and for your care. I think I can safely say we both appreciate it, very much." She glanced at Faorel, who nodded.

"Come, I must face my friends in the guild and see what amends I can make." She held her hand out to Faorel.

"Would you not rather I be a wolf?" he asked, confused.

"In light of Lady Elizabeth's predicament, I think not, my Guardian. It will do them less harm, and in some cases, some good, to see you as a man. Unless you've a reason I don't know about why you cannot be seen by them in this form?"

"None, Master, I thought only of your reputation."

"Oh, that. Well, I haven't one now. My former life is well and truly over, and good riddance. Besides, I was never fond of that set of dance steps to begin with." She shrugged.

A broad grin split Faorel's face, "I shall be very glad to be your Guardian, Master."

"I very much hope so," Althea smiled back.

As they approached the house, Althea paused. Faorel stopped only a moment later, feeling the tug on his arm.

"Master?"

Althea shook her head. "I think it would be better if you called me Althea from now on," her face clouded with worry.

"As you wish, Althea," he tasted her name, liking it.

She liked it too, for a smile lurked beneath her shadowed expression.

"I need to speak with the guild, Faorel. I am worried you may not appreciate how some of them may respond to me," she paused, "or to you, come to that. None of them will harm me, not physically, of that I am reasonably certain. So though I am loathe to ask this of you, I'd like your word that you will not let your protectiveness of me, your temper, get the better of you, no matter how sorely you are tempted," Althea continued to phrase her words carefully.

Faorel growled, not liking her request one bit.

"I will give you an explicit out, which I hope will console you at least for some small measure, and that is this: if anyone does attack me physically or magically, you are free to live up to your role as you see fit. I will neither hinder nor reproach you if it comes to that, however unlikely that outcome might be."

Faorel felt her steady gaze on him as his body fairly thrummed with tension. He was prepared for a fight, ready to protect her at any cost. After a few long moments, he met her eyes.

"Why, Master, would you ask this of me now?"

Althea smiled, glad to have a Guardian who could think as well as protect.

"I ask because I expect Peter to be unkind, and while the Durstons and the Weatherbys may still be my friends after this it is likely George will not. I have seen your reaction to Peter, when neither of you uttered a word, and fear an unnecessary escalation now. I expect both men to be unpleasant, actually, and I am asking you not to allow them to goad you." Althea's expression was open, pleading, worried. Faorel could not help but respond to it.

He cupped her jaw in both his hands to look into her eyes, his gaze unwavering.

"For you, this one time, I will be amiable. Short of true danger, I will neither bristle nor growl, and laugh off whatever slights they sling at us." He took his hands from her face and placed one over his heart. "My pledge to you."

Althea closed her eyes, relieved, then stood on her toes and kissed his cheek. "Thank you, Faorel."

Back on her heels, she squared her shoulders and took Faorel's arm. "Let's get this over with, shall we?"

"As you wish, my lady."

They strode in together.

"What kind of woman is she to spurn such a man?" George demanded, his voice carrying into the hallway as Althea and Faorel approached.

"I rather doubt she's spurned anyone," Mark denied.

"Peter has flown from here like a migrating bird, unable to bear the sight of her. Surely, she has toyed with him and rejected him. And for what?" George sneered. "For a legion of malformed creatures who can neither be seen nor spoken of in polite society," his own issues with Althea, and his inability to reconcile her magic with his parochial relations, spilling into his words.

"Malformed creatures?" Faorel whispered in Althea's ear.

"Before you are affronted, wait to hear what the others say," she jutted her chin towards the doorway.

"George," John warned, the insult to beings he would proudly call friends, if they'd have him, tripping the beginnings of a temper rarely raised. "My own gift may be paltry, but it outstrips yours by a considerable amount. I will thank you to be more careful where you place your insults."

Elizabeth's voice slid into the breach. "Gentlemen, please. Regardless of how any of us feels about magic," she paused. Althea assumed there was a *look*. "Your quarrel is not with each other, and I think you'll find that there is no quarrel at all, once Althea returns to explain herself." Elizabeth's Water flowed over all of them, soothing their hurts, smoothing over their tempers, and provided Althea the perfect opportunity to enter.

"Althea," Edna greeted her warmly. "What impeccable timing you have," her voice grew softer and each word came slower as Faorel followed Althea into the room.

"I'd like you all to meet Faorel, my elemental Guardian, whom I think even Mr. Hamlin will agree, however grudgingly, is nothing like a *malformed creature*," she barbed him, unable to resist defending the elementals, *her* elementals, despite her caution to Faorel.

George's lips went white with anger, but he said nothing.

"Your wolf?" Elizabeth asked, her eyes widening and her face paling slightly.

"Not at the moment, Mrs. Durston," Faorel spread his arms slowly and did a graceful turn. "Not so much as a tail, you see?" He gave her his most innocent expression.

Mark burst out laughing as Faorel dispelled the tension in the room. Soon the others followed suit, save George, who stood away from them all and glowered.

Elizabeth wiped the corner of one eye as she caught her breath from laughing. "Do sit down, sir, please. Consider yourself a welcome guest. I am suitably chided," the last few chuckles shaking her as she took her place near John.

Faorel turned and held a hand out to Althea, every inch of him a gentleman, to escort her to her seat and take his place beside her, everyone watching him closely for different reasons.

"If I may," Althea glanced from one face to another, each one nodding. "I'd like to acquit myself of the charges lately laid at my door."

George crossed his arms, a smug look on his face.

"While I don't know the particulars of what was said, I offer you the truth from my perspective."

She shared with them her overwhelming feelings of indebtedness, the contents of both letters she received, and how she had intended to deal with the situation, along with her reasons. Her summation was both fact and intent together, as she appealed to them for forgiveness over her deception and for the hurt she had caused.

"As for Peter," she paused, looking pointedly at George. "I gave him no declarations of love, nor he to me, no matter what he might have said. If he has left, it is because he chose to go, not because I have toyed with him nor spurned him."

Addressing the group as a whole once again, she said, "if it matters at all, whatever my intentions were then, whatever my private struggles, today the situation is somewhat different, and if I may still call you 'friends', I should welcome your counsel."

Althea sat back, letting her arm just touch Faorel, stealing a tiny comfort as she awaited their answer. Throughout her speech, Faorel remained neutrally attentive, balancing between his affection for her, his need to protect her from harm, his urge to be supportive, and their mutual need to mute their intimacy from her friends.

George stepped forward then. "For my part, you may not, Miss Chambers. You may not call me 'friend', for you have abused Mr. Croft abominably, and without remorse, and manipulated me into a similar state, all with no intention of reciprocating. I find you calculating and heartless, and I will thank you never to darken my company again." He bowed to the Durstons. "I will be leaving this afternoon, to save you any further discomfort. Thank you for your hospitality." With only a final scornful glance at Althea, George strode from the room, a man with terrible purpose.

Althea watched Faorel in her peripheral vision, dreading the fierce protector in him taking the lead. She need not have worried. His self-control was made of iron, and he kept only the slightest surprise on his face, and offered not a word.

To a one, they refrained from speaking, by silent implicit agreement wishing George well out of earshot before resuming discussion.

Edna's eyes rolled about the room, and then settled on the service in front of her. She reached for the pot.

"Tea?"

Althea stared at her friend who held a cup and saucer in the air, a mischievous fire in her eye.

Elizabeth broke first, a small noise, stifling a laugh. The rest snickered as tea was served.

"He did us a great service by bringing you to us, Althea," Edna spoke once everyone had composed themselves once more. "But I shan't say I care for his opinions at the moment," her implicit forgiveness and acceptance a balm to Althea's fears.

Mark looked at his wife in surprise at her restraint. He'd fully expected her fiery temper to be roused, either at Althea or Hamlin, though he would not have hazarded a guess at which.

"I quite agree with you, Mrs. Weatherby. Quite." He nodded decidedly.

Althea looked to the Durstons for their answer.

John looked to Elizabeth and they shared some silent signal between them. He turned to Althea and Faorel together, his gaze encompassing both of them.

"I can only speak for myself when I say I am just delighted to meet a Guardian. My tutor was a Master, but did not have a Guardian of his own, and could only tell me little of it, them, ah, you, your kind." His face scrunched up as he feared offending Faorel.

"The delight is mutual, sir, for I am glad to meet those who fought to rescue?" He looked to Althea for confirmation. She nodded. He turned back to John. "To rescue Althea, even if I know not yet what from."

John relaxed, relieved by Faorel's courtesy.

The words John chose left Althea afraid of Elizabeth's next words.

She need not have worried.

"My dear Althea, I am only too glad to call you friend. I daresay you've put up with much and more from us, and while we may not have been privy to your every secret, it was obvious that others caused you no end of discomfort, which I would have spared you, if only I could. I will suggest to you that you might spare yourself such scenes in future if you were to choose to share your burdens with those who care for you, but that is the end of it." Her next words were for both of them. "I shall only remind you that you are always most welcome at Longview."

The tension drained out of Althea and she lowered her eyelids slowly, then blinked.

"Thank you, all of you."

"Good," Edna dusted her hands. "Now that's cleared away, Althea, take pity on your companion and at least hold his hand, for he is desperate to console you."

"Edna!" Mark was shocked.

"Tosh. We are all friends here, and honest ones at that. If Elizabeth can offer suggestions, so can I," she gave him a mock-scathing look.

With the room distracted by Edna, Althea and Faorel did indeed arrange themselves more intimately on the settee without being indecent about it. Faorel squeezed her hand, making her smile.

"There now. Much better," Edna nodded her approval.

The matter of where Faorel was staying was a moment's confusion.

"He must have his own rooms."

"He cannot be separated from her."

"Then he could stay in her rooms, but only as a wolf."

"He cannot come out as a wolf, he'll frighten Elizabeth to death."

"As though he couldn't change back into a man in her rooms."

"My friends," John held up his hands to silence the room. "Althea is of legal age, and it is not for us to police her, or Faorel, in any case. He is her elemental Guardian, and whatever social conventions we might consider, do not apply here. Besides," a boyish smile crossed his face, "it is not as if we don't defy more than a few of those conventions ourselves."

Faorel squeezed Althea's hand again.

They prepared for dinner, Faorel with his back turned to Althea as the maid dressed her and set her curls. He stared out the window at the grounds beyond, keeping vigil for her safety while allowing for modesty.

"Done," said the maid, stepping away from Althea, looking very pleased with her work.

"Are you certain?" Faorel asked.

"Oh yes, quite, sir," the maid had a smile in her voice. "See for yourself."

Faorel turned to face Althea. His golden eyes glowed.

Althea stood still and straight, lifting her chin a fraction, ready for almost any reaction.

When Faorel continued to stare, Althea dismissed the maid with thanks. When they were alone, Faorel closed the space between them, taking both her hands in his and bringing her knuckles to his lips.

"You are magnificent, Master. Any man, any elemental, any Guardian, would be proud to serve you."

Althea tilted her head and looked at him through slit eyes. "Thank you, Faorel." She broke the mood with a shake of her head. "Shall we to dinner?"

He offered an arm and led her out.

While the others were intensely curious about Faorel, they were gracious about not prying, regaling him instead with stories of Althea's rescue and providing the particulars of how she became trapped in the first place.

"No wonder you knew so little of Guardians," Faorel remarked, looking to Althea. Turning back to the table he asked, "you mean to tell me my Elemental Master has been practicing magic for less than six months?" False shock shaped his face. When he looked to Althea again it was with mock disdain. "I am stuck with a virtual novice?"

Althea's eyes grew wide, then she pointed her utensil at him, wagging it like a finger. However sorely tempted she might be to banter with him, she feared accidentally commanding him or trapping him between careless words and his duty and desires. A sly smile told him she enjoyed the conversation and teasing, even if she didn't partake.

Both the Durstons and the Weatherbys delighted in the interactions between Althea and Faorel, wholeheartedly approving of Faorel's manners and playfulness. It was difficult not to like him, and like a dual pair of parents, they were glad to see Althea happy after being under duress for so long.

When dinner concluded, Althea offered to check the wards, thinking perhaps everyone would like a break from she and Faorel. Their disappointment at her offer was plain on their faces.

John rushed to suggest he check the perimeter, himself loathe to miss out on whatever was to follow, yet equally loathe to break up the party.

Faorel cleared his throat. "If I may?"

All heads turned to him as he turned to Althea. "There is no need to bundle up and walk the grounds unless you've a mind to. If you can tap the line beneath us, it will lead you to one of your wards. All are tethered together by a fine thread of power. You can trace that line all the way around the perimeter in a moment's thought, my lady." He glanced around, unsure if he'd just committed an offense.

Althea only smiled. She pointed to herself. "Novice." She pointed to Faorel. "Guardian." That brought the chuckles she'd hoped for.

"Can you help me, Faorel?"

He took her hand, closed his eyes, tapped the line and waited for her to follow. When she did, he went to the nearest ward and touched the line, making it sound, like plucking a violin string. From there it was a moment's race to circle back. Althea turned bright eyes on the room.

"All's well, what's next?"

When she and Faorel returned to Althea's rooms it was late, all of them prolonging the evening until even the most determined plead sleep. As he shut the door behind him, Faorel leaned his back against it, and closed his eyes.

Althea came up to him, wrapping her arms about his waist and peering up into his face.

"You were true to your word, Faorel, exceeding all expectation. Thank you."

He opened his eyes and looked down, meeting her gaze. "How could I not be when you were so careful to do the same this morning?"

Althea smiled her answer and rested her cheek against his chest.

"You are a treasure beyond all imagining."

❧❦

Breakfast came late the next day, the entire household of a mind to sleep in. Faorel and Althea remained within touching distance of one another the entire time, enchanting the guild with their quiet affection.

"I must reply to my aunt and uncle," Althea broached the topic once more, this time with full disclosure among them. She turned to Edna, "were you still intending for London?"

"It is our second home, my dear. And we should be glad to add a fourth to the party. In fact, her eyes narrowed, "it might be best that way."

Althea tilted her head in question.

Mark stepped in to explain. "You cannot traipse about the country with a man who is not your husband, and you cannot keep a wolf for a pet in the city."

Elizabeth smiled. "We might flout conventions, Althea, but not all of them, when so much ill could come of it."

Faorel touched his foot to hers, under the table, where no one could see.

"He shall be Faorel Gray, my nephew, and no tongue will wag over you travelling with an old staid couple and their nephew," Edna declared.

"Gray is such a plain name for someone so," Elizabeth paused, unable to find a suitable word.

John looked at her accusingly, suspecting the words she wanted to use, and suspecting she was a small measure bewitched by Faorel. After her jealousy over Althea's non-existent poaching, he was amused over the reversal.

"A name like 'Gray' won't spark any searching of the peerage for his origins.

Or if it does, the searchers will find so many, it will be impossible to tell which he is, and more importantly, nearly impossible to prove he isn't."

Althea sighed. "You're right, I suppose. But I can't say that 'Althea Gray' rolls off the tongue or inspires the sort of image one might expect of an Elemental Master." She shrugged. "But then, I don't imagine I often live up to expectations. Perhaps it is fitting after all."

It took a moment for the implications to sink in to the guild and to Faorel. Althea became engrossed in her breakfast, waiting for their reactions with concealed delight.

Faorel was the first to understand. "Althea, that is the most peculiar proposal of marriage I have ever heard."

Althea's face squirmed as she tried to hide a smile. She raised an eyebrow but said nothing, returning to her breakfast.

"Do you know what you are doing, Althea?" Mark asked, incredulous. "He's been your Guardian less than a week."

"Yet bound to me for life," Althea countered. "Besides, you said it yourself. I cannot traipse about with a man not my husband, or a wolf for a pet. Yet he must be with me." She looked to Faorel. "It is not as if the queen's law could bind you to me any more securely than you are already, after all. Assuming, of course, that you'll have me, Faorel. You haven't answered yet."

The table grew quiet, all eyes on Faorel.

"Are you certain, Master, that this is what you want?"

She wagged a finger at him. "Althea." She gave him a look. "If you wanted to, could you leave, remove yourself from my life, and go live yours in peace?"

"I don't want to," Faorel began. Althea held up her hand.

"But if you did want to, is it even an option?"

"No."

She turned to the table at large.

"Can any of you imagine a man so determined that he would pursue a woman always in the company of another man, or a wolf?" Various expressions answered her silently. Althea turned back to Faorel.

"Even if there were such a man, so determined, would you abide his company? His affections for me?"

Faorel bristled instinctively.

Althea held her hand palm up. "Thank you for illustrating my point." Althea stopped speaking then, letting them all come to their conclusions on their own.

Elizabeth composed her face carefully. "It seems to me," she said slowly, "that some people prefer a little romance before their proposals, some affection, some protestations of passion. You are being decidedly unromantic, Althea."

Althea grinned, then put on a show of being ever so put out, dramatically pushing back her chair, and falling to one knee with a flourish. Faorel turned his chair to face her, and she took his hand in both of hers, staring ardently into his golden eyes.

"Faorel, my Guardian, my life-bound companion, I come to you without dowry, family, or connections, save these here. You delight me at every turn, and surprise me at every opportunity. There is no other who could enter my life and change it as you have and as you will continue to do. Our life together will not be easy, but it may be easier to bear with growing affection between us."

Althea's words brought shining eyes in her friends, and a quiet stillness in Faorel. The emotion in the room grew too intense for Althea's comfort. She chose to lighten the atmosphere with her finish.

"Will you have me as your wife? Will you share your made-up name with me? Will you make me an honest woman, and protect me from the world's scorn, Faorel?"

He smiled at her sly twist of words, recognizing the playfulness as his own, and waited, certain she had not finished.

Althea sobered. "No other could offer me what you offer. No other could risk as much for me as you have risked already. You would do me a great honour, replacing the title 'Master' with 'wife'. What say you, my Guardian? Will you have me?"

No one breathed.

Faorel drew out the moment as long as he dared, then took mercy on them all.

"With all my heart, Master," Faorel lifted her hands to his lips, forcing her to stand.

Elizabeth threw her napkin into the air in celebration. "Hurrah!" She glanced about for a servant. "Cake! Punch! We must have something at hand to celebrate with."

The men laughed at that while Edna took a quiet moment to dry her eyes. When all had settled back into their seats and the general excitement ebbed, Faorel turned to Althea with mischief dancing in his eyes.

"You do know that Elizabeth said only that *some people* prefer romance. Neither she nor I said that *I* prefer romance."

Althea fought to smother a grin, convinced she was about to bear the brunt of his amusement as he continued.

"I would have agreed without the passionate and ardent entreaty, but you seemed so determined to do it, I hadn't the heart to stop you."

"Oh, hush, you," Edna tapped him lightly on the arm. "Let the women have their moment. Honestly," she huffed.

That set them all laughing again.

"Now I'm restless," Althea complained, unable to sit, stand, or pay attention to any one thing for more than a moment. She paced, sat, stood, and paced again.

"Perhaps a walk outside?" Faorel suggested.

"Perhaps a run. The horses have cut a lovely track winding all over the grounds."

In moments she had laced up her spell-breaking boots tight, and tied her cloak around her, Faorel only a step behind as she burst from the house and into the morning air.

"You might enjoy this more in wolf form," she said, turning to address Faorel only to find him already changed. "I might have guessed you'd anticipate me." She glanced around them for the elementals, finding them peeking around fence posts and over mounds of snow. "Hello, my friends!" She called to them. "If you are so minded, by all means, join us!"

She launched into a steady pace, the wind flying through her hair, whipping her cheeks and making her eyes water. Her heart began to pound and she took huge lungful's of air, relishing the freedom and the feeling of joy that made her so unsettled only minutes before.

The elementals paced her, flying and swinging from tree to tree lining the path, or diving into the snow to pop up ahead of her, only to dive back in again as she drew near.

Faorel remained at her side, his long, loping strides easy and graceful. His tongue lolled out, a happy-puppy look in his expression as Althea continued her rhythmic pace.

Half way around, Althea veered into an open field, the snow unbroken, and threw herself down to the ground to make a snow angel and rest a moment. Her elementals swarmed her as soon as she grew still, making her laugh.

"Hello, my friends, are you enjoying the day?"

"Delight-t-ted we arrre," trilled one of the bird-like elementals, "that-t-t you arrre well, Mast-t-ter."

Faorel flopped down beside her, pressing against her side as he kept an eye out for danger.

Althea reached out to touch him, resting her hand on his side, feeling his slow, steady heartbeat.

"I am more than well, friends. My guild friends have forgiven me, I've no more secrets to hide, and my Guardian has consented to be my mate."

"Guardians are difficult mates, Master," her favourite gnome warned.

"I am a difficult Master, so that is only fair," she quipped, undeterred.

"And if another Master challenges your right to have him?" The gnome persisted.

Althea sat up. "Someone can do that?"

"Yes, Master. One Master can challenge another if he feels the other does not deserve a Guardian, or out of jealousy. Either way, if the other loses the challenge, the Master takes the Guardian as his own."

Faorel growled, not liking the turn the conversation had taken.

"You'd rather I walk into a situation like that, not knowing what could happen?" Althea's tone sharp. "You'd rather I risk losing you, all because I am ignorant of the consequences?"

Faorel subsided.

"I'd rather not take the chance. Forewarned is forearmed, as they say. Thank you, friends, for your continued counsel. We shall be leaving for London in a few days, so if you've preparations to make, please consider beginning them soon." Althea stood, brushing herself off. "And now I am rested well enough to finish the track." She turned to Faorel, "shall we?"

They were off.

A bath and a braid and Althea was settled once again, serene enough to compose her letter to her aunt. She was grateful, pleasant, informative, and brief, finding it difficult to write to a virtual stranger. Giving the letter to the maid to post, Althea took herself to the music room to play.

She limbered up with scales and arpeggios until her fingers sought out other melodies, tripping around the keys with no particular tune in mind. Althea gazed out the window as her fingers wandered. She grew wistful at leaving such beautiful grounds, and such dear friends. Her hands found a minor key as sadness and loneliness crept into her thought. Mourning the loss of the Durston's company, mourning the horses, the greenroom, John's patient tutelage, mourning the maid who took such pleasure in piling and pinning her hair.

But I shan't be alone, for all that, and I can always return to visit, Althea chided herself, shaking off the mood. Her hand naturally changed key up a third, making her minor third a major root, as she contemplated London. The left hand hammered in the same way Althea imagined the traffic and factories would bang and crash, and the right hand chimed with chords of whistles blowing and bells ringing, and soon both overlapped into a perfect cacophony, a London street swirling around her.

Around both of us, Althea corrected herself, and now a new line emerged in harmony with hers, sometimes dark and menacing, others playfully dancing around her, a laugh in the choppy notes as one melody just managed not to crash into the other.

London fell away. The whistles and chimes fell away. The pounding and traffic fell away. Only the two melodies, single lines, no chords, remained, weaving between each other, then slowing into a languorous conversation, hushed and huddled together in private conference, then one single note as they met in the middle, one voice, one word, hanging in the air, sustained by the pedal and Althea's wish to let it resonate.

She took her hands from the keys and sighed.

Faorel was the only one in the music room, unable to abide by the ghosting the rest of the household adhered to, but he'd stayed out of Althea's line of sight and remained supernaturally still, muffling any noise he might make, with magic. When Althea sat back, he waited a few moments more, sensing she needed time to return to herself and be at peace.

"Well, my Guardian, did you enjoy that?" She asked, turning on the bench to face him.

"Yes, Master, very much. There is magic in your music, in the spaces between the notes. You paint a vivid picture with sound."

Althea smiled at the compliment. "Thank you for that. Perhaps we ought to rejoin the others now?"

Faorel rose fluidly, reaching for her hand. "With pleasure."

Inviting the local preacher to Longview, Althea and Faorel were married in the greenhouse, surrounded by elementals cleverly hidden among the foliage, and witnessed by their guild friends. The ceremony was small and brief, much to everyone's satisfaction, and all the household joined in the merry making afterwards.

It was late again when the household retired, and Althea and Faorel returned to their rooms.

"Well, the others can rest at ease now. Not a soul can accuse us of impropriety. There is, after all, nothing at all improper about a woman sleeping in the same room as her husband," Althea had stepped behind the screen to don her nightgown, still practicing modesty, despite her words.

"None indeed," Faorel murmured, staring at the screen with his head tilted. "Master?"

"Althea, Faorel, not Master."

Faorel ground his teeth.

"I shan't like to make that an order, however sorely you might tempt me." She stepped from behind the screen, unpinning her hair as she crossed the room.

Faorel stepped up behind her soundlessly and wrapped his arms around her waist. He leaned down and kissed her neck.

Althea smiled and hugged his arms.

"May I please you, wife?"

"Mm, you may certainly try," Althea teased, "husband." She felt more than heard the vibration of an amorous growl from him. For a moment she flashed back to her last days with the Wentworths and tensed up. Faorel froze.

"What is it?"

"I," she paused, "nothing," determined to push the memory away.

"Master, Althea, Lady Gray, Wife." Faorel spun her by her shoulders. "There is a shadow crept over you. This is not nothing."

"I thought the elementals might have told you already."

"Told me what?"

"Mind, they couldn't come very close to me then. They might not have known, unless John told them. But why would he?"

"Told them what?"

Althea sighed. "Perhaps we'd best get comfortable."

Faorel considered retorting with 'that's what we were trying to do', but couldn't find the levity. He sat down near Althea, she on the end of the bed, he on the chair at its foot. She took his hand and squeezed.

"There is a shadow over me, you said."

Faorel nodded.

"It was cast while I was with the Wentworths, after Aldergrove arrived. He was instructed to make me less than content. He obeyed."

Faorel's brow furrowed.

"You've heard most of this already, I know. What my friends did not mention, was that I was tampered with. Perhaps Edna didn't tell Elizabeth, I don't know," Althea would have continued had Faorel not jumped from his chair. A low growl, nothing like the sultry rumble only moments before, rattled in his throat.

"Tampered with." He stopped his pacing to look at her.

"Aside from a great desire for too many baths, it did not appear to do me much harm. Until now. When I would like to enjoy my beautiful new golden-eyed husband, but hesitate."

"You never shrank from me or withdrew when I touched you."

"You only ever touched me with affection and protection."

"And now? Was that not affection?" His eyes pleaded with her, afraid, hurt.

Althea stood, stepped in front of him, took his hands in her own and held them up between them, the only buffer between their bodies. She stood on her toes and turned her face up to him. He accepted the invitation and kissed her gently. She released his hands, placing her palms on his chest as he wrapped his arms around her in a protective circle and held her tightly, pressing her face into his shoulder.

She suppressed a bad moment where she could hardly breathe. He didn't deserve for her to lash out when all he wanted was to comfort her. But as he continued to hold her, the fear grew, as did the hurt, the anger, the humiliation, not just of her last few months with the Wentworths, but of a lifetime of slights and degradations.

A tear escaped first, then a sob.

Faorel locked his arms in place.

Althea tried to push him away.

He would not be moved.

She grew frantic, crying, pushing, wordless, beyond sense.

His marble body remained still and unyielding.

"Please," she whispered, her manic strength failing her, pouring out of her like so much mater. "Let me go," her lips brushed the fabric of his shirt. She hadn't the strength even to lift her head.

Faorel bent and kissed her temple. "Never, Master." He adjusted his grip to something more casual, more comfortable, now that her fit was over, and rested his chin on her head. "You are *my* Master. I shall never let you go. Least of all, when you need me the most." He kissed her head again. "As you do now."

"Faorel," Althea tried to argue. Her body gave the lie to her mouth, as she nestled more comfortably into him.

"No matter how unworthy they made you feel, no matter how unlikely they told you a match would be, you are cherished, Lady Gray, and infinitely lovable."

Althea chuckled. "You go too far," she reprimanded him.

Faorel snorted. "I do not go nearly far enough. Should fortune ever grant me the passing chance, I will go far enough for retribution."

His muscles tensed under her hands. Althea soothed them, caressing them gently but firmly, and sighed.

Faorel continued. "Remember that first morning, when you asked if enjoyed playing hide and go look with your maid?"

Althea nodded.

Faorel rested his cheek on her head. "I was not delighted by playing games. I was elated you chose a few more stolen minutes with me. I knew, as soon as you appeared in that grove that you would be a wonderful Master, someone I could serve with both joy and pride. Someone I could love with all my being, and never regret one moment of. Every second since, you have confirmed it."

Althea grunted.

"You said our life would be easier for the growing affection between us. Let us banish the shadows together."

And so they did.

Dawn broke over them, a tangle of limbs and bed sheets, as they lay exhausted. Althea nestled in closer, her head on his shoulder with a deep sigh of contentment.

Faorel kissed her forehead and laid back into the pillow.

"Well, Master, what say you?"

"Hmm," Althea purred and caressed his bare chest.

"Have I served you well?" The playfulness was back in his voice. He'd been deadly serious all the time he'd been caressing her, intent on banishing any shadow so thoroughly it could never return. A woman's pleasure was no laughing matter, especially if that pleasure had been broken.

Althea answered by squeezing him tighter and then going limp.

"Have you even an ounce of unsatisfied desire left in you?" He watched her slyly.

"Hmm. Not an ounce. Not a teaspoon." She stretched like cat and groaned softly. "Not a drop."

"Are you certain?"

"I am."

"I don't believe you," he kissed her. "Convince me."

"Will any of you be staying with John when we leave here?" Althea asked her elementals.

The wizened old elemental hobbled over to her, a sad look on her face.

"We cannot, Master."

Faorel squeezed her gently.

"Can you tell me why?"

"Mages are like flowers, and elementals like bees. We need the nectar of your magic to survive. If any of us stayed here, we would starve. He hasn't the magic to sustain even one of us." The elemental patted Althea's hand.

"You feed from us?" Althea's brow furrowed. "How?"

The old elemental made herself comfortable in Althea's lap.

"Magic is drawn to mages, to varying degrees. It flows to you in a torrent. It flows out of you through your music and the work you do with the plants. We absorb that, whatever is left over once your magical work is complete. We even feed from your wards, which is why you must check them daily and replenish them, Master."

"Why can't you feed directly from the magic I draw from?"

The old woman smiled. "Clever Master. You are a filter. Magic is raw, wild, and littered with all manner of things as it flows through the world. When you draw it, when it courses through you, as it must when you give it purpose, you purify it, tame it to your will, refine it to its essence, and that nectar is what we drink, what strengthens us. The taint would kill us, we cannot digest the raw ore of it. But oh," she closed her eyes as she hugged herself, "the sweet clean magic you pour into your work and beyond is a welcome offering, and a feast in our veins. Honey, liquid gold, warm and pure, coursing through us." She was in rapture.

Althea leaned back, into Faorel. "And you, my Guardian? Do you feast this way also?"

Faorel rubbed his cheek against hers. "A Guardian lives as a mortal does, on animal and vegetable. Though there is some exchange of magic, when necessary."

Althea sighed. "Poor John. It seems too cruel to deprive him of your company." She included all the elementals surrounding her in the statement. She hadn't noticed John creep into the sun room. Faorel had, but made no motion, trusting John as friend not foe.

"Ease your heart, Althea," he spoke as he cleared a corner, coming into view. "Much as your army has delighted me, amused me, and educated me, I am well-used to tending to my small magics in solitude." He addressed the elementals. "I thank you for your indulgence. Know that you are welcome here always."

A solemn moment passed between the elementals and John. An acknowledgement of a sort that Althea could not decipher.

"As for you," John pointed to Althea. "Your maid is already beside herself for the loss of you, and all the staff in mourning for your music. Though you are bound for London, I beg you to consider returning to Longview often, for I know Elizabeth will miss you more than she will say." He lifted his chin and looked to Faorel. "And you too, Rogue. Though you'd best keep to one woman and leave mine to me." He winked.

Faorel chuckled.

"I assure you, I have my hands more than full with my Master and wife."

Althea's jaw dropped open at the exchange. "Shocking! Truly, both of you." She looked from one to the other, seeing another silent exchange taking place.

"Cook has prepared lunch, and doubtless packed a basket to send with you for your journey this afternoon. We will have you on your way with full stomachs and in good time, if you'd deign to join us now." John bowed formally with a touch of the dramatic, then turned on his heel, allowing Althea and Faorel to follow in their own time.

Althea glanced around at her elemental friends.

"Is there anything you can do as a parting gift for him, my friends? Whatever magic I have is yours for the taking. I should very much like to leave him with something lasting for all he has done for me, for us."

The elementals conferred quietly then turned to her again.

"His wife," her favourite gnome spoke for the group. "She loves his roses, and the colour of orchids. Help us, and we can bring him sterling roses to give her. She will be glad to have them, and he glad to give them to her."

The others nodded. "As will we," the old woman added.

"Then tell me what I must do," Althea said.

Castalds

Part 4

London proved to be every bit as chaotic as Althea's music had promised. Althea longed to clap her hands over her ears to shut out the noise, so unpalatable was it after a lifetime of country living.

The carriage lurched, banging over a bump, and Althea reached for the side handle. Her gold band shone in the light streaming through the carriage window and caught her eye, making her smile.

Faorel, watching her, pulled her to him to brace her better than the coach handle would. She smiled her thanks up at him and settled in.

Edna leaned into Mark, infected by the quiet accord of the newlyweds. She sighed.

"We are quite the set. Newlywed couple and old married couple."

Mark kissed Edna's forehead. "And yet, our newlyweds still do not outdo us in affection."

"True affection ages like wine," Faorel agreed.

Althea glanced at her gold band again. Both hers and his were magically engraved with the word 'transcend', a command to become more than what each was alone, together. The rings were gifts from her elementals who both collected the gold from the earth and engraved them. Althea fiddled her fingers, getting used to the feel of it.

They arrived at Lt. Chambers home in the early afternoon, all of them glad for a chance to stretch and move about, though Faorel looked around dubiously. Two things disturbed him. The first was that there were far too many people around and any of them might harm Althea. The second was that there wasn't a scrap of yard, park, or green to be seen anywhere. If he wanted to be a wolf and take a run, this was no place to do it. Instinctively, he moved closer to Althea, gently pulling her to him with a hand at her waist.

Hannah Chambers appeared in the doorway while the luggage was being off loaded from the carriage roof. Elizabeth had insisted on making gifts of Althea's wardrobe, over any protestations.

"Welcome, all of you, come in, come in," she waved a handkerchief and disappeared inside.

Faorel grabbed their trunk in one hand, continuing to hold Althea close with the other. The Weatherbys sent their luggage on to the house where they would arrive later.

They climbed the stairs to the door and Faorel let go of Althea, allowing her to precede him while he stood between her and the street, guarding her. No one would get to her except through him. A middle-aged man took the trunk from Faorel, presumably to put in their room, and the party found Mrs. Chambers in the front room, waiting for them.

Introductions and pleasantries were exchanged, Mrs. Chambers disappointed to have missed the wedding, and soon they were all talking like old friends over tea.

"Oh, my Matthew will be sorely glad to see you, my dear. He misses his brother terribly, to this day, and you the spitting image. You have the Chambers' eyes, that's for certain true."

Footsteps out front alerted Faorel first of said uncle's arrival. He tensed beside her, his eyes darting from the window to the door. Althea clasped his hand, waiting for him to decide if friend or foe approached.

"And there he is now, just on time," Mrs. Chambers' joy at her husband's return plain on her face. "My, you are the jumpy one, aren't you?" She noted Faorel's reaction.

Mr. Matthew Chambers clomped in the door with a cut of meat dangling from one hand. Mrs. Chambers jumped up to greet him with a hug and kiss, and relieved him of his burden. "Your niece arrived while you were out, my dear, with her husband Faorel Gray, and their friends the Weatherbys."

Mr. Chambers stuck his head in the room and nodded his greeting to them all. "Delighted. Forgive me a moment, I shall return directly." He clomped up the stairs. Mrs. Chambers left to the kitchen.

"Fine wine," Mark said with a smile.

"Indeed." Faorel agreed, more at ease.

Over dinner, the Grays and Weatherbys recited the edited version of Althea's history.

"And here you are," Matthew smiled at Althea, accepting the tale.

"Yes, uncle, and very grateful to you and Aunt Hannah for having us."

"Tosh, child. 'Tisn't everyday a lost relation is found."

"You look a bit like him, you know," Matthew pondered her face.

Althea looked down, demurely. "I wouldn't know, uncle."

That inspired the few portraits of him to be found and family stories told.

"Your Da loved the sea," Matthew recalled. "He took me aboard his ship when he returned from his first voyage. He wasn't supposed to, mind. Him an ordinary seaman, and me just a boy. But he did it anyway. He was overflowing with energy, pointing out every wonder, telling of the salt wind on his cheeks as she cut through the waves." Matthew paused in the telling, considering his audience.

"He was quite special, was Edward," he let the phrase hang there, waiting.

Edna divined his meaning first. "As is his daughter. Takes after him that way." She looked significantly at Mark.

They dared not speak of magic openly. If Mrs. Chambers didn't know her husband's family had magic, or if the servants were unaware but within earshot, it could spell disaster.

"Actually, uncle, I was hoping you might also be able to tell me about my mother."

"Never met her, myself. What a dust up when Ed came home on leave, wed, and you on the way." His face darkened, remembering the last time he'd seen his brother. The joy of it overshadowed by the loss shortly thereafter.

"A friend of ours looked into the Fairchild's," Edna offered.

"Peter, I mean, Lord Croft." Althea stumbled.

"Peter, is it? My dear niece, what well-appointed friends you have made." Faorel grunted.

"Gave you a run, did he, Mr. Gray?" Matthew cast a knowing look at Faorel.

"Lord Croft thought the Fairchilds might have been related to the Duke?" Althea turned the conversation away from such dangerous waters.

Matthew nodded. "Might have. Fret not, Althea, the navy boasts some fine law men. We shall have them look into it."

The evening rounded out with cards and idle chat, all in the house retiring shortly after the Weatherbys left for their own home.

Faorel grumbled as they prepared for bed, his mood dark. He paced until Althea stepped in front of him, making him pause. She took his hand and led him to the bed, sitting down on its edge.

"I can think of a number of things that could be souring your mood, Faorel."

"Yes, Master?" His eyes glowed, no longer hidden by the tinted lenses that kept strangers from seeing his yellow eyes.

Althea counted them off on her fingers. "Strange city surroundings, too many people about, memories of Peter, memories of Wentworth, my uncle's taking a measure of you."

"Astute you are, Master," Faorel conceded.

"None of which we can do anything about," Althea raised an eyebrow at him, daring him to challenge her. When he didn't, she continued. "Yet there is this," she draped his arm over her shoulder. "Just now, there is only you and I in this room. We are together and safe as can be, which should bring you some comfort." She looked up into his face, inviting a kiss.

He accepted, the tension melting from him in moment.

The rumbling in his chest was not a growl.

"Come to bed, my Guardian."

Matthew did not exaggerate the navy's legal prowess. Before the week was out, they had all the particulars of Angelina Fairchild and Captain Edward Chambers.

"According to this," Mrs. Chambers pointed to one of the many documents splayed on the table, "you very well could be a Duchess, your grace."

Matthew grunted, his eyes scanning a different page. "Not sure you'd want it, highness. Looks as though all that remains of the duchy is a broken down barn of a building, and more debt than income, the last title-bearer apparently had trouble living within his means."

"A somewhat empty title, then," Althea concluded.

Matthew shook his head. "Worse." He held up the page. "According to this, if you take the title, you accept responsibility for the debt. No, niece, I suggest you let the crown take it, or the lawyers."

Althea sighed.

The Chambers misunderstood, Aunt Hannah looking sympathetic. "Oh, I'm sorry, my dear. I suppose you had your heart pinned on being a duchess."

Faorel laughed. "Forgive me, Mrs. Chambers, but I expect my dear wife is relieved. She was no small measure worried over the great mantle of responsibility."

Althea struggled to keep a grin from her face. "The dance, actually. The infernal dance of nobles more than daunted me."

Matthew grew thoughtful, taking Althea's measure as much as Faorel's in this first visit.

"Heavens, look at the time," Aunt Hannah exclaimed. "I am sorry to run out on you all, but I promised to call on Mrs. Kingsley this afternoon. Do excuse me." She bustled about and out quickly.

Matthew stared at the door after she'd left, then leaned in with sudden intensity, pitching his voice low.

"Althea, your friend said you take after your father."

"She did." Althea nodded.

"Have you the gift, then?"

A conspirators smile lit her face. "I do. Earth. Not Water or Air."

"Your aunt knows nothing of this. Not Edward's gift, nor mine. She wouldn't believe or accept magic even if we told her, so not a word of it."

Althea nodded, hoping her silence would grant her uncle whatever time he needed to speak his peace.

"How strong is your gift?" He pressed on.

"Strong, I've been told."

Faorel cleared his throat and leaned into the conversation, removing his lenses. "May I re-introduce myself, Mr. Chambers? I am Faorel Gray, elemental Guardian, and this is my Master."

"And wife," Althea chided.

Matthew's jaw dropped as his eyes grew wide.

"Strong enough, then." He turned to Faorel. "Trained?"

"Perfectly house trained, sir, I assure you."

Matthew stifled a chuckle. "Not you."

"In your own words, sir, well enough. Her education continues."

Matthew looked at both of them, one, then the other, then back. "You really haven't any desire for nobility, do you?" he was both certain of it and perplexed.

"Someday, when we are better acquainted, and when it is but a distant memory, I may tell you my feelings about nobility." Althea's tone was dark. "I shan't seek it if given a choice."

Faorel glowered. His intensity pushed Matthew back in his seat, even though he was not the target of Faorel's anger.

"So, niece, what would you seek, then?"

Althea shrugged. "As I have told others, the world is far greater than one small island. If there isn't room enough for Faorel and I here, I daresay there may be elsewhere."

"Without a shilling to your name, your grace?" Matthew prodded her.

"Without a shilling, Mrs. Gray, if you please. We are neither of us without talent, uncle. Nor above earning our keep. The question is only at what, and where?"

Matthew stared at them both, watching as Faorel drew up beside Althea, silently agreeing with and supporting her. *They stand together, in all things.*

"You have amazed me, niece. Raised by a nobleman, I expected you to be soft and privileged, with a sense of entitlement all out of proportion with your current circumstance."

Faorel tensed beside her. He would spare her the reliving of those life experiences that shaped her. Althea patted his hand. None of it was lost on Matthew.

"Perhaps my father's papers will offer us some options. Shall we continue, uncle?"

Matthew's gaze remained on them a moment longer before he returned his attention to the piles of papers. They were still reading when Aunt Hannah returned. She made some tea and joined them, without a word about Mrs. Kingsley, and the others were so engrossed they neglected to ask.

Hannah flipped a page over and exclaimed as she saw a bank note.

"My dear, you must see this," she handed the pages to Matthew, who read through them quickly.

Althea and Faorel stopped working through their piles and watched Matthew. His expressions left them in suspense.

"It appears," Matthew began, his eyes remaining on the page, "that my brother set aside some funds during his years with HRMs Navy. He named you heir, in the papers recently discovered, and pending my approval," he held up one page, "confirming that you are indeed Edward's daughter, the bank will release them to you." Finally Matthew raised his eyes to Althea.

"May I see?" She held out her hand for the pages.

Matthew handed them over and Faorel read over Althea's shoulder.

"Surely that can't be right," Althea murmured, for the first time seeing a possible future.

"It's no duchy, but it should see you settled comfortably, if modestly, niece."

Althea remained subdued through dinner, her mind churning over possibilities while her conscience plagued her for not sharing her thoughts with Faorel. He had as much right to the decision as she.

"Althea, dear," Hannah prompted her, breaking into her ruminations. "Perhaps you and Faorel would like to take a stroll, get some fresh air. You've been cooped up in here for days."

"Splendid idea," Matthew agreed.

Althea looked to Faorel, who nodded.

"Thank you, aunt, I think we shall."

Dinner was cleared away. Althea and Faorel were excused.

"We could take a house, oh, not in London, but a cottage in the country. Or travel. I could augment our income by becoming a tutor. Mind, I've no credentials, but I could manage music lessons at least." Althea bubbled over as they took a wide lane leading towards a main courtyard.

Faorel's eyes were everywhere. Every doorway, window, and shadow held potential enemies. He kept Althea close and towards the middle of the lane, discouraging anyone from snatching her away from him.

Althea noticed his tension and his hyper awareness.

"Perhaps this was not so fine an idea after all."

"Whatever pleases you, my lady." Faorel brought their knotted fingers to his lips, kissing her knuckles as he kept watch of her surroundings.

"Are you referring to our walk, or our future?"

An indulgent smile spread across Faorel's features. "Both. But if you would allow us to continue this conversation in a less exposed setting, your Guardian would certainly be grateful."

They'd come to the courtyard, in the center of which stood a large fountain. Hawkers were still about, determined to take advantage of every minute of daylight. Flower girls half-heartedly tried to tempt people into buying the last of their now-wilting blooms.

Althea drank in the sight of the water pluming and cascading from the upper tiers to the lower, fascinated. Faorel read her face and followed her gaze.

"Perhaps a few minutes near the fountain before we turn back?" He suggested.

Excited eyes shone up at him. "You don't mind?"

"How could I begrudge you this simple pleasure?" His eyes still darted around them, but his tone was sincere. "A few minutes, more or less, shan't make much difference to your safety, my lady, but may make much difference to your thoughts." He offered his arm. "Shall we?"

Althea fairly skipped beside him, eager to dabble her fingers in the water.

She sat on the edge of the basin, gazing up at the splashing water, seeing the sky through a myriad of crystals as the fleeting light caught in the droplets. Faorel's attention was divided between Althea and their surroundings, hence he noticed a familiar, if unwelcome face, before Althea did. When he tensed, her eyes flew to his then to where he was looking.

She sighed. "This can be such a small island at times," she said softly to him, quietly so only he would hear. She stood, brushing her skirts, and turned to face Peter Croft.

"Lord Croft, what an unexpected pleasure," she greeted him with a curtsey.

Peter bowed stiffly. "Miss Chambers."

"Mrs. Gray, actually, sir. I am lately married. Allow me to introduce Mr. Faorel Gray."

Faorel bowed as though to a lesser man. Althea withheld her reaction by will alone.

"You've," Peter sputtered, looking from Faorel to Althea. Interpreting Faorel's bow, Peter assumed she'd taken the duchy. He looked as though he'd tasted something sour. "Your grace," he said, a sneer in his voice as he bowed low and fled the courtyard.

Faorel growled. "No good will come of him."

"So much for the negligible difference of a few minutes," Althea took Faorel's arm as he stared after Peter. "Come, let us to my uncle's."

Faorel looked down at Althea, nodded curtly, and escorted her into the house. The Chambers were not in the front room, which Althea took as a blessing. She looked into Faorel's eyes as he slid off the tinted glasses. His eyes glowed yellow.

Althea stood on her toes to speak softly in his ear. He obliged her and bent down.

"You look positively savage, my Guardian. Would you consent to going upstairs to our rooms while I say our good nights?"

Faorel growled.

"I shan't leave the house. We are perfectly safe here. I promise, just a few words and I shall come up." She reached up and pressed a palm to his cheek. "Please, take the moment, Faorel. You need it. As do I."

He softened. "Always so careful. Never an order, never a command. Only a plea. How could I deny you?" He kissed her then, gently, with a thrill of hunger behind it. "Go," he tilted his chin in the direction of the back rooms, then smiled and shook his head at how she continually disarmed him.

Her eyes said what her mouth could not before she turned to look in on her aunt and uncle. She found them near the fire, he reading, her knitting.

Matthew looked up as Althea reached the threshold. "Had a nice stroll, did you?"

"We might have, but for an acquaintance come upon us."

"Oh?"

"Lord Croft, of all people, appeared by the fountain."

"You called him Peter, once," Matthew prompted. "You cannot expect old lovers and new to get on, Niece."

"He was never a love of mine, uncle."

"Perhaps he thinks otherwise."

"He can think what he likes, I am sure," Althea's patience wore thin. "There is still no excuse for such manners as he displayed."

"And your husband?"

Althea offered her uncle a look, her lips pursed.

Hannah heard the pause and looked up from her needles, Althea masking her face quickly with downcast eyes. Hannah glanced from one to the other.

"If you don't mind my saying so, Althea dear, he will need your assurances sooner rather than later. Confrontations of this sort tend to shake a man's faith." She turned to Matthew. "So don't you keep her late talking, husband. I'm to bed." She looked pointedly at Matthew.

He smiled at her. "I will be up in just a minute, Mrs. Chambers."

"See that you are." She nodded and left the room.

When she'd gone, Matthew went straight to the point.

"Bit protective, isn't he? Even for a Guardian? I saw how he reacted to me, and I am no threat. How much more to a discarded lover?"

"Uncle."

"Yes, yes." He waved her off.

"He is a Guardian. My Guardian. We are bound together no matter how anyone feels about it, especially those so wholly unconnected from us," Althea grimaced, thinking of Peter.

"I've seen men, jealous, over bearing, turn ugly over trifles, Althea. I shan't wish that for you."

Althea paused. "You are very kind, uncle. I thank you for how much care you and Aunt Hannah have shown us. Truly. Please do not fear for me. There is no place safer in the world for me than at his side. To that end, I bid you good night, and pleasant dreams." She curtsied and left the room to seek out Faorel.

She found him in their rooms as she expected to. He was pacing, and near flew to her as she entered. She pushed the door closed softly behind her and embraced him.

"Master," his voice was hoarse, laden with emotion.

Althea let the word pass and held him closer. "We are safe, Faorel. You and I, secure in this room. Not a soul to do us ill. Be at ease, my Guardian."

He held her tightly, making it hard for her to breathe. She stifled the fear that threatened to well up inside her. *No safer place on Earth,* she reminded herself. He relaxed his hold on her and buried his face in her curls.

"You could have had him, Master," he rumbled. "It is not usual for a Master and Guardian to mate. He could have been yours, and I just the wolf at your side."

Althea rubbed his back, offering simple comfort.

"I did not want him."

"You could have enjoyed his fortune, his connections, been among those others admire."

"I did not want those shackles."

"His position would have protected you."

"You protect me, Faorel. I do not want Lord Croft. I want you. It may not be usual, but you are not usual. You are far more than a wolf, Faorel. Far more than anything I could have imagined."

"It would be torture to watch you with him. But I would have endured it, for you."

Althea pulled away then, to look into his eyes. She clasped his face between her hands.

"You are not listening, Faorel. I don't want Peter Croft. I don't want nobility. I don't want to be tucked neatly away like a porcelain figurine. I want you. I want a wolf in my bed, a man by my side. We are bound and I am blessed. Of all the people in the world you might have chosen, you chose me. I am cherished all out of measure by a great and glorious Guardian. No one else could care for me as you do, protect me, as you do, love me, as you do. Discard this fear that I have made a lesser choice in you."

Faorel chuckled. "Perhaps you said that backwards, Master."

Althea tilted her head.

"A man in your bed and a wolf at your side."

Althea raised an eyebrow as a smile twisted half her mouth. "I did not inverse my words."

Faorel's jaw dropped. "Why, Mrs. Gray, you'll shock all and sundry."

"Only if you tell." She kissed him soundly then, awakening the passion he had smothered in his doubt.

ॐ

Peace reigned at breakfast. Faorel's fears assuaged, Althea's desires sated, and the Chambers sharing sly looks. As the dishes were cleared, Matthew leaned into the table.

"Althea, your aunt and I have been looking through our own papers, and found something you might be interested in."

Althea glanced at Faorel with a crooked smile and a raised eyebrow. Faorel grinned back and nodded.

"Lead on, uncle."

"We'd forgotten about it. Twenty years of it sitting out there, no children of our own to leave it to." Matthew shrugged. "We'd like to give it to you and Faorel now, if you'll accept it." He handed her the papers.

Althea read hurriedly and handed Faorel the pages, allowing him to take the extra time the tinted lenses required to read the small, tight lettering.

"A cottage, uncle? You have a country cottage?"

"We do. No knowing what state it is in. The locals may have taken care of it, or not."

"They may not welcome strangers," Faorel said mostly to himself.

Althea cast an indulgent look on her Guardian. "I am certain your charm will make us welcome wherever we go."

Faorel's eyes darted to hers as though he'd been stung. He nodded curtly and resumed reading.

"Our father left it to me when Ed died. He'd intended it for Edward. 'Tis only fitting it should go to you now."

"Uncle, this is far too generous," Althea began. Matthew interrupted her.

"Tut, child. You haven't the means to be proud. Take it. Take good care of it, and each other. Only promise me that you'll visit. You're all the family I have now, and the only piece of poor Edward that's left."

Althea's chest ached as she noticed how hoarse Matthew's voice became, and the shining in his eyes.

"Oh, uncle, thank you." She embraced him, giving him the opportunity to hide his expressions from her for a moment. When they parted, Faorel stepped up, offering Matthew a hand. Matthew clasped his hand and pulled him into a manly embrace, slapping his back.

"You are a very good man, sir," Faorel intoned.

"As are you. Take care of my niece. She will need it."

The men shared a look, dark, full of foreboding, with a promise to keep harm from Althea.

"You may want to visit the church, niece," Matthew hinted.

Althea tilted her head in question.

"To enjoy the only place for miles where more than two square inches of green can be found. You must miss the countryside, with all its flora and fauna."

Althea nodded. "What say you, Faorel? Shall we to the church?"

Faorel chuckled. "Always so careful. Yes, wife, to church with us." He offered his arm and they left. They avoided the busiest streets and the most empty for Faorel's sake. Empty streets made them prime targets for muggers, where no witnesses were about. The crowded lanes allowed enemies to sneak in, brought close by the currents and press of bodies, to slip away in a sea of faces, never to be found.

As they walked, Faorel asked, "what *did* transpire between you and Lord Croft?"

Althea stumbled on a cobblestone. "Not a thing, so far as I know, though everyone else seems to think differently."

She would have left it at that, but for Faorel's disapproving glance.

"Very well. He would never have even known of me, but for Mr. Hamlin's interest and determination. Honestly, I thought Croft took an instant dislike to me.

His distain was evident, and he claimed a certain satisfied air at triggering the curse to ensure he had the last word."

Faorel growled.

"'Tis past, my Guardian. Be at ease."

A subdued grumble reached her ears.

"The next time we met, I'd been with the Durston's for some time. He delivered the news about the Fairchilds. I recall he seemed out of sorts, but I had thought it was difficult travel telling on him."

"What time did he arrive?" Faorel asked, putting no great weight to his words, casting his eyes about for any signs of danger.

"Hmm? Oh, I suppose it was near dinner."

"When you were at your most ravishing." Those words Faorel dropped like a stone in a lake.

Althea shook her head. "You, my Guardian, are quite literally looking through tinted glasses. Thank you for the flattery, just the same."

Faorel snorted. "Dismiss it if you insist, but do not imagine a man with eyes would overlook you, regardless of a contrary first impression."

Althea sighed. "I never sought his good opinion, any more than I did Hamlin's. Nor did I consider either man in any light save that of someone to whom I owed a great favour I could never repay."

"Pray he does not feel the same," Faorel warned.

"Why so?"

"If you owe him, he may think it his due to claim you in whatever manner he chooses."

"He cannot. We have made that avenue impossible." Althea moved closer to Faorel, squeezing his arm.

"In the eyes of god, perhaps. Desperate men take desperate action, my lady."

They came to the church, finding it empty of parish or clergy, and stepped onto the grounds.

"He wouldn't dare, not with my army of friends no more than a wish away," Althea stooped down to where her favourite gnome appeared before them. He clamoured up her arm to sit atop her shoulder.

"He has an army of his own, Master, and he's whipped them into a fury."

"To what end?"

"To defeat you or claim you. He cares little which."

Faorel crossed his arms to look at Althea, *you see?* Written in the lines of his face.

"And how did you come by this knowledge?" Althea prompted the gnome.

"We've allies, Master, amongst other elements. And they with our opposites. When Masters look to wage war, we share what we know."

"Well then, friend, what do you know?"

The gnome laughed his silent laugh.

"Clever Master. He is obsessed and incensed at once. He's a coven of Air wielders at his home and has sent for them and all their allies to come to London. To find you. To take you."

Althea stumbled, catching herself on a headstone. She looked down. Captain Edward Chambers. Gone to the sea he adored.

"Oh," was all Althea managed, looking at the symbolic resting place of her father. She stared at the headstone, but spoke to Faorel and the gnome. "He could take you from me. Banish you from this plane. Enslave you to his will. Perhaps even turn you against me."

"No, Master," the gnome denied. "We are opposing elements. He has no power over us. Elemental wars have casualties, but we could neither be coerced nor enslaved."

"Except by more mundane means," Althea said. "Small comfort, that. But comfort nonetheless.," Althea continued to stare at her father's headstone, caressing its edge, as though in a trance. A chill wind blew over her as all the yard went still. A susurrus inside the breeze teased her ears.

"Master," a warning tone from Faorel.

Althea held up a hand. "Wait."

Faorel growled, unable to disobey her command. She would regret that later, but just now the whisper insisted.

It sounded like autumn leaves, dry and passing each other in eddies, a hollow whisper forming her name. "Althea."

Faorel looked around, seeking the caster of this unnatural wind.

"Althea," the wind called again, blowing against her skin, biting with cold.

"I've no quarrel with you," Althea declared.

A dry crackle of a laugh reached her ears. "Nor I with you, Daughter."

Just behind the headstone a smoky figure appeared. Faint at first, then gaining substance. The buttons on his uniform gleamed as they caught the light, as he faded in and out of sight, as though forcing the appearance by will alone, and that will insufficient against the forces of nature.

Only his eyes held their shape, light, and substance. Althea caught them, only to think she gazed into a looking glass.

"Father?"

"Aye, lass. Listen. You must away. 'Tis not honour to die in vain. Too much depends upon you. You must away."

"Father-"

"I must go, my child. You do exceedingly well. Have a care."

He vanished, as though the tide of the world pulled him under, his will no longer enough to withstand nature.

Faorel fumed silently where he stood, waiting.

Althea blinked, coming out of her trance. "Faorel?" She reached out to him blindly.

He came.

Reaching her side, he wrapped an arm about her waist and held her up beside him. He pressed his forehead to the top of her head, relief washing away his anger of a moment ago. He'd be angry later. Now was a time to be grateful.

"What did you see, Master?" asked the gnome, dismissing the tension between Master and Guardian.

"Didn't you see him?"

"No, Master. Only the mage sees ghosts, or calls them. That is beyond the power of an elemental."

"Not real, then." Althea's disappointment was palpable.

"As real as magic, Master."

"My father. He bid me leave this place. To run. Concede the field."

"Deny it battle." Faorel nodded, as though the wisdom were seasoned.

"I beg your pardon?"

"Deny it battle. When the enemy is too strong to be overcome, when challenging it will only mean your own destruction, no matter how tempted, no matter how baited the lure, deny it battle."

"He will target friends and family." Althea realised.

"Likely, Master," confirmed the gnome. "He is beyond reason and beyond measure in thirst for his revenge upon you."

Althea sighed. "Air is without reason. The wielders seek my destruction without prompt, without cause. First Aldergrove, now Croft."

"Caution, Master," Faorel's voice and word choice penetrated her thoughts. "That way darkness lies. Deny it battle."

Althea squared her shoulders, taking her weight on herself rather than leaning on Faorel, without breaking their embrace. "I am Earth. I abide. When all else flutters, burns, and flows in eddies and madness, I abide."

Elementals appeared from everywhere, then. They hung in trees, stood on markers, crested the ground in waves. They stood proud, challenge in their eyes, determination in their stances.

They reminded Althea of accounts of soldiers in the war, preparing for a hopeless battle, bravely facing their doom. Realisation dawned on Althea.

"Oh, no, my friends. No. I shall not, I do not ask that of you. I abide. But I need not insist on remaining here. I will not sacrifice you. You are far too precious. I shall not, we shall not partake of battle here." She glanced at Faorel, a mix of emotions wavering in his features. A twisted smile warped her lips. "Lord Croft has lost the battle before it begun. It did not survive even the first engagement. What war can he wage if his opponent has vanished?"

Faorel passed his free hand over his face.

She let him compose himself and looked to her army.

"Tell me, friends, if you can, is it true you can travel leagues at the speed of thought?"

Grins appeared among them.

"May I take that as a 'yes'?"

Some of them nodded.

"Then if I may beg a favour of you, any of you, I should like to know the state of my uncle's cottage. Is it habitable?"

Silent laughter resounded among them.

"Perhaps I should rephrase the question," she addressed the gnome on her shoulder.

"I know what you are thinking, Master, 'Is it habitable to humans, or only bugs?' We are not quite so elusive as that, however tempted we might be to tease."

Althea smiled and looked at him expectantly.

"If it is not now, it will be when you arrive. Fear not, Master, we shall make you a sanctuary. Plan your travel."

"Thank you, friend. What boon can I offer you in return?"

"We do not bargain with Masters, Master. We serve whom we wish, when we wish, out of love. That is all." He waved his arm out to the gathering before them. "As you can see, we have much love for you."

"Then I am much blessed and grateful. Thank you."

"My Lady Gray," Faorel found his voice and composure once more.

Althea turned to him, delight in her eyes, as joy and rightness with the world filled her to overflowing.

"Yes, my Guardian?"

He swooped in and took a kiss that stole her breath. She turned her body to face him, clasping her arms behind his waist, taking as much as she gave.

The elementals approved quietly.

Faorel's hands came up to clasp her jaw as their lips parted. "A treasure and more, my Master."

"A delight and more, my Guardian," she replied.

"I don't understand your haste, niece," complained Hannah. "You've only just returned and now you dash off once again? It is all so sudden."

Matthew comforted Hannah as they sat in the parlour while the maid packed their things.

Althea spoke as close to the truth as she dared, without mentioning magic.

"I fear what scenes may arise if Lord Croft and I should meet again, scenes that might be unpleasant to more than just myself. I shouldn't like you to be included in anything so," she paused, searching for the right word, "distasteful." She made a face.

Faorel laughed.

"Mrs. Gray, you have the most magnificent expressions."

Hannah watched them both and could not help but be charmed.

"You will write, won't you?" Hannah conceded the field, and switched to pleading.

It was Matthew's turn to laugh.

Hannah gave him a disapproving look then dismissed him, turning back to Althea. "Won't you?"

"Of course, aunt. How could I not? I shall keep you abreast of all the goings on in the home you have so graciously bestowed upon us."

Faorel gave her a squeeze of approval.

They began their journey that afternoon, stopping at the Weatherby's for tea on their way out of town.

Edna and Mark were only too glad to receive them.

"You know," Mark sat back in his chair, considering them. "You are far too sensible for a girl of twenty." He waved a sandwich at her.

"One and twenty, as though that makes all the difference." Althea rolled her eyes at her own insistence. "One quickly learns to accept what one cannot change, else fall into madness and despair."

"Deny it battle," intoned Faorel.

Althea nodded. "Just so."

"And how shall you like being mistress of a country cottage?" Edna asked, sipping her tea.

"I've no idea, I'm sure." Althea admitted. "Though I have great expectation of felicity, all things considered," she indicated Faorel.

Joy lit his eyes at her words. His playfulness returned once they'd made the decision to leave London behind.

"Town did not suit either of us so well as we might have hoped," Althea continued. "Though we wish you both all the joy to be had of it."

"Fear not on that account, Althea," Mark assured her. "My Edna has plans every day for weeks, if not months."

"Which include answering letters from you, I might add." Edna warned.

"We should stop to purchase a large quantity of writing materials before we leave, Lady Gray." Faorel teased.

"Already done." Edna answered. "How better to ensure your correspondence than to equip you handsomely? You have no excuse now, my dear." Edna winked at Althea.

"Incorrigible," said Mark.

"Generous," countered Althea. "Thank you."

Before they were ready to part, the carriage was ready, packed tight with their belongings, and Edna's gifts. Althea and Faorel sat inside while the driver managed the horses.

"Well, Lady Gray. What make you of your choice?"

"Hmm. Which one? We've had no few of late." She teased him, knowing full well what he was asking. She nestled in close to him, and heard an answering rumble in his chest, making her smile.

"Poverty."

"Ach. Such an ugly word for what we have, and not the least bit accurate. We have all the world to explore, and a place to hang our cloaks at day's end. What more do we need?"

Faorel gathered her close. "All I need is here in this carriage."

"Just so."

❧❧❧

The cottage was as sound as a horde of elementals with a will could make it, which was to say, impregnable. Not only that, but it was immaculate. Being Earth elementals, they had but to call, and every mote of dust, every leaf, every stray bit of debris would glom onto them until they either absorbed it into their form or took it outside.

The furnishings were sparse, only a bed, a kitchen table and four chairs, and a pair of low benches throughout.

Despite the Spartan trappings, Althea was delighted as she moved from room to room, spinning around, her arms wide, drinking in their modest abode.

"Can you believe it, Faorel? A home of our own."

Faorel leaned against the doorframe, watching her with delight.

"Let it not be said that we live extravagantly at the expense of others."

Althea cast hurt eyes at him. "You wished for more?"

"Oh, no," he rushed to reassure her, closing the distance between them to clasp her hands. "No, my lady. Not for myself. For you."

Althea's face shaped into an rare expression, one of disappointment. "You know that antique chairs, damask, and silk are not for me. Look around," she turned them both to face the kitchen, "here is where we will learn to fix our own meals, with no one to condescend, no servants to adjust our actions and speech in front of, no one to judge or demand." She walked them both to the bedroom. "Here is where we will sleep, intertwined, husband and wife, Master and Guardian. Where we will do more than just sleep, with only generosity between us."

She spun to encompass the house and yard, "this is our space, to live as we will, to grow things, to build a life together." She faced him. "Our life together has only just begun. This place is an apt reflection of that. Only see the potential, Faorel."

"Just as your uncle was stunned, so too am I reminded what the trappings of privilege cost you." He bowed low. "Forgive me, Master."

"Wife. Althea. Lady Gray." Althea insisted.

Faorel's eyes sparkled as he stood straight. "As you wish, wife." He kissed her soundly.

He jerked away suddenly, his wolf hearing picking up footsteps on the path leading to the door. In another three heartbeats, Althea heard it too. She grinned then went to the door, waiting for the hesitant knock before opening it.

"Good afternoon," Althea managed around her excitement.

"Good day, I'm Mrs. Miller. My husband Gregory, and I, live just down the lane. We saw your carriage pass and thought you might appreciate a welcome."

Faorel stepped up behind Althea while the woman spoke, his tinted glasses hiding his eyes, one hand gently resting on Althea's hip, companionable rather than possessive.

Althea glanced up at Faorel then back at Mrs. Miller.

"How kind of you. Do come in. This is my husband, Faorel Gray, and I am Althea." They stepped aside to invite Mrs. Miller to enter.

She appraised their space quickly, impressed with the condition it was in. "No one's been here near twenty years." She seemed slightly awed.

"Our friends knew we were coming and did what they could." Althea said.

Faorel smothered a grin at how quickly Althea adapted to telling truth without speaking of magic.

"Well," Mrs. Miller huffed, slapping her lap. "No doubt you've not a crumb to eat, arriving just today. Will you accept an offer of supper with Mr. Miller and I?"

Althea dropped into a low curtsy, "we should be delighted, Mrs. Miller, thank you."

Mrs. Miller watched Faorel, whose attention was all for Althea. As Althea straightened, he took her hand, knotting their fingers. When she looked at him, he stood straighter. Like a magnet near its polar opposite he seemed pulled towards her.

"Newly married, then?"

"Indeed."

Mrs. Miller nodded. "Enjoy it." She might have said more, but held her tongue as a dark look shadowed her eyes.

"We aren't the kind to borrow trouble, Mrs. Miller. Each day has more than enough of its own."

Mrs. Miller nodded again, approving of them both. "Whenever you like, we will be glad to have you. Turn left past your gate, we're the next on the right. Mind you don't stray too far from the road. We've wolves nearby." Mrs. Miller warned.

Althea suppressed a smile. *If only you know how near.* "We will be careful, Mrs. Miller. Thank you."

Mrs. Miller nodded again and let herself out.

Althea stepped out onto the back porch to drink in the yard.

"Well, my friends, are you here?"

They appeared slowly, cautiously, as Faorel stood behind and to the side of Althea, on guard. She fell to her knees rather than tower over the elementals as they approached. "Why so shy, my friends?"

"Too many eyes, Master. Your arrival has not gone unnoticed."

"I should expect not. Mysterious occupants of a house abandoned twenty years. I am sure every detail will be recounted."

"Yes, Master. It begins even now."

"What about magic? Are there any other wielders about?"

"No, Master, but a few are sensitive. They might see us, might not. Might recognize something in you, might not."

"Might burn her or lock her up as mad, might not." Faorel growled.

Althea turned to Faorel. "Is it being a Guardian that makes you think that way? Or did you think that way before?"

"Does it matter?" Faorel asked, his eyes scanning the area.

"I suppose not." Althea shrugged. To the elementals she said, "is there more?"

"Aye, Master. Much. We've harvested for your larder. Nought we can do about meat," the elemental looked to Faorel.

"I might be able to do something about that," he replied without looking at either of them, his tone flat.

"There's wards and all to set, and a fouled area near. Miller and Baker are good friends to make."

"And Peter's war?" Althea prompted, not interested in the items to settle in.

"He's no notion you've left, Master. He is too busy planning and gathering resources."

"I pity those near him when he discovers our absence."

"Aye, Master."

"Are we safe, for now?"

"Aye, Master."

"Thank you, my friends. For all you've done for us, and for your counsel."

"Master?" The elemental defied the dismissal.

Althea looked at the creature with care in her features. He seemed hesitant, almost afraid. She hoped to dispel that with her open countenance and interest.

"What troubles you?"

The elemental looked down a moment and then peered into her eyes with fragile hope. "Set your wards?"

Faorel's head whipped around then, making the elemental flinch.

"It's all right," Althea said to both of them, with different meaning for each. "Simply done, my friend. Only let me get my shawl and we shall set them now." She glanced at Faorel. "That should satisfy both of you."

Faorel nodded curtly while the elemental looked relieved.

"Thank you, Master," he vanished with a pop.

Althea blinked. "I've never seen them do that before."

Faorel held up a hand, silencing her and looked to the treeline. A young boy appeared, parting the foliage to peer at them. He wore greens and browns, camouflage for the woods. A small bow was slung on his shoulder. A poacher. Faorel lifted his chin, acknowledging the boy. He approached.

"Excuse me, Master," he spoke to Faorel. Althea suppressed her grin at the reversal. The boy deferred to Faorel, not to her, gave him the title Master, not her. She waited, letting Faorel handle the situation.

"You normally hunt these woods?" Faorel asked, indicating the bow.

The boy blushed.

"No sense denying it. You may have been clever enough to leave your kills there where we can't see them, but your bow gives the lie."

"Aye, sir." The boy looked down, certain of a reprimand.

"Good hunting?"

"Aye, sir," the boy said more softly than before.

"Enough for us both?"

The boy perked up then, lifting his chin to look into Faorel's face. "Aye, sir."

"You know how to husband the game?"

"Sir?"

"No yearlings. No new mothers. Nothing carrying."

"Aye, sir."

"Good. Abide by that, and we've no quarrel. Understood?"

The boy's grin split his face. "Aye, sir!"

"Good lad." Faorel nodded. "I am Faorel. This is Althea, my wife. Mr. and Mrs. Gray when others are about."

The boy flashed them a huge smile. "Michael Brandon. We've the farm bordering your woods."

"That's supper you've left in there?" Faorel nodded to the trees.

"Aye, sir."

"Then you'd best get it home before it gets dark."

"Thankee, sir." Michael sketched a poor bow, more of a bob, and raced away to his catch.

Althea stood and stepped up beside Faorel, sliding her arm through his. "Another conquest, my love."

Faorel looked at Althea in shock and delight.

She leaned her head against his shoulder.

"You've never called me that before. Always 'Guardian' or 'husband'. You chose to wed me for convenience, or because I would be too inconvenient opposite a suitor."

"Who told you that?"

"You did."

"I only posed the questions."

"But-"

"What is between us is between us, and not for public consumption. All those questions and their answers were true, but were not why I asked you to marry me. They were the logic I used to justify my choice, to convince all of you of what I knew the moment you took human form."

"And what was that, Lady Gray?" Faorel trembled ever so slightly.

"That you were the stronger part of me, a part missed, ached for, but never defined. That I would no more live without you than cut out my heart. You gazed at me with your beautiful golden eyes and I was lost within them." Althea smiled at the memory. "You were so concerned I was disappointed."

"You pulled your hand away."

"For fear of letting on how you transformed both of us in that instant. Fear of you knowing how moved I was. How vulnerable. How taken with you. I loved you in that moment, and every moment after. But let a young woman speak to anyone of love, and suddenly all caution is voiced. All obstacles laid. I took the shortest route to securing you in the eyes of the world as I could think of, playing the cold, logical, world-savvy ward."

"All this time?"

Althea laughed. "Not so long a time, Faorel. Not compared with your time waiting for your chance to become a Guardian."

"Then Croft and Hamlin?"

"Never had much chance before I met you. None after."

Faorel whipped around, holding her tight, pushing her up against the house, kissing her passionately.

Althea responded with interest.

"You," he began when they broke for air.

"Loved you then and now with all my heart, Faorel." Her eyes were soft as she gazed up at him.

"I wasn't the only choice that was simply easier than being a single woman?"

"You are the only choice that would make me whole, assure my joy. You are the best creature in all the world I have ever met, with more true nobility, honour, valour, and grace in one whisker than ten 'good men' combined."

Faorel pulled her close, resting his head atop hers. "Master of my heart." He smiled, content with all his being for the first time.

"My love." Althea squeezed him gently.

"You fooled us all," Faorel accused lightly, pulling back only far enough to look into her face.

"A lifetime of practice. Besides, you are distraction enough to bring an elephant into a room without anyone remarking on it, your care for me, brighter than the moon. Who would notice if my gaze or touch lingered next to that?"

"They thought you indifferent, resigned."

"They were meant to."

"I couldn't reconcile you at all."

"Perhaps you will now."

Faorel pulled her close once more. "Yes, Master," he teased.

Althea heard the smile in his voice, as she lingered in his embrace.

"Shall we see about setting some wards, my love?"

"Yes," Faorel said decisively.

"Can we use the same method as checking the wards at the Durstons?"

"We could, but for initial setting, it is best to know the land by sight and feel." Faorel released her then offered his arm. "Shall we?"

"Yes, I think we shall," Althea linked her arm in his and they set about walking the perimeter.

They'd walked some distance before Faorel resumed the conversation. "Besides, I'd like to see what our friend was worried about when he suggested the wards."

Althea's eyes were everywhere, learning this new space that they had become caretakers of. She set the wards with Faorel's help and anchored them in place. She fed them and tuned them to recognize Michael as well as themselves, that she might not be alarmed by one poor boy supplementing the dinner table for his family.

"The Brandon boy is going to worship you, you know that," Althea mused.

"Then we shall have one more ally in the event of trouble," answered Faorel with satisfaction.

Althea smiled and shook her head at Faorel's defensive mind. Then, without warning, Faorel shifted into a wolf and took off running. Knowing him as she did, Althea took a glance around, found no better place of cover than the dense foliage she was in, and sat down. She formed a wish for an elemental and the old woman appeared beside her hand with a soft touch.

"Master?" The elemental whispered.

"Trouble, but I don't know what kind. I daren't move. Faorel would not look kindly on me putting myself at any more risk than I am here, and he would not have left me here if he didn't think it was safe enough, for now."

"Aye, Master. Wish for more of us. We will watch out for you both."

Althea did, and in a moment a horde of elementals appeared to her magical senses, but not to her physical ones.

"Eyes other than yours are near, Master," the elderly elemental explained.

Althea sat still, hoping to avoid being seen by those other eyes, trying to imagine an excuse for being out in the woodland on her own, in case she was discovered before Faorel returned.

One of the elementals turned into an animal known to lead hunters away from its young, and began making enough noise to get attention, squawking, rustling the leaves and branches around it. Althea listened in horror as the cries grew more distant.

"He'll be shot, or captured," she whispered to the elderly elemental.

"Shh, Master. He will be fine. We can pop away quicker than an arrow, and can trip a trap without being caught in it."

Althea remained where she was, keeping company with her elementals until Faorel returned, loping along a deer trail as a wolf. He glanced about and shifted back into man form.

"Althea?" He spoke softly, concern laced in his voice.

"Here," she stood carefully, her elementals giving her room.

Faorel's golden eyes grew wide as she seemed to appear from nowhere, a screen of leaves and branches melting from in front of her.

"Did you do that, Master?"

"No," said the wizened elemental. "We did. Then was not the time for teaching," her gaze dared Faorel to say different.

Althea stooped down to offer the old elemental a palm up. When the woman climbed on, Althea lifted her between her and Faorel. "You certainly are fierce, aren't you?"

"We will look after you, Master."

"So I see. Thank you for your quick thinking and your protection."

"Only don't complain when you reinforce your wards tomorrow, and that is thanks enough," grumbled the woman. "Finish your perimeter. The danger's not passed yet," and she vanished.

Faorel held Althea a moment. "Thank you, Master," he murmured into her hair, in case other ears were near.

Althea squeezed him in response, feeling exposed and under scrutiny. She took his arm and resumed their walk more briskly than before. They tied the last ward to the gate opening onto the front path from the road, closing the loop. Althea traced the route magically, sounding the lines and then reached for the power she so rarely sought to harness, but which flowed around her constantly. She poured it into the circuit, making it more than just a warning to her that the area had been breached. She strengthened it to actually bar entrance for anyone magical who was not friendly, be they human or other.

Faorel watched her in surprise, his eyes hidden by the lenses of his glasses in case anyone came upon them. Before he could ask her about it, she did one more thing, she did a magical wash from the edges inward to the center. The wards would do no good if something unfriendly had been inside before she closed the boundaries. To her great relief, all was clear and she pulled Faorel along, into the house before speaking.

"Where did you learn to do that, my lady?" Faorel asked, trying not to use the word 'Master'.

Althea looked suddenly tired, a wan smile on her lips. "I didn't. But it seemed right, somehow," she shrugged. "John did say I was a natural at defensive magic. Perhaps this is what he meant."

Faorel stepped to her side to support her as she swayed.

"That's no small magic you just did. Not so great as creating a Guardian, but then you were fed and rested, today you are not." He led her to a kitchen chair which she collapsed into gratefully.

"Our friends claimed the larder was stocked. Would you be so kind as to look and see if there might be something to replenish me, my love?"

Faorel smiled at her care. Even exhausted and drained magically, she was wary of accidentally issuing an order.

"With pleasure, my lady." He bowed himself out and went in search of something suitable. When he returned she accepted his bounty with thanks and fell to.

"How did you know to stay in the woods?" He asked as she ate.

Althea offered him another soft smile. "My Guardian would only leave me in the safest spot he could find. Coupled with the company of my clever friends, it seemed wisest." She took another bite, chewed, and swallowed. "Besides, if you returned and I was not there, you would have been frantic. I didn't see any point to alarming you unnecessarily." She put one hand out on the table for him to hold.

He reached for it and squeezed it gently.

"And you?" Althea asked. "Did you find anything in your chase?"

"A scent, which I lost, and a glimpse of a shadow, no more."

"Then whomever it was is both clever and quick." Althea sighed, the delight of their new home already diminished by unknown foes. "We've only just arrived," she began to complain, then stopped herself. "Never mind. Thank you, Faorel, for hunting the woods."

"I knew you would make a marvellous Master."

Althea rolled her eyes but smiled. The colour returned to her cheeks. She stood up slowly, testing her body's reaction. Finding it solid, she nodded. "Now, we have a dinner engagement, my love. Shall we?"

Faorel argued, knowing her to be safer inside the perimeter than outside, but unable to say what their intruder was. It wasn't until Althea pointed out that they were expected, and would have to send word if they weren't to make it, and in that case, Faorel would have to go, leaving her unattended, that he relented.

"Take whatever form suits you best for the walk, Faorel. Only be sure the Millers don't see you as aught but a man," she kissed him to take the edge off her teasing. The passion he responded with surprised her.

"If I didn't know how terrible consequences could be, I might invent a scare or two, just for that enthusiasm afterward."

"Don't even jest about that," warned Faorel with a growl.

Althea looked appropriately contrite. "I'd never hurt you or make you afraid for me Faorel. Not purposely," she reassured him. She leaned in again and kissed him tenderly, a silent promise that he melted under.

"I pity her," Mrs. Miller said to her husband after the Grays had left.

Mr. Miller took a pull on his pipe, blowing out smoke rings. "Why, Mrs. Miller?"

"She's obviously come down in the world. That gown and her manners mark her as nobility, if ever I've seen it."

"And have you? Seen nobility?"

"None such as she, dearest."

"Well, you've done your neighbourly duty, and satisfied your curiosity as well. That shall be the end of it, I should think."

Mrs. Miller looked askance at her husband. "Did you not enjoy them?"

"Oh, he made love to us very well indeed. But she was a bit standoffish. I can't see them being separated for any length of time, so there's no point in me cultivating a friendship with him if she must be endured. I think only of you, Mrs. Miller, burdened by a young snob of no consequence."

"Hmm," Mrs. Miller made no more reply, instead turning to the window to watch the Grays make their way down the lane.

Althea and Faorel walked home in companionable silence, Faorel with the basket of gifts from the Millers on one arm and Althea on the other. He kept her close, though he took the road side, staying well away from the hedges that lined the lands bordering the path.

"Well, Mrs. Gray, what say you?"

She leaned her head on his shoulder. "I say we have done more than enough for one day, and I am ready for some quiet time with my Guardian. And you?"

"Master, I-"

Althea hissed. "No more of that. Not in public."

Faorel looked at her in confusion.

"Between the Brandon boy, and our unfriendly shadow, we have been watched and perhaps even heard. We cannot afford," she left the rest of her reasoning unsaid, a cold prickly feeling of being watched tingling up her back. "Please, Faorel, let us only hurry home."

Faorel read her tension and nodded, picking up their pace and holding her closer.

They reached the house without further incident, much to Althea's relief. Once she was inside the wards they'd set, Faorel turned to go back outside. They shared a look and Althea nodded, silently agreeing to stay inside while Faorel ran the grounds. She waited in the kitchen, watching out the window for sign of his return.

Out of habit she wished for an elemental to keep her company. Her favourite gnome appeared.

"Well hello, my friend," Althea greeted him warmly. "I did not recognise the elemental who came to us earlier. Glad am I to see your familiar face."

Her gnome smiled and bowed, sweeping his blue cap off his head with a flourish. "Always at your service, Master, if not always seen." He winked at her.

"Should I wish for more of our friends to join us? Or are we safe enough to only want ourselves for company?"

"Your walls are good, Master. Nought wishing you ill can enter."

Althea slouched down, crossing her arms on the table and resting her chin on her arms. The gnome stepped back until Althea could focus on him properly without being cross-eyed. He laughed his silent laugh at her.

"I don't suppose you have any notion of who our unwelcome watchers might be?"

The gnome looked pained, "Master, I, we," he stammered.

Althea looked at him with pity and concern. "Don't fret, dear one. 'Tis no fault if you don't know. You may be pure magic, but I doubt that makes you omnipresent." She offered him a crooked smile and relief washed over him.

"Master, we don't know this territory. We can move quick as thought, but like thought, we tend to routes and ruts. Of those of us who stayed near you all your life, few ventured here and the local elementals don't know you as we do." He dropped his eyes, staring at the table top. "We are failing you."

"Nonsense," Althea placed one finger under the gnome's chin to raise his gaze. "You could not fail me if you tried. Just as you are not omnipresent, I doubt you can see the future. Who of us could have known we would end up here?" She raised an eyebrow.

"There may be a solution, Master."

"Oh? I would welcome your advice."

"Alliance."

Althea tilted her head.

"With the other elements."

"Is such a thing possible?"

"Aye, Master. 'Tis rare for us to ally with a Master not of our element. Alliances haven't been seen in a long time. But 'tis possible," he shrugged. "We are all drawn to power, every kind of elemental."

"But I've never seen the other elements."

"We only show ourselves where we are welcome. They are curious, and we speak of you, of your kindness and care. They only await your invitation."

"Indeed?" Althea's eyebrows rose. "What sort of invitation might I offer them?"

"You may not be able to forge an alliance with Air, because you are opposing elements, but," the gnome shrugged, "the others are drown by tokens of their own element. Cleanse a pool and the water elementals may come. Light a magically imbued candle, and Fire may come."

"Oughtn't I worry they will alight our home?"

The gnome laughed his silent laugh. "No more than you worry that we will track mud everywhere."

"What of my Guardian?"

"What of him, Master?"

"Will he not be hurt that I sought additional allies?"

The gnome looked behind him, out the window. "You might ask him yourself, Master. He comes."

Althea looked over the gnome's head and spotted a lupine shadow approaching. She stood and opened the door for him to enter. Once it was shut behind him, he shifted back into man form and looked pointedly at the gnome.

"Welcome home, Guardian."

Faorel offered him a bow. "Thank you for keeping my," he paused, "wife company, the word 'Master' almost audible in that pause. Where are the rest of you?"

"Only a wish away, Guardian. She did not need an army within your home, the barriers set are more than sufficient when coupled with your diligence." The gnome returned the bow.

"Thank you for your company and your counsel, my friend."

"We live to serve, Master," the gnome dove into the table top and vanished.

Faorel turned and wrapped his arms around Althea. "What counsel did he offer, my lady?"

"He suggested allies."

"Wise."

"Elemental allies," Althea clarified.

"Indeed?"

Faorel's body language told her nothing. He neither tensed nor relaxed.

"He claims I need only provide a small offering and I might earn an audience."

"With other elements."

"So he said."

"Well, Lady Gray, you've done quite enough magic for one day. I think we should make a different kind of magic as we seek our bed. Time enough tomorrow for offerings and invitations." He kissed the top of her head then tilted her chin up with one finger to kiss her mouth.

He was insistent, hungry, almost feverish, the events of the day, including the threats to Althea's safety, fueling his passion. Althea was breathless trying to match him, surprised and delighted by his eagerness.

When he scooped her up, one arm behind her knees, the other under her arm, she squeaked and then laughed.

"To bed, with us, Mrs. Gray."

"Yes, my love," her eyes sparkled, knowing how those words would thrill him.

⇛⇝

Althea stretched in the bed as she woke, groaning in pleasure as her body recounted the evening's passion. She turned a smiling face on Faorel only to find him watching her with amusement in his eyes. He ran his hand over her body, making her twist like a cat under his attentions.

"Good morning, lover," Althea purred.

"Good morning, Master of my heart," he kissed her.

"I think I shall like this married life we've begun."

"I do hope so, Lady Gray."

She touched her nose to his and rolled away to rise from the bed.

Faorel caught her waist and pulled her back to him, burying his face in her neck. "What is your hurry?" He growled. "Not a soul waits on us or for us today."

Althea was persuaded to stay.

When their day finally began, both were buoyed up and excited to begin building their life together.

"I promised you meat for the larder," Faorel reminded her.

"Only be careful not to get yourself shot. Our neighbours are watching for wolves, dearest."

Faorel laughed. "Do you not think I can hunt as well as a man as I do as a wolf?"

Altheas' mouth dropped open, her cheeks reddening.

Faorel kissed away her embarrassment and left the house, trusting that she would stay within the wards until he returned.

Althea busied herself with unpacking their few belongings and writing to their friends and family on the exquisite paper Edna had provided. Though they'd only arrived yesterday, there was still much to tell, and she was certain at least one of them would be concerned over their arriving safely.

Althea felt especially guilty about Elizabeth, who'd only heard the barest word of their arriving in London, and none of the events since. Althea filled the pages with descriptions of London, their journey, their new home and neighbours, and promised to write more once they'd settled in.

She sat back in her chair and took a deep breath, enjoying the quiet domesticity for a moment. Her favourite gnome chose that moment to appear on the table.

"Master," he bowed.

"Hello my friend, how are you this fine spring day?"

"Well, Master, thank you."

"To what do I owe the pleasure?"

"Some of the other elementals and I were wondering if we might offer you and your Guardian some gifts?" He looked hesitant.

"You have given us much and more already, my friend. We couldn't ask it of you."

"But Master, you are not asking. We are." Pleading hope lit his face.

"Well then, we can only be gracious and accept, with much gratitude."

The gnome clapped his hands in glee and spun around, then disappeared into the table top.

Althea shook her head at his antics and began folding up her correspondence to post. She'd just finished stacking her letters neatly when Faorel returned, a brace of rabbits slung over a shoulder, and a pair of pheasant hanging from one hand.

"I see you were quite successful," Althea praised him, despite the concern on her face.

Faorel's self-satisfaction evaporated at her expression. "What has happened?" he demanded, dropping his kills to the floor.

Althea's face softened. "Nothing, love, I simply haven't the first notion of how to prepare either of the selections you've brought." She looked at him sheepishly. "I ought to have learned more from those friends in service that I made."

Faorel kissed her cheek and retrieved the meat. "If that were the worst of our troubles, we would be fortunate indeed, my lady." He turned towards the larder to prepare the meat for storage. "We shall both learn much in the coming months."

When he returned he sniffed the air. "You've had a guest in my absence?" When Althea didn't respond, Faorel elaborated. "That gnome of yours has a distinct if subtle smell."

"Ah, yes. An offer of more gifts from the elementals. I haven't the slightest notion what of."

"What of your Allies?"

"It seems to me that first I should introduce myself to the locals of my element."

"Wise, my lady." Faorel nodded, then indicated the stairs into the cellar. "Where better than a room carved into the earth?"

Althea nodded and preceded him down the stairs. "Not to mention, an easily defensible location, not visible to any unfriendly eyes."

"You learn quickly, mm, Lady Gray," Faorel stumbled around the 'Master'."

Althea spread a found tarp on the bare earth floor and settled herself atop it, pooling her skirts around her. She wished for local Earth elementals, sending it out as a general invitation. Faorel stood in the doorway, barring any less magical being entrance.

In a moment, faces, heads, bodies, began to flow through walls and push up from the floor.

"Hello," she greeted the group.

A chorus of murmured 'Masters' echoed in response.

"Thank you all for taking the time to meet with me and my Guardian. I haven't much notion of the protocol of a new magic wielder entering territory."

A mole-like creature stepped forward to represent the group of local elementals.

"There is no protocol, Master. You call, we answer."

"Only if you choose to, at least in my case. I do not like the slavery implied in my title. I would like all of you to hear this from my lips that you might believe the other elementals if you hear them repeat it: I will not command you, or coerce you. While I accept the title, I would much rather be a friend than a Master. Is that understood?"

The tension in the room plummeted.

Althea's face squirmed with a suppressed smile. "You didn't believe the others when they told you about us, did you?"

The mole looked bashful.

"Do not be alarmed. I understand many Masters take themselves rather seriously, and have a narrow notion of what you all are like. With their legacy, I can understand how you might doubt a stranger's contrary words."

The mole looked from Althea to Faorel.

"My Guardian. Faorel Gray. Wolf, man, Guardian, elemental, husband, all in one magical package.

Faorel sketched a bow but said nothing.

"Master?" The mole man turned back to Althea.

"Yes, friend?"

"You have much power."

"I have been told so, yes."

"We are starved here. It has been long since one of your kind has taken residence in this area."

"But I thought you could travel anywhere in the blink of an eye?"

"When we are fed, yes. But some of us grew too weak to travel far, and no magic near enough to reach."

Althea was horrified. "Bear with me but a moment, little ones. Let us take care of your hunger before we do aught else." Althea gathered the power that swirled around her and spun it into threads of light, twisting it to flow from her hands into a growing pool in front of her.

"Eat, my friends. Take your fill. I only hope you are not like humans, who sick up what they eat when they are starved."

The mole cast a grateful and amused look at Althea before falling to the feast she offered.

Althea kept spinning the magic as she sent out a general call to any Earth elementals who were hungry. It was a no-strings invitation to come feast until they were sated. Some faintly faded creatures drifted into the room. If they were elementals, they looked as though they should belong to Air not Earth, as they were little more corporeal than smoke.

Althea continued to spin as she watched the elementals numbers increase and their bodies straightening up and filling out before her eyes. She spun faster. Faorel watched her with pride and love in his eyes, if he chose to keep his expression stony.

Before long the ragged wispy creatures that surrounded her resembled the army she'd met first at the Durstons' home. The pool of refined magic began to grow as their hunger slackened. Althea slowed down her spinning to a steady pulse and looked them over.

"I must say, you all look the better for a meal."

"Master," they chorused as one. In one gesture she'd won their loyalty. Part of her was delighted. Another part saddened that so small a gesture could win them so securely.

"What would you have of us, Master?" The mole-man asked, prepared to answer any command.

Althea shook her head, an indulgent smile on her lips. "Not a thing, my friend. I only wanted to introduce myself to you all, and offer my friendship."

She decided against forming any new alliances today. The magic she'd spun had drained her, and it seemed right to simply offer them all this gift.

Smiles and nods of approval were shared among them.

"Are you all sated? Are there more of you in want of a meal?" She asked the group at large.

"There are others, Master," the mole-man replied.

"If I feed the wards, will the others be able to reach them?"

"Yes, Master."

"Good. Dinner's on." She winked at the mole and flooded the perimeter, recalling Faorel's lesson in plucking the line like a violin string. She hoped the gesture would somehow resonate in the magical realm and alert the other elementals of the wards.

"My lady," Faorel watched her wilting beneath the strain of so much power coursing through her so quickly. His voice held warning.

Althea looked up at him with tired eyes and nodded.

"My friends, my Guardian is warning me that I will be no use at all to you if I work much more magic today. Will this sustain you until I recover?"

A flurry of sounds of agreement and dismay filled the room.

"Fear not, I will continue to feed the wards. You shan't starve again on my watch," she reassured them, misinterpreting the source of their dismay.

"Master, we fear for you too. You are rare. You will be a good Master. We do not want to lose you so soon after finding you."

"You are very kind. All of you. Thank you. I think I can safely say that my beautiful Guardian will do whatever it takes to make sure that does not happen."

Faorel nodded.

"Thank you for answering my call, friends. I think I must put myself in Faorel's very capable hands to help me replenish myself."

Another round of 'Master's and the elementals flowed away from her, into the walls and floors they came from.

"Neatly done, my lady," Faorel approached, offering her a hand up, which Althea gratefully accepted.

"Thank you, love. May I ask you to help me as I told the others you were fully able to do?"

"My careful wife," Faorel smiled. "I am delighted to serve you." He put an arm about her waist and led her upstairs to the bed. "I will return shortly with just the meal to brace you." He kissed her forehead and left to rummage the cupboards.

He returned with a full meal set on a splendid wooden tray, darkened from much use. Althea did not recognize it. As she fell to, her eyes caressed its lines, noting every detail.

"Where did you find this, Faorel?"

"I thought it was yours. Another gift from your generous friends."

"Our generous friends," she corrected him. "No, I don't recall either the Durstons or the Weatherbys including such a lovely piece in our baggage."

"Perhaps it was your other friends?"

"Oh," understanding dawned on Althea. "Is this what they meant?"

Faorel nodded. "Elementals can craft many things, my lady. Some more elegantly than others. Always using materials of their own element. I would expect to see more like this going forward." He indicated the tray.

"Then I must find a way to reciprocate."

"I think, Mrs. Gray, that is just what they are trying to do. Power wielders are notoriously selfish and demanding. Those characteristics generally increasing with the amount of power they can control. Make no mistake, control is very much what they seek. You, being one of the strongest power wielders in quite some time, could command legions of elementals."

"But the gnome said,"

"He gave you an incomplete truth. Because you did not bind them, they can come and go as they please. Any Master can bind the elementals as he chooses." Faorel touched her hand. "They come to you not only to feed, but because they esteem you. Most Masters must perform elaborate rituals, with carefully baited traps, which hungry elementals are drawn to out of desperation."

Althea looked horrified. "I don't understand."

"Power pulses around you, and you refine it unconsciously, scattering it for the elementals to come across as a squirrel finds nuts. Most Masters hoard power and hide the refined magic in strongholds, starving the land, the elementals. Those wise enough, flee before they cannot. But the smaller and younger ones do not always understand soon enough, and become trapped, like those you met today. When the wielder finally puts out a portion of magic, the elementals are too hungry to care about the trap. The Master binds the elemental and garners himself a slave."

"Despicable," Althea spat, leaning back into the pillow.

Faorel smiled, his expression soft. "You will upset more than a few Masters and elementals with the liberty you give to your 'friends', my lady."

"Let them be upset. I won't bind them to my will."

"As I am bound?"

Althea winced.

Faorel moved the tray to the floor so he could lay beside her on the bed. He wrapped his arms about her waist, pulling her close.

"I would not be bound to any other," he murmured to her, the word 'Master' whispered into her hair. "If given a choice, I would choose you."

"I love you too much to disbelieve you, Faorel. Selfish of me, but so it is."

"Then be selfish, for it serves us both very well."

When Althea recovered from the magic she'd wielded to feed the local elementals, she decided to send her invitations to the water elementals next. She and Faorel had discovered a small pond on their lands that was long overdue for some tending. They spent the better part of the morning dredging any number of foul items from it. Althea insisted Faorel stay away from any water deeper than his waist. When he argued, she waded over to him and embraced him, whispering in his ear.

"The elementals told me, Guardian wolves can't swim, dearest. Your body mass is too dense. I won't lose you to carelessness."

"But I should stand here and lose you?" He demanded, cross at her logic.

"You shall not lose me. Unlike you, I can swim." Althea kissed his cheek and waded back out to the middle, swimming when the water grew too deep.

When lunch time arrived, both of them were pleasantly exhausted and the pond was restored. As they ate their packed lunch, Althea sent a magical pulse through the ground and water, removing any blight or decay that remained.

She leaned her head on Faorel's shoulder, resting a moment before chasing the pulse of magic with an invitation to the water elementals to come enjoy the pool.

"A fine invitation, my lady," Faorel commended her, taking a holistic view of the morning's work. He tensed.

"What is it, Faorel?"

"It may invite more than just those you intended."

"Nothing unfriendly will get past the barrier at the perimeter."

"That barrier is steadily weakened."

"And steadily replenished."

"There are others who could cross."

"Mm. We haven't been here long enough to make any enemies."

She nestled close to him to rest and watch the pond to see if any elementals would show themselves. Before long both of them were sound asleep in the spring sunlight.

While they slept, Althea's call was answered. The water began to shimmer and ripple with the movements of elemental otters and undines. They gathered and frolicked in the pool, and then began to assemble around the sleepers, waiting patiently and quietly. One elemental reached for Althea, only to be yanked back by his neighbour.

"Don't be a fool. Can't you see that's a Guardian beside her? Touch her and he will destroy you without thinking, and nought any of us could do about it."

The offending elemental bowed and stepped back, ashamed.

Across the circle another conversation took place in gurgling tones. "You've heard the tales the Earths tell. Both new and local now sing the same tune of her."

The other nodded. "What Master works this hard for anything other than gaining power?"

"If you believe the others, this one."

"Believe your own eyes. She and he did this for us. Not her elementals. She asked no favours, made no commands. She mucked her own way through that foul bog."

"Quiet now. They stir."

Althea blinked herself awake slowly, while Faorel came awake all at once. Seeing they were surrounded he shifted to wolf form and growled.

The elementals all stepped back, widening the circle.

"Faorel, if they meant harm, they could not be here." She tapped the lines underneath the wards making them sound, proving they were still in place.

Faorel growled but sat down.

Althea addressed the water elementals. "Forgive us for such cold welcome. We were startled."

The elementals waited.

"I hope the pond is to your satisfaction. We wanted to make a small pocket of sanctuary for you."

Again they waited. Faorel grew restless.

Althea guessed some ceremony might be involved, magic words to allow them to talk to her. She didn't know what either might be. She reached for Faorel, running her hand through his fur, seeking comfort and guidance.

"My love, can you help me?"

He whined and bumped her with his shoulder.

She tousled the fur on his head with a laugh. "I suppose not."

Turning back to the waiting Waters, she lifted her chin and looks passed between them, as though she'd confirmed their suspicions.

"Allow me to begin again. I am Althea Gray, Earth, and this is my Guardian, and husband, Faorel. We welcome you to our pond, and hope you will make free of it."

Looks of shock and wonder that followed her introduction, making Althea smile. She held her tongue, hoping one of them might now choose to speak.

Finally an otter waddled forward.

"Thank you for your gift and your welcome, Earth Master," he bobbed his head.

"You are most welcome. I hope it pleases you."

"Why should you care to please us?"

"A friend once told me there was little enough comfort in the world. Even less for magical creatures." She shrugged. "It seemed only right to change that in any small way I could."

The otter looked around the circle at his peers.

"We agree. But your kind do not bring comfort," he challenged her.

"I hope you will find that not to be true in this case."

Her favourite gnome appeared at her feet, tunneling up from underground, surprising all of them.

"Master," he stopped, seeing the ring of Waters surrounding them. He looked about in confusion, recognizing a containment circle when he saw one. His Master might be oblivious, but the Guardian was not, however little he might be able to do about it. When the gnome's eyes lit on the otter his face broke into a relieved grin, and he trotted over to stand before the Water.

"Old friend, I am glad to see you again."

The otter remained guarded. "We were invited, Earth."

The gnome looked past the elementals to the pond beyond.

"So I see. And you've accepted, if not graciously. What do you mean by surrounding my Master, ready to attack?"

"These lands have been barren for no small time. The sudden appearance of magic smelled of a trap."

"'Tis no trap. Haven't you heard us speak of her? 'Tis a gift. One of many she is like to give. Where is the trust, Water?"

"Trust is earned."

Faorel growled, making the gnome look over his shoulder at the Guardian.

"I believe he agrees with you. Surrounding them is not going to help his temper."

The otter relented, waving a paw to dismiss the circle. Some of the elementals gathered behind him, the rest went to play in the pool. The gnome nodded then came to stand beside where Althea still sat.

"Thank you, friend, for your intercession. Can you stay? Or have you other business to attend to?"

The Waters that remained watched closely and were stunned by Althea's interactions with her elemental.

"I am glad to stay with you and your Guardian, Master."

Althea offered him the palm of her hand and he scrambled up her arm to her shoulder. Faorel, no longer pressed to guard her on all sides, moved to stand beside her, completing the uniform front.

"Well, this was far more confrontational than I hoped. I understand you are guarded. History has taught you much. I respect that. I think we shall leave you now to enjoy the pool. Perhaps we might meet again another time." Althea began packing up the remains of lunch slowly, dismissing the water elementals from her thoughts, and deliberately not looking at them.

"Faorel? Would you be so kind as to join me?" She asked as she stood, the gnome still on her shoulder. Faorel offered one last growl to the water elementals then took up his position at her side.

They left the elementals and made it back to the house safely, despite Faorel's growling and the prickle of danger that crept up Althea's spine.

She fell into a kitchen chair with relief as Faorel circled her and sat down at her feet. Althea chose not to press him. The gnome nestled closer into Althea's neck.

"That was a close call, Master."

"So I gathered. I mistakenly understood they would be curious and friendly, open to an overture of friendship."

"So we thought too. We did not think they were as starved as our kin were."

"We might have."

"Yes, Master," the gnome spoke softly, feeling rebuked.

Althea lifted her shoulder slightly, giving the gnome a gentle squeeze. "We are all safe now, thanks to your intervention and Faorel's intimidation. No harm done."

"Master."

"Thank you for your gift, by the way. That wooden tray is lovely."

"Our pleasure, Master," he hugged her neck then scrambled down her arm and dove into the table.

"Well, my love," she wrapped her arms around Faorel's neck. "I am for a bath. That pond was foul, and half of it is in my hair and clinging to gown and skin." She kissed his furry cheek.

It wasn't until after Althea had dressed again and was re-braiding her hair that Faorel made an appearance, still in wolf form.

"Something still troubles you?" She pet him like a dog, scratching behind his ears. "Do you need to go out and hunt it? Or are we safe enough in here?" She brought her face close to his muzzle and stared into his glowing golden eyes.

Again she was pulled into their depths, surrounded by his Guardian magic, pulled into a sea of amber, not knowing which way to turn or look, for it all seemed filled with light, blinding her. As she became aware of her heartbeat the magic receded and Faorel the man knelt before her, his head in her lap.

She stroked his hair and caressed his neck, waiting for him to speak or move.

He shuddered under her hands and wrapped his arms around her legs, squeezing tightly. She leaned down and pressed her face into his neck, breathing in the scent of wolf, moonlight, and magic. He groaned as though in pain. She held him tighter, reaching down his back to surround him, and kissed his exposed neck. A low growl escaped him. She kissed him again, savouring the taste of him on her tongue, turning comfort into something else, hoping to distract him from the dark fears the encounter reawakened in him.

Before long he succumbed, taking his passion to their bed until Althea was pleasantly exhausted. He spoke not a word throughout, and only after, when she was curled up at his side, her head resting on his chest, did he find his voice.

"I failed you, Master."

Althea's hand caressed his body.

"You did not. I am perfectly sated," she deliberately misunderstood him.

"I should have,"

"No, love. You did everything right. We are home safe, which I believe is an indicator of success in your line of work." She kissed his chest. "No 'what ifs' today. No failures. I might have anticipated, but did not. When we invite Fire, I think I shall simply leave the offering for them and return to it sometime later, to avoid a recurrence of today." She interspersed more kisses among her words, hoping to distract him.

"You are too great a Master to lose so soon," Faorel sounded pained. "I waited so long for you to appear."

"You have me, body and soul, love. I am here in your arms where I am meant to be. Your thoughts linger in *then* and *there*. Perhaps they might be better employed *here*, *now*," she chided gently.

Faorel kissed the top of her head. "Always so careful, Lady Gray."

He felt her smile against his chest.

Althea and Faorel began introducing themselves to their neighbours, stepping outside the wards to become acquainted with the area. The Brandon's were good folk, living up to the impression their son Michael had made. For the rest, they were like any other community, some traditional, some progressive, some loud, some quiet. While they formed no close attachments, they were universally welcomed.

More elemental gifts appeared in the house. Food magically appearing in cupboards. Furniture of a rough sort, later refined, began to fill their rooms. Dishes and other assortments came to hand when needed. Althea remained grateful, relieved that the small income from her inheritance would not have to stretch as far as she originally thought.

Their alliance with Fire went much more smoothly than with Water, and soon they were saved from the burnt suppers Althea produced as she learned to prepare the kills Faorel brought home. The salamanders were only too glad to cook once Althea promised them whatever leavings they could find. They greedily sucked the drippings from duck right out of the air as they twisted around it.

When the fire elementals began ornamenting the woodwork throughout the house, Althea was certain their alliance was sound. Water still kept its distance, but any day that brought Althea or Faorel out towards the pond found elementals splashing and swimming.

Althea's letters to and from her guild friends settled into a quick rhythm. Only her insistence that they not alert Peter to her whereabouts kept them from visiting. Elizabeth offered aid in winning the water elementals in the form of speaking with her own to pass the word of Althea's character.

"They might believe one of their own more readily," she wrote.

They were quite settled in when Faorel's gift arrived. A great carriage pulled into their small drive, astonishing Althea as much as it did the neighbours.

Faorel slid his glasses into place smoothly as the driver hopped down from the carriage. Faorel stepped out the door to direct the men into the house.

A small piano forte was quickly set up and tuned in the front room which now sported comfortable chairs and a number of shelves, littered with Altheas writing supplies and the few books she'd managed to obtain.

Althea stood amazed throughout the endeavour, watching Faorel handle the men with deft ease. Faorel escorted the men out and returned to find Althea sitting speechless across the room from the piano.

"Well, Lady Gray, will you play for me?"

"How did you manage this?"

"The elementals and Mr. John Durston helped a great deal."

"We can't possibly afford it."

"Fear not, Master of my heart. All is taken care of and well. Now, will you play?" He reached both hands out to her. She placed hers in his and he gently pulled her out of the chair and over to the new addition to the room.

She sat down and stroked the keys lovingly, not sounding a note, only appreciating its beauty. Faorel settled into one of the chairs and waited, watching as various elementals appeared outside of Althea's line of sight, to listen. He even spotted a water elemental in the vase of flowers, as it looked out at Althea.

Power gathered around her as she prepared to play, and the elementals, sensing the gathering, came to drink their fill.

She began with scales and arpeggios, fearing she'd lost her technique during her musical hiatus. She feared for nothing, as her fingers remembered what her mind forgot. Soon the house was ringing with chords of joy as her hands tripped up and down the keys, giving voice to all she could not say.

A pattern emerged, repeating in the background of her playing, reminding Faorel of the routine they'd found living in the country. They rose for breakfast and walked the perimeter, replenishing the wards. He hunted, she maintained her magical offerings to all three elements. He returned, they prepared his finds for the cold room, visited the neighbours, stole delicious hours. Dinner and quiet companionship in the evenings, including another perimeter walk and the comfort of each other's arms at day's end all formed the pattern of their life.

She trilled through the elementals, the notes gamboling as her Earth's were prone to do. Fire drove hard and fast as both chords and running notes. Water gurgled darkly in a minor key, wary and distant.

She mimicked the neighbours conversation, some droning slow notes out of time with the rest, some trilling of high chatter from the more excitable ladies. Even Michael Brandon's voice made its way into her playing as a tenor leaning toward a bass, his youthfulness warring with his desire to seem adult in front of Faorel, his fellow hunter.

The elementals drank it all in as power swirled around Althea. Even the water sprite seemed delighted with the feast, near dancing within the confines of the vase it inhabited.

Faorel sat watching them all and glowing with pride at his gift and his Master's obvious joy at being reunited with an old friend.

Althea told the whole story of their life at the cottage with her music, winding it down and shifting into her feelings for Faorel. He didn't recognize it at first, the tones coming slowly from her, hidden beneath a continuous running line of everyday distractions. It pulsed steadily, a constant companion, rooting the rest. When it pulsed, gaining in speed, consuming more of the sound, he smiled at her aural description. Laughter and joy tripped through the higher notes as the lower grew faster and more insistent. When the chords crashed in climax and release, he felt unknown tension drain from him as she settled into a more sedate pace, the sound languid and sated, then lyrical and peaceful.

She let the last notes fade into the room before turning in her seat. The elementals fled before she moved, that she might not know she had an audience. All of them left with smiles, looking brighter and more substantial than when they'd arrived.

Faorel let them have their secret and let his relaxed body language speak for him. Althea's eyes danced with light as she looked at him. She caressed the keys once more and then came to sit in Faorel's lap, wrapping her arms about his neck and kissing him soundly.

"You are far too good to me, Faorel."

He pulled her head into his shoulder and held her gently, saying nothing, not wanting to spoil the moment by arguing with her.

Part 5

Althea's next letters from the guild and her aunt were disturbing. Faorel found her in the kitchen when he returned from the hunt. Her face was pale, one hand over her mouth as the other hung limply from the table's edge. Her eyes were wide and shone with unshed tears.

"What's happened?" He demanded, dropping his kills and coming to kneel at her feet.

Her eyes continued to stare at nothing as she gave no indication she'd heard him.

"Althea," he raised his voice and grasped her face with both his hands, turning her head to look at him. "Althea, please, what's happened?"

She blinked, forcing the tears from her eyes. They slid between his fingers and her cheeks.

"Lord Croft has finally finished amassing his army, and discovered our absence. He is incensed. Rather mad, according to the Durstons and the Weatherbys. He attacked my Uncle Matthew."

Faorel drew Althea to him, surrounding her with his strength and comfort.

"All survived, but my aunt cannot understand what afflicts him, and he cannot say. The dark side of Air, apparently, involves the trappings of madness. Noises no one else can hear. Insomnia as the voices whisper terrible lies to the victim. I should be glad I was only cursed and not driven to madness."

Althea broke down and wept, clinging to Faorel, burying her face in his chest until his shirt was soaked through with her tears. She howled with grief and impotence. Once she'd cried herself out and pulled away, Faorel searched her tear-sore face.

"Is there nothing we can do?"

"I cannot take the elementals to war. I won't sacrifice them to Peter's overweening pride and delicate ego."

"What element is your uncle?"

"Water, like my father."

"You are certain he is not Air?"

"Yes, why?"

"Wish for your gnome, lady love," he gently dried her face with the corner of his shirt.

Althea barely formed the thought and the little man appeared on the table, without any of his usual theatrics.

"Master?"

Althea looked to Faorel, who then turned to the gnome.

"How close are Matthew Chambers' elementals to him?" Faorel demanded.

The gnome looked to Althea. "Master?"

"It's all right. Please, if you can, answer him."

"Not near so close as we are to her."

"Can they not withstand the attacks of Air?"

Understanding dawned on the elemental. "So. You have heard." His voice held mourning, whether for Matthew Chambers or out of empathy for Althea, they could not tell.

"Please, friend, what can you tell us?" Althea begged.

"Master, the Air are too many and too strong for your uncle's elementals to withstand. They will not sacrifice themselves to a losing battle on his behalf. 'T'would serve nothing but to diminish their numbers. He might do better were he nearer to the sea, rather than that accursed city." The gnome shrugged. "But that's nowhere near certain either, besides, they won't move him in his condition."

Faorel turned back to Althea. "Have they a cellar? A room below ground?"

"I don't know. I think, maybe." She hesitated.

"They do, Master," the gnome offered, anticipating Faorel's next words. "We might not do better than his Water, despite the earthen room."

"What would it take to increase your odds?" Faorel growled, frightening the little elemental into cowering.

Althea interceded, offering a sheltering arm around the gnome.

"Please, if there is something you need from me, name it. I cannot go to London to take up Peter's war, but I must do something."

"Master, we are but small creatures. His Air are no larger, but they are many."

"And you would be lost in battle, which I will not abide. I won't ask it of you."

"There are larger elementals, Master," the gnome looked in agony, as though betraying a great secret. "They keep to one place, rather than travelling as we do. They are loathe to stir."

Althea nodded. "Explaining why I haven't met one, and why neither of you spoke of them until now." She thought a moment more. "Is there such a one in London?"

The gnome winced. "Aye, Master. But he is angry and sick from all the

144

poison man has fed the Earth."

"Can we feed him? Heal him?"

The gnome twisted his cap in his hands, a grimace on his face. "He can feed from lesser elementals as we feed from you."

Althea grimaced and Faorel grew quite still.

"That is no better than sending you to war."

"We can carry power, Master," the gnome offered. "If enough of us arrived at once, with pockets of power to give, he might not devour us."

"Might." Althea dropped the word like a stone. "Have you a protocol around message bearing? Would he guarantee your safety under any banner?"

"No, Master. Only a direct meeting between you and he could protect us, and that only if you mark us as yours."

"Mark you?"

"Claim us as most Masters do, binding us to you."

"No."

"Master,"

"I said no. I will not make slaves of my friends. How can I meet with him if I cannot go to London?"

Faorel cleared his throat. "The same way you lay and sound the wards, my love. Lay a line to London, then sound the line. He will hear and answer no matter how cross he is."

"I can push magic into the line."

"Yes," Faorel answered, pride in his voice as she understood.

"Will you help me?" She asked both of them.

"Yes," they replied as one.

The elementals formed a relay, giving Althea beacons to follow when building the line. They kept their distance from the Greater Elemental's lair, at Althea's insistence. She did not want them close enough for him to consume, which only reinforced their love for her. She made them abandon the line before she laid the remaining length to where she sensed the elemental. They gathered around her and she twanged the line.

A tendril of power reached back for her. Faorel growled as he snatched her away before it grabbed her.

"Sick does not mean weak, I see," Althea kissed Faorel in thanks for his quick reactions.

"Who disturbs me?" A voice demanded, the sound resonating along the line beneath their feet.

"I do. Althea Gray. Earth Master." Althea's voice rang with authority she never used.

"Master, are you?" The Greater Elemental was condescending and greedy at once.

"Aye, and I have a boon to ask of you."

"Why should I believe you?"

Althea recognized the test and shot a surge of refined magic up the line. "Because I can give you more of that."

The magic disappeared, consumed by the Greater Elemental.

"Tasty, but not enough to prove you are a Master, nor enough to earn a boon from me."

Althea looked to her little elementals for guidance. They fixed their eyes on Faorel.

"His presence proves you are a Master."

"No. I won't put him in danger any more than I would you."

While she argued, Faorel grasped the line. "Faorel Gray. Guardian to Lady Gray." He sent his own signature up the line to the elemental. The elemental surged back along the line, seeking to grasp and trap Faorel, out of hunger and greed. Althea threw Faorel off the line with as much physical strength as magical, keeping the Greater Elemental from touching him. Her fury and fear blazed around her in a magical pulse, making Faorel and the elementals squint.

A chuckle resonated from the line. "A most feisty Earth, Althea Gray. It has been long since a Guardian walked our island. Longer still since one of your power appeared."

"I hear they have poisoned you, poisoned your home. I can cleanse both, if you will help me."

"What bargain?"

"Banish the Airs that plague Matthew Chambers."

"And you will feed me?"

"Yes."

The line grew quiet as he considered. Faorel sat stunned, still recovering from Althea's protective reaction. He held his head and kept his eyes fixed on the ground as he fought to manage the headache her blast of power gave him.

"Agreed."

Althea answered by gathering power and pushing the magic up the line to the elemental. She began to hum, her mind fixed on the task, the notes dark and determined. The magic flowed stronger. She continued for a handful of minutes, then stopped.

"A worthy offering," the Greater Elemental claimed, "though not enough."

Althea heard his greed.

"You shall have twice that again, and no more until you stir yourself for Matthew Chambers," she answered.

"Fair."

She pushed the magic up the line twice more, growing weary as she came to the end.

"There. That's all I have to give you until I hear he is no longer plagued."

"I shall honour our agreement, Master Gray." The Greater Elemental released the line. Althea took back the wards, retracting the line back to her perimeter. Her elementals swarmed her as she collapsed. Faorel remained incapacitated as they brought her food, drink, and blankets to warm and restore her.

"Thank you, friends. Is there anything you can do to help my Guardian?"
They plied him with much the same.

Althea dragged herself to where Faorel was recovering.

"Remember this," she said to him, anger burning in her heart and voice.
"For the next time you are tempted to do something so unnecessarily foolhardy."

Faorel growled.

"Growl all you like. Risking yourself for the sake of my credentials is not the
same as protecting me. I need you. Every day I need you. I won't say I'm sorry,
and I won't have you endangering yourself when it is not necessary."

Faorel grunted, subsiding, then reached for her. Her anger burned out at his
simple gesture for comfort, leaving her exhausted. She curled up with him,
surrounded by elementals, to recover from their encounter.

"I can see why few would seek out such a creature," Althea groaned. "I
much prefer the company of my smaller friends. Will you watch over us, dear
ones? I fear neither my Guardian nor I are up to watching for danger at the
moment."

Her favourite gnome waddled up to her face and patted her cheek.

"With pleasure, Master. You need not have asked."

⌒∽⌒

News arrived, in the form of a letter from Aunt Hannah that Uncle Matthew
was quite restored. His affliction left him all of a sudden, much to the amazement
of both physician and friends. He could not speak of that time, claiming he had
no true memory of it, nor of its cure.

"I shan't care," wrote Aunt Hannah, "so long as he is himself again."

Althea made good her word with the Greater Elemental, cleansing the area
surrounding him, and feeding him enough power to heal himself. She and Faorel
had no misunderstandings when they made contact the second time, each wary
of the Greater Elemental's devious nature.

Again the magic wielding left her drained. Again Faorel tended to her, a
most attentive caretaker. His job was made easier by the help of the elementals.
Both Earth and Fire helped gather and prepare the treats best suited to replenish
what she'd spent in converting raw power into magic. Faorel was as affable with
them as with the guild, and laughter rang through the house, carrying up the
stairs to where Althea was tucked up in bed.

She smiled as he entered carrying a tray of treats. The smell alone made
her stomach growl and her mouth water.

"You do know how to make a tempting presentation, Faorel."

"With aid, my lady."

She cast him a smoldering look. "You need no aid to tempt me."

Faorel stared at her, disbelieving, and laughed. "Really, Althea, you will
shock the neighbours if they hear you."

She stretched languidly. "I told you before, what is between us is not for

147

public consumption. I rather like having you all to myself."

"And having your way with me, too."

She purred. "Yes. Yes I do. Now, if you would be so good as to hand me that delicious smelling tray, so I can get my strength back, I may be able to show you, rather than tell you."

"Yes, my lady," Faorel replied with a grin.

It was a few more days before Elizabeth's letter arrived, warning them of Peter.

"He's reacted rather badly, I'm afraid. Bad enough that you should elude him, but for your uncle to make so miraculous a recovery, and you nowhere near. I shudder recalling his rage as he demanded an explanation of John. He claimed the area stank of Earth, and since John is the only Earth in your acquaintance, to Peter's knowledge, he assumed my dear husband was responsible. Lord what a mess he made of the house, winds blowing like a desert storm, furniture and all flying about."

Althea envisioned the havoc wreaked upon the Durston's home with a sigh. All of Elizabeth's lovely things, smashed and broken. She continued reading.

"Fortunately, John has neither temper nor fear, and his quiet dignity only made Peter feel foolish, like a child in tantrum. He didn't apologize, mind, but the winds stopped. Peter sneered something about the strength of John's powers and stormed out of the house, and good riddance, too!"

"Oh dear," Althea commiserated with her friend. "Such a to do. I must get that from my father," she mused.

Faorel stepped up behind her and kissed her neck. "Or your mother. I daresay her abandoning family and estate to move cross country was no less upsetting than your father's sudden marriage."

Althea leaned back, pressing her head into Faorel's shoulder. His eyes were scanning the page in her hands. He growled.

"Peter Croft, again."

"Yes."

"That man is a plague."

"Indeed. As the locusts to Egypt, so is he to our tranquility. I cannot say I have it in me to be amiable to an Air wielder after my dealings with Aldergrove and he."

"Not even a madman could fault you for that, love," he kissed her cheek. "What now?"

She recapped Elizabeth's account thus far. "She offers us warning." Althea read the remainder of Elizabeth's letter aloud.

"Take care, both of you. It was Peter who uncovered the information about you and your family before, doubtless he shall do so again. It is only a matter of time before he discovers your location. Your saving grace is that his army has disbanded, the elementals seeking wielders a touch more sane than Peter appears to be."

"Be well, my doves. Yours, etc."

Faorel paced, restless, the protective instincts of the Guardian warring with his target being out of reach. Althea did not attempt to calm him.

"How well stocked is the larder, my Guardian?"

Faorel lurched to a halt, caught off guard by Althea's question. He turned to her, confused.

"My lady?"

"It might do to add a rabbit or two, don't you think? A good hunt, the chase," she swallowed, "the kill," she finished with a slight grimace.

Faorel's eyes glowed, blood lust growing within him. He growled savagely, shifting as he did, until the growl finished with a wolf's snarl.

Althea stood and opened the door for him. He sped out without a backward glance.

"No point warning him to be careful," she said to herself as she closed the door. "With his instincts in such possession of him, he'll sense danger long before it senses him."

If only that had been true.

Some weeks passed before the trouble began. Invitations to dinner grew less frequent, and their own invitations were declined with regret. It wasn't until the evening Althea and Faorel met the Brandon boy while they were walking the perimeter, discreetly replenishing the wards, that the truth of the situation came to light.

Elementals were not to be found, which was Althea's first clue that something was amiss. While she didn't form a wish for them, invariably, they would appear. Either her gnome would meet them and climb onto her shoulder for their walk, or others would peek out from behind leaves and branches, playing a variation of hide and seek with them. None appeared now.

Althea kept up her quiet conversation with Faorel, exchanging a look. He nodded, both acknowledging her silent observation and agreeing with her strategy to pretend as though nothing were amiss.

"I can't help but wonder why our welcome has chilled among our neighbours," she continued. "Though I can't say I regret having more of you to myself." She gave him a sly look as she made room between them, in case he needed to shift or move quickly.

"Lady Gray, whatever their reasons, it is they who are deprived of your company." He froze, holding a palm to her. She stood still and silent, waiting. Faorel listened, cocking an ear to a direction ahead and to the side of them. Someone waited just off the path, hidden from view, if not from wolfish hearing. Faorel sniffed the air and a small smile spread across his face.

"Michael, its Faorel. Please come out." Faorel's voice carried the weight of authority.

Some rustling, and the boy appeared, looking sheepish.

"I wasn't eavesdropping, Master Gray, honest."

Althea remained a step behind Faorel, again allowing him to take charge of the situation. 'Master Gray' could easily handle one small boy.

"You were waiting for us."

"Yes, Master Gray." The boy twisted his hands, nervous.

"To what purpose?"

"As it happens, just the same thing Mrs. Gray mentioned as you came near, sir."

"Go on," Faorel encouraged, crouching, rather than looming over the boy. Althea suppressed a grin at seeing Faorel emulate her tactics with the elementals.

"There's talk, Master Gray, that there is a monster about. That it comes out at night. That it arrived about the same time you and Mrs. Gray did." Michael continued squirming, shifting his weight from one foot to the other, glancing about. He continued. "I told my Da it wasn't true, what people were saying. That you and Mrs. Gray wouldn't have anything to do with a monster. He said there was no monster. Just a very large wolf."

Althea winced inwardly, but kept her face still.

"Ma told me to stop hunting on your grounds, until the wolf was killed, but Da pulled me aside later and told me to keep hunting so long as you allowed it." He made eye contact with Faorel for the first time since he'd appeared. The tinted lenses disguised Faorel's eye colour, but not his gaze.

"You have been careful to abide by our agreement, husbanding the game responsibly. I see no reason why you shouldn't continue helping me manage the population. So long as your family allows it." Faorel fed Michael's words back to him with a wink.

Relief washed over Michael as he let out a held breath.

"Thank you, Master Gray."

"Michael?" Faorel added as the boy turned to leave.

"Yes, Master Gray?"

"You have nothing to fear from this oversized wolf, if indeed it exists."

"Sir?"

"It is probably a story. But if it isn't, you still do not need to be afraid."

Michael's confusion was written in his scrunched brow, but he was too polite to voice it. "Yes, Master Gray."

Althea and Faorel waited until they were safely within their own walls before discussing Michael's revelation.

"A very large wolf about, at night?"

"Yes, my lady."

"But you are here at night."

Faorel dropped his gaze to the floor.

"Aren't you?"

"Some nights, when the moon is bright, and you sleeping sound, I shift to patrol the grounds. I don't need as much sleep as you do. A gift of being a Guardian."

Althea sat down.

"Have you found anything on these patrols?"

"Sometimes I am certain enemies lurk just beyond the wards, but they are like that first intruder, a hint of a scent, and a shadow."

"Yet you did not mention them to me."

"While you are within the perimeter, they cannot harm you. When you are outside it, I am with you. I did not want to alarm you with suspicions I could not even prove to myself."

Althea remained silent for a time, reasoning things out internally before responding to Faorel.

"Are the elementals aware of your nocturnal activities?"

"Yes. They often accompany me."

"And have they sensed these enemies?"

"Yes, my lady."

"Yet they too have said nothing to me."

Faorel remained silent.

"You asked them not to."

Faorel did not look up.

"I see."

Althea took a deep breath. "How very fortunate for both of us that I know how tightly you and I are bound."

"My lady?"

Althea's voice was tight, riddled with conflicting emotions. "Keeping this secret, and involving the elementals in it feels rather like betrayal. Only the knowledge that you and I are bound for life is tempering the feeling, and that, not very well."

"My lady," Faorel paused and came to sit at her feet, looking up at her. "Master of my heart, I would never betray you. I thought only of sparing you needless worry. You feed the creatures of three elements daily, bargain with a Greater Elemental, fear for family and friends both, and care for home and lands no less than I . You have more than enough without the burden of a Guardian's duties as well." He pleaded with her, having slid his glasses into a pocket when they arrived home. His eyes were large, their amber colour like fresh honey. The pain in his face was too much for Althea.

She reached out and cupped his cheek in her palm. He leaned into it and closed his eyes, hoping for forgiveness.

"A Guardian's duties, you say. You might outline those in more detail for me one day."

Faorel whuffed into her palm and kissed it. "You are most careful when you have strong feelings, Lady Gray."

"Hmm?"

"Careful not to command. Careful with your power. Careful with your words. Rather singular of you, actually. Few could boast that control."

"Few need to." She lifted him up from his place at her feet. "My knees ache for you," she explained.

Faorel swooped in for a kiss and spun her in a circle, overcome with emotion as he sensed her forgiveness.

"Don't rejoice just yet," she warned. "We still have trouble to attend to." She squeezed his hand to soften her words, then wished for her gnome to appear.

"Master?" The little man stood on the kitchen table.

"Welcome, friend. I hope we are not disturbing you."

"No, Master. You have never called for me specifically. I am curious."

"I wonder if you can help me reason out a puzzle?"

The gnome looked worried.

"Fear not, little one. I shan't push you for anything you cannot give."

He relaxed marginally.

"Faorel has told me of your nightly patrols. It seems the neighbours have noticed him. Let us assume the threat you all felt was not imagined. How should we proceed?"

The gnome looked to Faorel and back to Althea. "Master, the threat is not imagined." He looked at Faorel again. "You know what claws at her barriers."

Faorel sighed. "Tell her."

"And rouse a Guardian's anger?" The gnome said, incredulous. "Thank you, no."

"Would you prefer a Master's anger?" Faorel's eyes pointed to Althea.

"Earth Masters are rarely out of temper."

Althea composed herself as they spoke around her.

"Please," was all she said, or had to say, her tone spoke volumes.

"Master, 'tis shadow elementals which seek you. They are as starved as all other elementals in the area. They know you've the power. Even more delicious if they can turn you, make you a Dark Master. The brighter your soul, the greater the treat for them to corrupt you."

Althea turned to Faorel. "You were trying to tell me without telling me."

Faorel looked down. "Yes, my lady."

"Can they take down the barriers?" She asked the gnome.

"If enough target the same spot at once, perhaps."

"Can they feed from it?"

"No, Master. They can only destroy, not consume what you have built."

"Feeding them is out of the question. No matter my pity for them, even I am not so foolish as to strengthen my enemies. Leaving might spare us the attention of these particular creatures, if they are so starved that they are trapped here, but other shadows elsewhere will be no less tempted." Althea paced as she reasoned aloud.

Faorel growled at her words, not liking where her thoughts turned to.

The gnome shrank under Faorel's anger.

Althea paused and looked at them both.

"I suppose there is more?" She raised an eyebrow at them, deliberately not demanding their response.

Faorel growled again. "You might as well tell her, gnome."

"Master, you can banish them. Just as a failed Guardian is demoted to a lesser creature, so too can shadow elementals be returned to a prior state to be redeemed."

"I sense a warning."

The elemental sighed, wishing she were less astute. "Yes, Master. It is dangerous. To banish an elemental takes great power, and your intentions must be entirely for its own good, else you chance corrupting yourself and making them much stronger at once."

"Will it hurt them, this banishment?"

"You must divide the shadow from the elemental, Master. Yes, it is painful. While you work they will cry, bargain, plead with you, curse you, all to tempt you into stopping. They will cry for others to save them. You could be swarmed and consumed by them."

Faorel continued where the gnome left off. "The kind of Master who enjoys the pain of others, enjoys breaking and banishing elementals, is too easily tempted to become a Dark Master. There is another trap. Just as zealots enjoy exorcising "demons" from those who do not conform to their faith, so too can good Masters grow heady with the power and become like the inquisitors who hunt the possessed."

"No one is incorruptible," Althea summarized.

"You cannot mend the world, Master," the gnome said, sorrow plain in his features and his voice.

"Perhaps I'd best sleep on this. Are we safe enough, for now?"

"Aye, Master."

"If Faorel does not patrol for a few days, will aught be amiss?"

"No, Master."

"I don't suppose you could patrol for him?"

"We could, Master."

Althea faced Faorel. "Will that serve until we get the neighbours sorted out?"

Faorel was not pleased, but nodded.

"If you and others would be so kind, we would very much appreciate your help with the perimeter, my friend."

The gnome perked up, glad to have something to do to serve her. "Yes, Master."

"Please try not to be seen," Althea begged. "I don't know how I could explain all of you."

"Worry not, Master. We shall take care of it."

ཚོ྾ཚ

Faorel's welcome in the village grew colder. Women were seen to pull their children closer, men stepping in front of their women. Althea saw how it hurt Faorel, though he never complained. His tinted lenses might hide his eyes from others, but Althea could feel his muscles tense when any of the little slights the villagers offered reached him. Despite this, he was always amiable, playing his role, taking the lead while his dutiful wife stood just behind and to the side of him.

For her part, Althea pretended to notice none of it, neither the villagers fear, nor Faorel's strained feelings. She took his arm and pointed out any little thing that took her fancy. She leaned on him with smiles and care, her eyes wide, her cheeks flushed with excitement. Let the village think her silly, she did not care. It gave Faorel an opportunity to smile at her, laugh at her, lean on her in return. Let them see how kind and generous he was with his adoring wife. Perhaps then the rumours would stop. Perhaps then, they would hesitate to connect 'monster' with 'Faorel'.

They returned home from one such outing with an armful of goods and Althea collapsed into a chair in the sitting room, worn out by the performance for their reticent neighbours. Knowing nothing pleased him so much as serving her, she feigned more hurt and exhaustion than she felt.

"Come, my love. I need you," she held out her arms, inviting him to her. Inwardly she winced at the command. Thoughtless words. But it was not a distasteful command, nor of long duration. She would forgive herself for it in time.

Faorel obeyed with joy and concern both.

"What is it, Master of my heart?"

"I think I very much need the comfort of your heartbeat in my ear, the safety of your arms."

He sat with her, letting her curl up against him.

"I would sit with you like this for hours, if you wanted it, love," he kissed her head. "If I thought you needed it." He called her bluff.

"I need you every day, Faorel." She refused to relent, knowing it was he who needed the comfort she was determined to give. If nothing else, she would show him that she did not fear him or think him a monster.

"What are you up to, Lady Gray?"

She snuggled in closer. "Not a thing," she purred, feeling her own tension draining away, tension she hadn't realised she carried. "Any day you are a part of is better than every day you were not. I am determined not to take you for granted."

He nuzzled her head, then rested his cheek on it. "It is the children that bother me most," he said, his own burden easing with Althea in his arms. "The adults, well, they don't know any better. But children still have their instincts, their innate sense of good and evil."

"Little Michael Brandon, who has met you, knows you for the good man you are."

"The pinched look in their tiny faces is almost unbearable."

Althea squeezed him gently, offering support and comfort, and hoping to distract him from his current train of thought.

"Then we shall not go to the village anymore. The elementals keep us more than well supplied. Whatever else we need, I can send for by post. Doubtless the

Durstons or Weatherbys can advise us of connections."

"And deny you what little society this village offers? No, my lady, we cannot. 'Tis too cruel to ask of you."

"You are not asking, and neither am I," her implacable determination crept into her voice. "I can't say I care for people who believe idle gossip and nonsense, thank you."

Faorel laughed, another measure of tension draining away. "Hardly nonsense. I *am* a wolf, after all."

"Perhaps, but you are many other things besides. They are fools not to see it."

He wrapped his arms more tightly around her, pulling her closer.

"Have I told you today that I love you, Althea?"

"You tell me every day without words, dearest."

Days passed in relative peace. Althea was playing at the piano forte when a fire elemental appeared, spinning in fast circles above her hands. She gasped and played a sour chord as the salamander surprised her.

"Hello, friend, you startled me. Are you all right?"

"Message from Master Weatherby," it hissed.

"Please, continue. I am listening."

"Peter's found you. Beware," the salamander said nothing more but continued to spin in agitation.

"Thank you. Did she say anything more?"

"He's mad, Earth Master. Only the shadowed will serve him."

"I understand. Thank you. Now what can we do to ease your heart? You seem quite upset."

"We, too, fear for you, Earth Master."

"You are very kind. All of you are generous and kind. We appreciate the friendship you extend to us. Truly," she watched as he spun a little slower. "But you are dimming, little one. I won't have you trapped here if a storm is coming." She spun magic to feed him. He writhed in hungry pleasure at her gift.

"You must conserve your power, Earth Master, as he amasses his."

Althea smiled. "That may be the wise thing to do, but it is not the kind nor right thing to do. I shan't have you trapped here, nor any of the others. Would you be so good as to warn them for me? The wards should have more than enough power to feed you all well enough to get away."

"Earth Master, you cannot face him without elementals."

"Let me worry about that. I would be grateful if you and the others found safety before dear Lord Croft arrives."

"But Master, he is already here."

Althea closed her eyes for a moment. "Please, if you care for me, take what you need, warn the others, and get far enough away to be safe."

The salamander spat a tiny flame at her and then popped out of existence. Behind her, Faorel growled.

She turned to face him. "Nothing's crossed the wards. There is still time."

Faorel shifted into a wolf and snarled at her, his yellow eyes glowing with Guardian magic. He walked to the doorway and sat down, barring her exit.

"Oh, I shan't go, is it? What will you do, sit on me if I try? Bite me?"

Faorel growled.

She came to him and sat down in front of him, dangerously close if he'd been an ordinary wolf. He could maul her face and throat without hardly stretching out his neck.

"Faorel, love," she reached a hand out to scratch his shoulder.

He growled.

"Please, dearest, listen to me just for a moment."

He grumbled then subsided.

"I have been learning from you all this time. Peter has seen my wolf, and he has seen my husband, but nothing he's seen will make him put those things together and come up with 'Guardian'. Come with me as a man. Let him underestimate you. Keep the element of surprise on our side."

Faorel's chest rumbled with something less than a growl.

"You are afraid I am going to order you to stay behind, that I am so stubborn as to face him alone, because I sent the fire elemental away. I am not so foolish as that. But I must face him. Come with me, my love, as a man. Let us see how Lord Croft fares against Master and Guardian, united."

Faorel's muzzle shot forward and he bumped his nose to hers. Then he shifted, becoming a man, crouched before her. When he spoke, his voice was hoarse.

"I had hoped to have more time with you, Master."

"Fear not, my love. Our time together is only beginning." She kissed him lightly, then moved to stand.

Faorel grabbed her and kissed her with passion, hungry, crushing her arms in his grip. As he pulled back, still holding her, he said, "so you'll never forget." His eyes blazed once and something inside her shifted. "I love you, Althea Gray."

He stood, looming over her, seeming larger than usual. He offered her a hand up, pulling her to her feet.

Althea sent out a warning to any elementals in the area to flee if they could. Her gnome appeared at their feet.

"Why do you reject us, Master?"

"I don't. I fear for you. Save yourselves if you can. I can't bear the thought of you being hurt or worse."

"We will not abandon you, Master. We live to serve, no less than your Guardian, even if we are not bound."

Althea sighed. "Very well then. To arms, my friend. The fight comes to us."

The gnome transformed into a fierce creature, fingers growing to claws, teeth growing to fangs, and horns appearing everywhere on his body.

"Yes, Master," he said with vicious delight. Then he disappeared.

"Do I want to know what becomes of an elemental who loses a battle with a shadow elemental?" Althea turned her face up to Faorel.

"He becomes shadowed and turns on his Master."

Althea scowled. Her wards blazed a warning at her in that moment, deepening her grimace. She began spinning power into magic to reinforce the barrier.

"He's here."

They went to the door and looked out to find Peter standing at the gate, just outside the magical boundaries Althea had erected.

He looked wild, winds whipping about him, his hair flying in all directions, his skin chapped by his own element. His clothes were worn, uncared for. His eyes were wide and held no small measure of madness. Althea stared at him, amazed by his transformation. She kept her face still, refusing to betray her feelings, and stepped outside, Faorel only one step behind.

"Fine barrier you have here, your grace," Peter snarled, unable to cross its threshold. All around him the winds whipped in fury, creating a storm for miles around.

"Not *your grace,* thank you. 'Mrs. Gray', if you please."

"You declined a duchy for this?" He waved his arms and the winds battered at her wards, unable to penetrate them. "Fool!"

"What can we do for you, Lord Croft?" She said, continuing to channel power into the perimeter.

"You passed up the title and fortune of being Lady Croft for him? For this squalor?" Peter continued, now screaming to be heard over his own conjuration.

Faorel growled, Peter's words touching too close to his own feelings and insecurities.

"I've no need for either, Lord Croft." Althea answered only to allay Faorel's fears. "What is it you want here?"

Peter's fury spiked at her wards, creating thunder where none should be. Althea winced at the noise.

"I've occupied your elementals elsewhere, Althea," Peter gloated, both at his success and at using her Christian name, denying her the respect she was due, and undermining her position of authority.

Faorel growled at Peter's familiarity.

"I will break your wards and kill you, Althea. You've cursed me to love you." He threw power at the barrier. Althea felt it as a physical blow, but held her ground without betraying it. "I cannot sleep but to dream of you." He hammered the boundary again. Again she reinforced the shield. "I am consumed by thoughts of you with another man, and here you are, making those fears come true. Whore." He blasted the wards again.

Althea felt them begin to weaken, no longer able to refine the raw power swirling around her, but remained determined to stay inside the perimeter. Until Peter broke the circuit, there was nowhere safer, and he would expend much power in trying to smash the shield, leaving him weakened when he finally did break through. As worried as she was for her elementals, she pushed them out of her mind, focusing on her own battle and trusting them to theirs.

"Weeks I have been here, planting seeds of distrust among your neighbours. I didn't want to hurt you. I just wanted him gone. How better than a village lynching, born of superstition? He should have left. You should have sent him away." Peter attacked the boundaries again.

Althea decided to push his rage while the boundary still stood between them.

"I would never send away my dearest love," she spun to face Faorel, wrapping both arms around him to kiss him passionately, surprising him. He clutched at her, fear for her warring with his Guardian's instinct to neutralize the threat at the gate, but she would not be denied, and her desire was not feigned.

Peter screamed where he stood, whipping the air into an even greater fury to batter the protections she'd spent months reinforcing. Lightening crackled around him, while inside the perimeter, all remained still and serene.

When Althea disengaged from Faorel, he gasped for air, both stunned by her passion and stunted by her sudden withdrawal. He reached for her and she twisted so that he stood behind her, clutching her close.

"You've bewitched him no less than you have me. Yet he tastes you, and I do not. It shall not stand, Althea. He shall not keep you. You'll be mine, or you will be dead."

Althea rolled her hips against Faorel, a look of delicious pleasure on her face. "There are other outcomes, *Lord Croft*," she distanced herself from Peter using his title with disdain. "Much more pleasurable outcomes."

Faorel was shocked by Althea's tactics but hid it by nibbling her neck and watching Peter through her hair, playing along.

Peter was incensed, and redoubled his efforts at bashing in the wall of power that stood between he and his prey.

"I will take every person, every elemental, every friend and neighbour who might support you, away from you, Althea, dear. Then it will be just you and I. We shall see how proud you are then."

"I'm afraid you tried that already. It hasn't worked." She taunted him.

"My lady," Faorel warned, his mouth still at her neck, and his voice barely loud enough for her to hear.

"Trust me," she replied as softly.

Faorel nipped her gently.

"Even if you could remove my allies, you still can't reach me." She stepped forward, out of Faorel's embrace to stand mere feet in front of Peter. She pouted at him then batted her eyes. "All that power, and still so impotent." Her eyes changed, her expression smug and mocking.

Whatever sanity he might have had, fled him then, and he turned a berserker rage on her, crashing down on the barrier. It was then that Michael appeared on the edge of their woods, inside Althea's wards.

Michael ran towards them, calling to Faorel. Althea backed away from Peter to stand near Faorel, both of them warning Michael to stay back as he warned them of the approaching storm. Between all the dust and debris Peter had kicked up, and Althea blocking Michael's line of sight, he had no idea that the source of the storm raged at their gate.

The series of events that followed remained a blur to Althea, her brain unable to process what her eyes recorded, as it all seemed to happen at once.

Michael raced into the space between Peter and Althea, Faorel behind her, just as Peter broke through the wards. Peter launched himself forward, throwing a blast of magic towards Althea, not caring that Michael stood in the way.

Faorel moved with Guardian-enhanced speed, shoving Althea to the ground as Peter laughed, shrieking, his voice shrill and hoarse at once.

Faorel launched himself forward, wrapping himself around Michael and rolling, taking the boy out of harm's way, then popped back to his feet just behind Peter and spun him around with a snarl. A heartbeat, no more, and Faorel shifted to a wolf and tore out Peter's throat with his jaws.

Peter went down without a sound. Faorel savaged his body, tearing out large chunks of flesh and organs, spitting them out on the ground. Now Faorel's fury matched Peter's, and he tore the body to shreds, while all around him, Peter's winds dropped, and everything carried by them crashed and floated to the ground.

Michael cowered, his back turned to Faorel, unable to watch his friend and mentor.

Althea vomited on the grass then crawled over to Michael to comfort and console him.

Elsewhere, the elementals banished Peter's shadows and celebrated their victory. No few of them were injured. The battle was brief, but furious, lasting only the length of time between the barrier coming down and Peter's death. Like Althea, they chose to remain within the safety of her perimeter and let the shadows wear themselves out attacking the wards until the circuit collapsed.

Althea held Michael to her chest, keeping his eyes away from Faorel, while she watched in horror. The man she loved, the Guardian she trusted, was indeed a monster.

࿇

Faorel's rage outlasted Peter's body, and he lifted his bloody muzzle, searching for new prey. His eyes glowed with Guardian magic and anger.

Althea held Michael closer and stared at her Guardian in both defiance and fear. He took one step towards her and she lifted her chin, a protective instinct for Michael forcing her to warn Faorel away. He gave them up and raced into the woods instead.

"Come, Michael. You are all over with dirt and I shan't send you home like this." She stood, clasping his hand and led him into the house where she proceeded to wipe his hands and wash the dirt and tearstains from his face. She brushed his clothes, casting dirt and dust everywhere, for once trusting the elementals not to mind cleaning up after her.

Part of her mind had run screaming into an unknown corner. What remained was focused on the smallest details, the most mundane of tasks. If she could have seen herself, she would have been shocked by her own tear- and mud-stained face, and the pallor that fairly glowed underneath. Her clothes were torn and wind-whipped, her hair a tangle beyond hope. Her wide eyes spoke volumes, and Michael shared her fellowship in shock and fear.

Althea brewed tea, without the help of an elemental, and they sat in mutually agreeable silence for some time before Faorel returned, once again a man. He opened the door, startling them both from their individual far-away places. They both turned wide eyes on him, making him wince. His gaze flicked to the cold, untouched tea in Michael's hands and then back to both of them.

"Michael, 'tis time you were at home," he suggested gently. "I've told them you had quite a shock, and they are expecting you."

Michael looked to Althea who nodded. "You'll be fine, Michael. Go on."

"You're the great wolf," Michael accused Faorel.

"Now is not the time, Michael. We will speak of this later."

"But,"

"Go," Faorel said gently but firmly.

He stumbled out the door, his movements stiff and jerky, as though he was only emulating walking from pictures he'd seen.

Faorel closed the door and stood just inside the threshold, waiting.

Althea didn't look at him. Couldn't. She stared out the window for some time. Faorel remained a sentinel, hardly breathing, still and silent. Althea took a deep breath, pushing herself up from the table.

"I'd best see to the elementals," she said aloud, without looking at Faorel. She stepped out the back, avoiding the massacre in the front walk, and called for them, Earth, Fire, even Water, if they were so inclined.

The ragged mass approached, disheveled and almost transparent, at her feet. She sat down carefully, wary of doing them any more damage than she had already. Without a word, she began spinning power into magic and pooling it in front of her for the elementals to eat and restore themselves.

Again her mind focused on the small task, ignoring all else. She spun without a sense of time. It could have been minutes or hours, she could not tell.

"Were any of you lost to us?" She asked finally, as the pull on her magic weakened.

"No, Master," her favourite gnome climbed into her lap. "With Fire on one side and Water on the other, we were too many and they too few. We are only weakened is all."

Althea nodded. "Small mercies, for which to be grateful."

"And you, Master? Are you lost to us?"

"I am here."

"You did not fare well." It was a statement and accusation at once.

"You shall have to speak to Faorel about it," Althea began to tremble, her shock overtaking her will.

"We have already, Master. You must go to him."

"No," her voice was flat, without inflection.

The gnome placed his tiny hand on hers, stilling her spinning, as all the elementals had fed.

"We are well, Master. Our kind, and generous, Master, tending to our hurts before her own. Our enemies are dead or gone."

Althea took a deep breath and stood carefully, cradling the gnome in the crook of her arm. The other elementals drew back to give her room.

"Master," the gnome persisted.

"The barrier is down, the wards must go back up." To the group at large she said, "thank you all for protecting us, for fighting where we could not. Please accept my apologies for all the harm you took in doing so. I will do all I can to repair the damage. Be welcome here, to anything that you fancy, you've more than earned it." She began walking to the edge of the property, the elementals parting before her and melting away to wherever they went when they were not with their chosen Master. The gnome remained in her arms.

"Master, you have healed us. Now you must go to the Guardian. He needs you."

"I must put the wards back up," her blank expression and halting steps made their progress slow.

"Master, you know these lands. You can reach out with magic and restring the perimeter from here."

"I must," she paused, her exhaustion washing over her and breaking her single-minded focus. "Yes. You are right." She reached for the power that flowed around her, finding it sluggish and thick, her hands and mind both fumbling with its unwieldy bulk.

"Spin, Master. Just spin the magic," her gnome prompted her.

She did. As her mind clutched at that task, she remembered how to line the wards and did so, sounding them once the tail met the mouth.

"Nicely done, Master."

"Thank you, friend. I could not have done it without your help."

The gnome crawled up her arm to her shoulder and hugged her neck. "You are a very good Master, Master. It is our joy to help you."

Althea closed her eyes, savouring this small comfort, offered by one who should rightly resent her. She felt unworthy.

"He loves you still, no matter what you saw. Even in that terrible moment, he loved you. He will perish without you, Master. He is a Guardian. Bound to you, no matter what either wills. Make it right." The gnome whispered the last in her ear, acting as her conscience, holding her to her duty.

A shadow of a smile brushed Althea's lips, wan and tired.

"I could fault you for cruelty, but it wouldn't be true. Go on, my diminutive friend. Find your haven to heal your wounds and be safe."

The gnome squeezed her neck again and then dove from her shoulder down into the earth.

Althea swayed on her feet, drained by the magic she'd poured into the elementals and the wards, exhausted by the battle and her shock and fear. She fell against a large rock just off the path, sitting on it awkwardly. Her eyelids grew heavy and her eyes burned with unshed tears.

"Master? May I help you home?" Faorel appeared from behind a tree, moving silently, meek in his request, his voice soft and pleading.

Althea's hand flew to her heart, a surge of adrenaline racing through her blood as he startled her. "I thought I warned you, if you continue to scare years off my life, ours will be a short partnership." Her words were light, but her tone was lead.

Faorel wavered between a smile and shame.

"Please, Master, may I help you home?" He repeated.

"Leave off the Master, Faorel." She winced, hearing the command only after it fled her lips. She held a hand out to him. "If you would be so kind as to let me lean on you, I should like to find a bath and clean clothes."

Faorel approached her slowly, not wanting to frighten her again, nor remind her of his terrible speed.

He crouched under her arm, taking her weight and lifting her to a standing position with gentle grace.

Althea began to tremble.

"Mm - my lady?"

"Please, just help me home, if you've the strength left to do so."

Hurt, sad eyes looked at her as he scooped her up and carried her into the house. She shook even more in his arms than by his side. If Faorel were a wolf, his ears would have been flattened to his skull, his tail slung low. He deposited her in the water closet and left, closing the door quietly behind him.

A salamander attended her, heating the water, offering small flickering light to make the shadows dance around her.

"Something lovely about firelight, Earth Master," the salamander hissed. "Flattering."

Althea watched the play of light and shadow on the wall, and leaned her head back. "Yes, friend, it is beautiful. Thank you for keeping me company and attending me so faithfully. You are very kind."

"Gentle Master."

One of the local Earth's appeared at Althea's feet.

"Master, I've brought oils to loosen your tangles. May I work in your hair?"

"Heavens. You all must be as tired as I, yet you spoil me."

"Elementals recover quickly at the hand of a good Master," the salamander said, his voice crackly.

"With my thanks, both of you," Althea nodded.

The Earth elemental was both gentle and thorough. Althea sighed as the knots were worked out of her tresses and her skull. While her eyes crossed in bliss, she spun a garland of magic for each of them to take away and keep until they needed it.

The salamander brought her a set of the guild's lounge wear, warming it while Althea towelled off. She slipped into the clean, warm, comfortable garb with a sigh. "Your generosity is beyond repayment, I'm afraid," Althea savoured the moment.

The earth elemental chuckled. "Master, you pay in advance."

Althea smiled and nodded, unwilling to argue, too tired to say any more.

They left her then, to face Faorel and whatever else the evening entailed.

She came into the kitchen and froze in the doorway. Before her was a banquet laid out on the table, the seat at the head vacant, but set for the guest of honour with the best of everything. Most of the foods were those to replenish her after using so much magic. The rest were her favourites, placed there to tempt her into eating if she balked.

Elementals swarmed the kitchen as Faorel brought the last dish to the table. He placed it and stood to the side like a servant, waiting.

"The elementals and I," he began, then stopped, unable to continue.

"Yes, I see. Thank you all. You are far too kind."

The elementals bobbed their heads and vanished.

Faorel pulled out the chair for Althea to sit. He sat to her left, passing her whatever she wished for, neither of them saying anything more than was polite.

Althea glanced at him surreptitiously, noting he was impeccable. Not a drop of blood or spot of dirt anywhere on him.

When her belly neared full, he plied her with every dish at the table, trying to tempt her into one more bite, solicitous that she should not sicken from using so much magic.

"I cannot manage another morsel." She leaned back from the table, "though it was all utterly delicious. Thank you."

"A pleasure, my lady."

Both remained careful with their manners, neither broaching the subject of the battle. The silence that followed filled the room, the space between them growing infinitely larger.

"I should walk the perimeter," Faorel said softly.

"The wards are quiet. The elementals tell me there are no enemies left to be about."

"Still,"

"As you wish."

Faorel rose and left, a pall over him.

Althea sighed and took herself to bed. Time and rest might do what she could not.

They passed a number of days in polite silence, Althea regaining her strength and reclaiming those parts of her mind that had fled during the attack, Faorel keeping his distance, mostly absent, if always nearby.

"Master," the elderly elemental appeared on the shelf near Althea.

"Hello, friend. To what do I owe the pleasure?"

"Master, your Guardian is unwell." The elemental squirmed, trying to find a way to deliver her message without disregarding the authority of a Master.

Althea offered the elemental a palm and carried her to the chaise, where she sat down.

"Can you tell me, wise one, what is wrong?" Althea asked carefully.

"He should be elated and proud, insufferable. He fulfilled the highest and most dangerous duty of a Guardian, and he did so without hesitation. He should not feel remorse and shame for what he is."

"Yet he does."

"Yes, Master, because of you. Because of your fear of him. Because you see only the vicious part of the Guardian, and not the rest of the man, the elemental, the mate he has always been." The elemental was passionate and out of patience with Althea.

Althea sat quietly, thinking over what her elder elemental had said.

"He did just what he is meant to do, and you punish him with distrust, withdrawing from him, making him wish he could disappear. Then he berates himself for being selfish, for even thinking of abandoning you, as if he could." The elemental snorted. "He is torn to pieces, and will become dangerous if you do not fix this."

Althea sat up straighter, accepting the rebuke.

"How should I fix this?"

The elemental gave her a disgusted look. "Hold him, praise him, welcome him, thank him, as you thank us. Appreciate him as you do us."

"How can I? All I can see is blood lust and the gore when I look at him."

"Look harder," the elemental scolded and vanished.

Althea had the remainder of the afternoon to consider what the elderly elemental had said. No other elementals appeared, as though by unanimous consent, avoiding her until she made amends.

Among her other revelations was that the elementals would leave if they were displeased with her, as they appeared to be now. It left a sour taste in her mouth, knowing she was in the wrong and paying the price for it.

She paced. She occupied herself with useless, mindless tasks. She berated herself. She silently wished the elementals were not right.

She took all her pent up and conflicting feelings to the piano and pounded them out, all of them muddled together in an ugly mixture, filling the air with dissonant chords of tension and pounding bass lines. Shrill squalling of the higher notes grating on the ears. The longer she played, the fewer conflicting notes appeared, until thirds and fourths replaced seconds and sevenths. The lines grew melodic, wandering in major and minor key alike. By the time she'd finished, every emotion had been purged, and what was left was a quiet serenity.

She turned in her chair after the last note faded away to see Faorel standing in the doorway, leaning against the frame. She smiled at him, glad that her wish to make amends should be granted so readily. She stood and approached him, standing just far enough away to grant him his space, should he deny her and refuse her apology.

"Hello, my love," she began, in the hopes that he wouldn't rebuff her.

His face and eyes were both neutral and bland, his turmoil suppressed.

"I heard you playing."

"Indeed?" Her face twitched, she looked uncertainly at him.

"All that crashing about was frightening and familiar at once."

Althea winced, fearing she'd done more harm.

"Then the crashing stopped, and what followed gave me hope I had thought gone."

Althea winced again, this time at the depth of harm she'd caused. His sense of loss was far greater than she'd realised. *Too selfish to see what I was doing to him*, she berated herself.

"You drew me in, when I was determined to let you alone, to keep my distance." He reached out, hesitant, to touch her face. She leaned in, closing the distance, giving him silent permission.

He dragged his knuckles down her cheek then cupped the side of her face, stroking her cheekbone with the pad of his thumb.

"I thought I had lost you," his voice was hoarse.

Althea closed her eyes and leaned into his palm, lifting her chin a fraction.

"After you'd done such a thorough job of saving me? That hardly seems fair."

"I agree," he whispered, afraid.

Althea opened her eyes to see what Faorel had concealed. Hurt, anger, frustration, all cast shadows in his gaze.

"I was cruel, unthinkably cruel. I won't make excuses, for there are none. I am utterly in the wrong and I am sorry, Faorel. You did not deserve it."

"I cannot be timid when it comes to your safety. I cannot fear your reproach when you need protecting. You said so yourself. Yet you looked at me as though I am the monster the neighbours claim I am."

Althea remained silent, listening, waiting, certain he was not finished, and knowing she deserved to hear him.

A tortured sound escaped his throat.

"I am a monster. You do well to stay clear of me." He cast his eyes down, turning his face away from her.

"No."

Althea gently pulled his chin around, forcing him to look at her.

"No. You are not a monster. You are a Guardian. You are brave. You are fierce. You are loyal. You are kind, and you are generous."

"You saw," he interrupted.

"I saw a man using every possible method to save a child who could not defend himself. I saw a Guardian doing what his exhausted Master could not, to make certain the danger was eliminated."

"You cannot pretend, cannot sanitise what I did."

"But I can put it in context, and I can remember my promises to you. That passionate fury is part of you. A part I would do well to be grateful for. I love you Faorel. All of you."

"You didn't seem to."

"That is my failing. Not yours. Can you forgive me?"

He pulled her to him, wrapping his arms around her and pressing her close. He said nothing, only held her tight and rested his cheek on her head. She breathed in the smell of him, her heart pounding hard enough for him to feel it battering her ribs.

"Oh, Althea, I could face a hundred Crofts, and never be afraid. But your countenance struck such fear in my heart as I have never known."

"Let us hope there are not even ten such men in the world as Lord Croft."

"Indeed." He kissed the top of her head then pulled her close again.

Althea sighed, relieved and comforted, savouring her Guardian, hopeful that she could make amends.

"Perhaps we should walk the perimeter?" she suggested.

"The perimeter is fine," he said over her head. "There is another form of exercise we are sorely in need of." He pulled away to cup her jaw in both hands and kissed her soundly.

"Yes," she breathed when he released her.

In the coming weeks, the village welcomed them again, no longer spurred on by Peter's malicious rumour mongering. Faorel forgave them graciously.

Not a word was said about the mysterious disappearance of the stranger. The day of the great storm was remembered and the stories retold, with no mention of Peter, his departure lost among tales of felled trees and roofs in need of repair. He'd paid his bills and claimed to be journeying on to meet with an old friend who went unnamed. Althea and Faorel were content to let the matter drop, as it seemed no matter at all to the village. His remains had been disposed of by the elementals and that was the end of it.

As for the Brandons, they were Faorel's staunchest supporters. They didn't believe a word of Michael's tale as far as Faorel being a wolf was concerned, but they did believe Faorel had saved the life of their son, and were the first and loudest to invite the Grays to any gathering. Michael seemed just as willing to accept the altered version of the attack and so he too sought out Faorel, with as much or more hero-worship as before.

All seemed to have returned to normal for Mr. and Master Gray, with the elementals flitting about them whenever no other eyes were near, including the Water elementals. Althea's prompt attention to their hurts after the attack had won them over completely, and now they could be found peeking out of every body of standing or flowing water.

Only one matter was left to attend to, and that was to inform their friends, the guild, as to what happened. They dared not tempt their good fortune by committing the events to paper, so they planned a visit with the Durston's, hoping to arrive before the first of the season's snow. They packed up the house, leaving it in the care of the elementals until they returned and journeyed east to where their friends awaited their arrival.

They were welcomed and greeted by all the household with much enthusiasm. Once in the parlour they were regaled with stories of the past months and told to expect the Weatherbys in only a few days' time

"Our stories shall have to wait, then," warned Althea, "that we might not bore you with the retelling."

Elizabeth's look of exaggerated disappointment had them all laughing.

"Well, whatever might have transpired, you look to have weathered it well." Elizabeth commented.

Faorel lifted their knotted fingers to his lips, kissing Althea's knuckles. "We have."

"If you cannot share your news, then you must share your music. Will you play for us, Althea?"

Althea smiled at the flattery.

"If you insist."

"I do."

Soon it was just as it had been, servants perched on anything that would hold them, all hanging on every note, as Althea trilled and pounded through the stories of their cottage home, of London, of their negotiations with the Greater Elemental. She neglected the story of Peter, of the damage between she and Faorel, and skipped around to the neighbours, Michael Brandon, and the offerings to the elementals.

She ended with the frolicking of the water elementals, their story playful and full of laughter. She turned to see Faorel staring at her, a smile on his face, and love and pride in his eyes.

"Will it do?" She asked him.

"Aye, lass. That will more than do," called the butler from the hallway. He stuck his head in the room. "How we have missed you, Mrs. Gray. Welcome back."

Althea's cheeks flushed. Faorel answered for her.

"Glad we are to be back, sir, and thank you." Faorel tipped his imaginary hat.

The butler nodded and vanished.

They emerged from the room a few moments later to the applause of the Durstons.

"I see you have made use of Faorel's gift, for I swear you've grown even more skilled since the last time we heard you," John said.

"You are too kind," Althea demurred.

"Best get used to the praise, Mrs. Gray, for this is only the beginning."

Althea cocked her head quizzically.

"Oh no, if you are to withhold your stories, we shall withhold our surprises as well." John's eyes sparkled with mischief and delight.

"Surely the offering just now must merit a hint?" Faorel played along.

"Not so much as a whisper," John shook his head.

Dinner passed companionably, followed by Althea and Faorel walking the perimeter and reinforcing the wards. Althea insisted, claiming her debt to them still unpaid.

Elizabeth nodded sagely, recognizing both Althea's determination and her need to spend time with Faorel unaccompanied.

"They've grown closer since last we saw them," Elizabeth said to John after the Grays had left.

"I should hope so. Time together will do that." John replied.

"Trials together, perhaps. Time alone could not have done that."

"Very perceptive, Mrs. Durston," John kissed her cheek. "I sensed a change in our Althea, but it is something only another Earth would notice." He warmed his tea and sat back down. "Some trouble has forged her magically. She is refined, somehow, no longer a cloud of raw power."

"I'd worry about her if it weren't all past," Elizabeth mused.

"Ah, but it is passed."

"Hmm."

The next day, John invited Althea to the greenhouse while Faorel went hunting and Elizabeth tended to managing the house.

Althea moved about, praising the changes he'd made and marvelling at the sterling roses. She traced some of the magic work he'd done, her mouth forming a silent 'oh'.

"You have a deft touch, John. I could never do something this delicate, this intricate."

"Comes of having only small amounts of power, my dear. One learns to do tiny magic and make the most of it. A concept you are rather familiar with, I sense, making the most of something?" He raised an eyebrow, inviting her to share.

"I suppose so, though, I am not near so careful as you are. Not a speck of magic is left to fly about loose." She glanced around the sunroom. Much as she admired John's work, she couldn't help but think of hungry elementals, and the way most magic wielders hoarded magic for their own use.

John let her ignore his invitation and began telling her of some of the improvements he intended to make. Althea was attentive, laughing where she was supposed to, commiserating when expected, the perfect audience. It seemed as though only moments had passed when Faorel tapped on the outer door before letting himself in.

"Hello, dearest. Good hunting?"

"The Durstons have the finest grounds in all of England, I am certain," he came up to her and kissed her lightly then stood beside her, one hand on her waist.

"We like to think so," John agreed. "Shall we?"

Before long, the Weatherbys arrived and Althea was able to tell them Peter's story, at least her part in it. She only grazed Faorel's part in it, not wanting to share unless he wished to, saying only that 'Faorel dispatched Peter, and as far as the village was concerned, the man had left peaceably'. She leaned closer to Faorel in an attempt to show her support.

"But he did not 'leave peaceably', did he?" Mark prompted.

Faorel answered. "I am afraid he was dispatched rather permanently, which is why we came to tell you in person. Such a thing cannot be sent by post."

An uncomfortable silence settled among them.

"I'm afraid he was quite mad." Edna dismissed the tension. "His own would have had to put him down if you hadn't. Seems to me you saved them the trouble, and who knows how many innocents besides." She absolved them and passed sentencing on Peter in one statement, calling an end to it.

Both Althea and Faorel visibly relaxed. They had both feared the guild's reaction to Peter's demise, and the repercussions.

Mark chuckled. "Thought we'd string you up, did you? Let us tell you our stories of the late Lord Croft in the time since last we were together."

And so they did. Peter had attempted to not only gather his elementals in London, but every magic user he knew as well. His staff had little choice. Either obey or seek employment elsewhere. Some did just that. The majority of those who abandoned Peter were among those who had accompanied Peter to Briardowns originally to investigate Althea's situation. They tutted and shook their heads at Peter's obsession with her, and then resigned to find work in other houses.

Peter's neighbours noticed the changes in him before he went to London, and not a one faulted the servants for leaving, accepting them into service readily.

Peter's cries to his magical friends were met with reproof, and he was strongly encouraged to leave off this fool's errand and return to his home and duties. No one came to his aid which only incensed him further. Letters flew like pigeons among the guilds, even a gathering held to discuss his fate. In the end they decided he was no more than a nuisance, and surely the Grays could handle it.

When he attacked the Chambers, no one could prove anything. Though many had their suspicions, suspicions alone are not enough to put a mage down. Since Matthew Chambers made a full, if sudden, recovery, the greater guilds again stayed their hands. After all, no lasting damage had been done.

"Perhaps it would be better if he simply disappears. He left your little village with his coat and hat and was never seen again. Travelling, perhaps. Missing, presumed dead. A mystery, but a minor one," Elizabeth suggested. "Perhaps the storm got him." She shrugged.

"Agreed," nodded Edna, looking to her husband.

Mark nodded then slapped his lap. "Well that settles that. What else have you?" He looked at Althea and Faorel expectantly.

They obliged the group with tales of Althea's attempts at cooking, and the antics of the neighbours. Laughter abounded through dinner, and long into the evening.

When they all sought their beds, Althea suggested a ward-walk to Faorel.

"Not tonight, my lady. Let us replenish them from here, and take ourselves to bed as the rest have done. You are more than done in, I believe."

Althea's lips twisted into a half smile. "Sometimes I think you read me too well." They recharged the wards and went to their rooms.

Faorel stepped up behind Althea, pulling her close to whisper in her ear.

"Besides, I should like you to spend your remaining energy in much more pleasurable pursuits."

❧❦

"We have a guest arriving today," John announced at breakfast.

Edna glanced at her husband and then at the Grays. "And what are we, then?"

"Chopped liver," quipped Faorel with a sparkle of mischief in his eye.

"Family," said Elizabeth, a pointed look on her face.

Faorel sat back, Elizabeth's single word robbing him of any flippant response. Althea patted his hand.

"She's right, dearest. We are all the best sort of family. The family we choose."

Faorel squeezed her hand in response.

"A guest, you say?" He cast an innocent glance at John, as though the interlude had not happened.

"Aye. He is an old friend of mine. We went to Oxford together. He went into a rather different vocation that he initially intended."

Althea buttered her toast, listening, but not with the anxious anticipation John hoped for.

"He comes for you, Althea, so you need not look so calmly disinterested about it," John scolded.

Without a pause, Althea looked up, meeting John's gaze, and said, "I have trouble enough with one man in my life, without wishing for another, John."

Edna choked. Mark patted her back.

A slow smile spread across Althea's face as she continued. "I am a more than happily married woman. You should turn your match-making skills on someone much more in need of them than I." She cast a sly look at Faorel, to see the giddy grin on his face at her praise.

"Althea," Elizabeth filled the space between them. "Daniel is coming to assess you, not mate you."

John changed approach. "Have you any long term plans?" He posed the question to both Althea and Faorel.

170

Faorel looked to Althea. "To be wherever she is." He shrugged. "What else is there?"

John nodded then looked at Althea expectantly.

Althea spared Faorel a loving look before facing John.

"The same."

"Would you consider sharing your immeasurable talents with the world, rather than a handful of households?"

"Teach?" Althea asked.

"Perform." John answered.

Althea paused. "I've never thought of it," she confessed.

"Daniel would like to hear you play, to see you, see how you respond to an audience. He spends his time matching entertainers to venues, and often finds there is a niche of venues for which few entertainers are suited. You may just be one of them."

Now Althea put down her food and sat back.

"Has he magic?" She blurted suddenly.

Elizabeth laughed. "Have you become a magic snob, my dear?"

Althea looked at her, confused. "Not at all. I simply do not want to inadvertently slip if he is not."

"He is not," John answered here, bringing her attention back to himself.

"I shall have to find my lenses," Faorel commented.

"Not right away, I think," John squinted his eyes. "You see, one of the reasons he is coming is that he is intrigued by the idea of a woman accompanied by a great gray wolf."

Elizabeth paled. Faorel noticed immediately.

"And where would he get such an idea?" Faorel challenged John, distressed by Elizabeth's obvious fear of him.

Mark, noting all the expressions at the table, chimed in.

"From John, no doubt. People like Daniel often look for something to draw people in. Lady Gray, Wolf Woman, or some such."

John cleared his throat. "Yes, well, that is for him to decide."

Edna smirked. "We might find you a great red cloak. Let you be known as Red Riding Hood."

Althea held her tongue.

Faorel turned to Elizabeth. "I couldn't distress you so, madam. Be at ease. Intrigue or not, I shan't be a prop that awakens your greatest fears," he assured her.

"Oh, I am certain we can arrange it so that everyone can be comfortable," John dismissed Faorel's concern with a wave of his hand.

Elizabeth ignored her husband and gathered her courage. "We only meant to show you an option, Althea dear, in the event you hadn't already made plans."

"For which we are both grateful," Faorel answered before Althea could open her mouth.

"Indeed," was all she said.

Daniel Adams arrived that afternoon. Elizabeth and Edna kept out of sight, letting the men, and wolf, handle the introductions.

"My word, what a large beast he is!" Daniel exclaimed, laying eyes on Faorel for the first time.

Faorel growled softly, prompting Althea to lay a hand on the back of his neck.

"Not the finest word to use, Mr. Adams. I'm afraid he has quite the vocabulary and he is not over fond of that particular description."

Daniel paled and took a step back, realising the danger of an unhappy wolf.

"I beg your pardon, sir."

Faorel slid his front feet in front of him, lying down.

Althea watched Daniel's calculating expression as he considered them both.

"Your wolf alone would be a draw, never mind your gift for gentling him."

"Or her musical talent," Mark reminded them all.

"Yes. Yes, of course," Daniel nodded. "Will you play, Mrs. Gray?"

"I would be honoured," she curtsied.

Daniel looked about him. "Where is Mr. Gray? Is he not here?"

"He will join us after the performance," Althea replied casually.

"I see."

Althea assumed her post at Elizabeth's piano forte, Faorel sitting beside her bench seat. The men took up positions in the first row of seats in the music room, while the remainder of the household, wives included, gathered in the hall to listen.

Althea took a brief amount of time to warm up before launching into her father's tale of being at sea. The roll of the waves, the roar of the wind, the perfect joy of being just where he was meant to be: at sea. Her fingers trilled the calls of birds and drummed the beat of the rowers and waves resonating in the hull. She mimicked the piper with a nautical tune, a bare motif among all the other voices of the ship and sea.

Her melodies spoke of the anticipation of some unknown destination, of the roll and heave as the ship crested one wave falling into the trough only to rise to the crest of the next. Just as the journey began to lose its sense of delight and forward motion, Althea clanged the chords like a bell. Land. Shore. They'd arrived.

She mimicked the flurry of activity as the crew prepped the ship for docking, while eagerly stealing glances to the port. The tempo slowed, as the ship slowed, not wanting to crash headlong into shore. The tension brought by the sighting of land was peeled away slowly, and the melody grew ever slower, until the ship nestled into the dock. It resolved on a soft major chord that bobbed a few times before coming to a close.

The silence that followed made Althea nervous. Faorel, sensing her tension, put his head in her lap and looked up at her with glowing yellow eyes.

She smiled and patted his head, and waited for Mr. Adams' evaluation.

"Mrs. Gray, forgive me. You left me bereft of words."

Althea patted Faorel's head and stood to walk around the piano and face them. Faorel followed and sat at her side.

"Remarkable does not even begin to describe it," Daniel offered.

"You are very kind, sir. We thank you," Althea nodded, indicating Faorel.

"I believe the ladies await us with refreshments," John said as he stood. Mark and Daniel followed suit. "Althea, perhaps you'd like to see to your wolf and invite Mr. Gray to join us?" He suggested smoothly.

"Thank you, I think I shall. If you gentlemen will excuse me?" She led Faorel up the stairs to their rooms, where he could shift in peace.

"An interesting choice," Faorel commented as he reached for his tinted glasses. "Why the sea?"

"I was thinking of my father, it seemed fitting somehow."

Faorel kissed her cheek. "And so it was. Shall we?" He offered his arm and escorted her back downstairs.

They joined the others, and once the rituals of pouring tea and piling plates with dainty sandwiches were complete, Daniel effervesced with ideas and excitement.

"The Great Gray," he dubbed them. "Referring to both the great talent of Lady Gray and the great size of the gray wolf who accompanies her. What say you?" he glanced around the room.

"Don't look at me," Mark put up his hands. "I haven't the first notion of what attracts an audience," he protested.

"Ah, but it is far more than that," Daniel claimed. "We shall not be hawking on street corners to entice people into a hall. We will cultivate an appetite among the nobles, make a visit from the Great Gray a symbol of prestige, something to covet, vie for. They will not perform just anywhere, for just anyone. No," he shook his head. "They will only play for the most discerning."

Althea kept quiet, allowing him to spin his vision. Faorel watched her, taking his cue from her to wait and see what this Mr. Adams proposed.

John took the role of Althea's spokesman, negotiating on her behalf.

"Just what would that entail, Daniel?"

Daniel waved his hand as though clearing a bad smell. "Oh, very little on her part. Maintaining an air of aloofness when in public, and largely staying out of public view. Creates an air of mystery if she is seen but rarely. What does she do in all that time? People will ask themselves. Does she play every hour of the day, mastering her art? They might invent scandal or fantastic notions, filling her time in their imaginations."

"With seeds planted by you, one presumes?" Edna asked innocently.

"One reaps what one sows," Daniel splayed his hands. He looked Althea over with a critical eye, making Faorel uncomfortable. "We must consider costuming," he said abstractly, as though looking at a doll and not a human being.

Althea cringed inwardly. Their small income would not support grandiose gowns or anything of the sort. "Bit restrictive with the piano forte, though," Daniel continued. "Can't just carry it about with you and play at a moment's notice."

Althea held her tongue. She hadn't a fiddle to play, no matter how proficient she might be, and knew a proper violin would cost as much or more than costuming. Still too dear for her and Faorel.

"No mind," Daniel decided, taking a sip of his tea. "Another spin we can use to our favour, adding to the delay in her performances. Only those nobles serious enough about music to keep a piano forte will be worthy of their attentions." He resolved the matter neatly, without Althea having to mention her other talents, much to her relief.

"What of compensation?" John asked, taking the role of negotiator.

"Hmm? Oh, sixty/forty, for me, after expenses." Daniel said distractedly as his mind flitted from one possibility to another.

"Seventy/thirty," John countered, "for them. They are not your only client, Daniel, and there are two of them to one of you."

"A man has to eat, John," Daniel complained.

"Two have to eat," John said, nodding towards Althea and Faorel.

"Very well," Daniel sighed. "Fifty/fifty, but that's as low as I can go."

"You forget, I roomed with you at Oxford. I know how low you can go."

Daniel cast him a warning glance, not wanting tales of youthful indiscretions trotted out.

"Sixty/forty, for them," John offered. "That's more than fair."

"'Tisn't," Daniel paused. "But I'll take it."

Faorel watched them with amusement. A combination of schoolboy rivalry and genuine respect coloured the dynamic between the two men, despite the business at hand.

"Done," agreed John. He turned to Althea and Faorel. "Will you shake on it?"

"My talented wife has the final say, Mr. Adams. If she agrees, so do I."

Althea stood and offered her hand to Daniel. "Agreed."

"Done and done."

The next days were filled with plans and preparations, including commissions for performance attire that was shockingly simple.

"She must stand out from her audience," explained Daniel at the questioning looks he received from the guild. "I have seen her among you fine gentlemen and ladies, her manners are impeccable, and by them she will blend beautifully among her patrons, bridging the visual gap we shall create. I hope you are not over fond of colour, Mrs. Gray," he turned back to Althea. "For I am in mind to drape you in silvers and charcoals to add to the drama of your name."

Althea dipped her head shallowly. "I will defer to whatever you see fit to do,

Mr. Adams. Even had I a lust for colour, my public appearances, by your own estimation, will be few, leaving me an abundance of private time in which to indulge, were I so inclined."

"Just so," Daniel nodded. "Champion. I foresee an easy alliance among us, Mrs. Gray."

"I certainly hope so."

As Althea and Faorel walked the grounds in the evening, replenishing the wards, her elementals flocked to her.

Faorel indicated them with a tilt of his chin and his darting eyes.

"Not only your element appears this evening, my lady."

Althea welcomed them all with a smile as her favourite gnome tugged at the hem of her cloak. She scooped him up, depositing him on her shoulder where he settled in.

"Word of you travels, Master."

"Oh? And what word is that, my friend?"

"That you will travel, and your coming should be looked on with favour."

Faorel rumbled, pleased and amused. "You once claimed a quiet life, my love."

"As subtle an 'I told you so' as I can imagine," she bumped him as they walked.

"Shall I hope for a warmer reception than our last?" she asked her gnome.

"Yes, Master, and a greater demand for your help. Many are as trapped as those you lately liberated."

"Then we shall do what we can to repair that situation. Only," she paused, both Faorel and the elementals waiting for her to find words for the puzzle only she could see. "Is there aught any of you might be able to do to guide these poor creatures?"

"Guide, Master?"

"At present, my only thought is that the best opportunity to spin magic will be while I am performing. If the audience were to see any of you, it could spell trouble."

Her gnome shook with silent laughter. "There will be many times and places for you to work magic, Master. Fear not. Besides, we are ancient, older than man. We have hidden among you beyond remembering. No trouble will come of us."

Althea relaxed then. "I shall make a reputation of myself with odd eating habits." Althea's mind jumped ahead.

"Doubtless, Mr. Adams can manage that too," Faorel said, amusement in his voice.

"Indeed. I am sure you are right, love," a contented smile settled on her face.

Faorel studied her a moment. "Any other mage would be daunted, my lady. The number of trapped elementals, the amount of power to spin with no hope of personal gain, either would be a burden too heavy to bear."

The elementals of all three elements watched Althea carefully, measuring her response.

She turned her peaceful countenance up to Faorel and then to the group at large and shrugged.

"It feels right to help where I can, no less than at our cottage, or that grumpy, devious Greater Elemental. If they are wounded or trapped, and I have the means to help, then I must. You will all save me from taking sick from it, I am sure, so there is no harm to me, and much gain for them, for all of us."

Her gnome hugged her neck. "Our very good Master."

Althea chuckled and squeezed him gently with her shoulder. "My very good friends."

☙◦❧

While Althea's costumes were being made, Daniel made good on his promises and began stirring up word of the Great Gray among the nobles. He began with the barest of hints, playing coy when they pressed him further. The air of mystery around him deepened, as tiny details and rumours of a fantastic new musician began to circulate.

Daniel planted false rumors as well. Tales of exotic origins, of the ability to commune with animals as a Doctor Hunter was rumoured to do, helped fuel the gossip and anticipation. It was only a matter of time before the high society would clamour for proof of this mysterious personage.

When the costumes neared completion, Daniel chose a near-worshipped society matron to host the Great Gray's first London performance. That esteemed lady was guided to invite only a handful of the most discerning of the peerage to her intimate affair, with promises that she would be credited with introducing this rich, new, talent to the London season.

As the day approached, all in the Durston's home felt the rising anticipation, and Althea's tension. She could not hide it from them, nor did she try, choosing instead to show her misgivings to her friends, as she had not following her rescue when both Mr. Hamlin and Mr. Croft vexed her.

Elizabeth found her sitting alone in the parlour one morning, Faorel having gone on a hunt, or at least, a run. She sat down beside Althea, as Althea gazed out the picture window, seeing nothing, nor noticing Elizabeth's arrival.

Elizabeth patted her hand and then clasped it lightly, gently bringing Althea out of her ruminations.

"Share your burdens, Althea dear," Elizabeth invited, her tone soft and reassuring.

Althea offered her a sheepish expression. "What's to tell that you don't know already?"

"I don't know what about this troubles you so, for you keep it locked behind your teeth as though you are a stone statue."

Althea winced, not at Elizabeth's words, but at the fears that clawed at her.

"I haven't the first notion of how to be a performer."

Elizabeth's face held chiding. "Have you not been performing most of your life? Dancing steps, as you call it, for all to see, regardless of the truth of the matter?"

"You make me sound like a great deceiver."

"You hid the truth of your situation from more than a few, as I recall," Elizabeth reminded her, still holding her and, and bouncing it gently once.

"That was not by choice," Althea defended herself.

"Oh, I agree, you were backed into it, rather effectively, but it was a choice," she held up her free hand, forestalling Althea's rebuttal. "Not one I would have decided differently on, my dear. I am not accusing you. Only reminding you that you have the experience and the skill to do again what you have done already."

Althea sighed. "I know that dance, those steps. It was abundantly clear what I had to do. This?" She paused and closed her eyes. "This dance I know not at all, yet I must play the tune for it, rather literally."

Elizabeth looked long at Althea, a thoughtful expression shaping her features. "It is, therefore, your dance to create, as you see fit. Give yourself to the music, the story, the notes, all else will unfold as it should. Now," Elizabeth stood, smoothing her skirts. "Enough of this brooding. Your doting Guardian will return soon, John is holed up with his magical workings, and your elementals, I am told, seek an audience with you in the hothouse."

Althea's face held an open question.

"Alliance," Elizabeth said, being deliberately cryptic. "I must say, it is rather disturbing to cast a circle of calling, and have the roles reversed, where mage becomes messenger, and elemental the Master."

Althea sucked in her lips. "I had no idea they would do that, Elizabeth, I am,"

Elizabeth silenced her with a look. "No apologies from you. You cannot help what you are, nor would I wish you to, for you are my dear friend, and I love and cherish you in all your imperfect glory. Go," she made a shooing motion with her hands. "They wait for you."

Althea bowed her head once and went.

"Master," her elementals called together as she entered the greenhouse. Althea stepped only a few paces into the room before they near swarmed her in excitement, all of them speaking at once, the cacophony of their voices overwhelming her ability to understand any of them. She waited for them to settle, a warm smile on her face at her army of friends.

Only one of the bird-like elementals kept his distance, perching on a tree branch, and watching the scene as he picked and preened at his feathers. Althea fixed her gaze on him and the others soon quieted, noticing her gaze. They parted before her, defining a path to the tree.

She trod carefully and lightly to where he watched.

"Good afternoon, feathered one. How fare you today?"

"Verrry well, Mast-t-ter, and you?" His elemental stutter a welcome sound in her ear. All the other elementals stayed silent for their exchange.

"Delighted and confused at once, I'm afraid. There are so many more of you here than usual."

"We came t-t-to tell you of yourrr assurrred and imminent welcome in that foul cit-t-ty," the elemental replied.

"How many trapped or poisoned?"

"Many."

"Imminent, you say?"

"Yes, Mast-t-ter."

"I suppose we should pack."

"Yes, Mast-t-ter."

"And most of you will not be coming with me."

"No, Mast-t-ter."

"So is this an impromptu going away celebration?"

"Yes, Mast-t-ter." The elemental bobbed his head.

Althea glanced at all the hopeful faces around her.

"Well then, allow me to get comfortable, and we shall see about a feast to tide you all over in my absence, shall we?"

Smiles broke out everywhere and in moments, Althea was settled in, surrounded by and covered in elementals, all seeking a place as near to her as possible.

She began spinning the strands of magic for them to feed on and to take away with them, focusing by singing softly to them. They drank in music and magic both, lounging and soothed by her gifts. When Faorel came in, they did not even stir, except to make room for him near her as he fitted himself behind her, taking the place of the tree she leaned against as her back rest. She smiled her welcome at him, her notes not faltering as they fitted their bodies together. Even he was soothed by her gifts and the sea of tranquility and air of satisfaction around her.

When every elemental was strewn with garlands of magic, her melodies ran out and they sat in silence for long moments afterward, no words or gestures needed. One by one, the elementals came to touch her and then move away, disappearing in the foliage, saying farewell, until none remained.

Faorel wrapped his arms around her middle and squeezed her gently while kissing her neck. "A fine gift, Lady Gray."

The elementals named the timing perfectly, for the post arrived next day that they should begin their London journey immediately. Althea dashed off a brief letter in response, making the postman wait to take it, telling Adams to expect them only a day behind their letter.

"Give them half a day, and my whole house will begin mourning your loss, Althea," John admonished her. "For it shall only take a half day for all your things to be packed and preparations made for your departure."

"You are too kind," Althea demurred, choosing not to dispute his claim.

Elizabeth sat back in her chair, considering their guests. "You do have a pattern of leaving in haste. Not one for long goodbyes, are you?"

Mark chuckled, "takes after her sea-faring lineage. They rarely have notice and no time to linger." He changed his voice to mimic her Uncle Chambers, "the tide waits for no man," he quoted, making Faorel laugh.

"A truly cunning imitation, if ever I heard one."

Edna snorted. "That might be fine, but for the fact that she is not a sailor, and has no tide to catch." She rolled her eyes. "Really, Althea. You must plan your travels better in future."

Althea heard the teasing in Edna's voice and strove to look contrite, despite her amusement.

"And so I shall, Mrs. Weatherby. I am rightly chastened."

They spent the evening in quiet companionship, all of them seeking to distract Althea from her coming adventure, and maintain the mood of peace her elementals had created.

She and Faorel prepared for bed in their room, and Faorel nestled in behind her as they crawled into bed. "I like your chosen family. They are good people."

Althea's smile came through her voice. "Our chosen family. And yes, they are."

Another chorus of reminders about correspondence, another carriage ride, another wall of cacophony, and they were back in London. All of Faorel's previous impressions of the place still held, the crowding agitating his protective instincts, making him wary and curt.

Daniel arranged their living arrangements, while John arranged their arrival. The main carriage would deliver Mr. and Mrs. Gray at some non-descript inn and deliver their belongings to another. They would pay for the night, and once all were asleep, Faorel would shift into a wolf and Lady Gray and her wolf would be picked up by a grander carriage and taken to their long-term residence, where their luggage was already waiting, dropped off by its own second carriage earlier, thus establishing the mystique Daniel had created.

They would have the day for final fittings on Althea's costumes, and otherwise to spend in leisure indoors, and the evening would bring Althea's debut.

Her attire for the performance arrived just after dark, accompanied by a long leash and well-crafted collar for Faorel. Daniel delivered both personally, announcing that he would escort them to avoid any misunderstandings along the way.

Faorel growled at the collar and refused to wear it until Daniel demonstrated how it was designed to snap open if tugged on.

"Mrs. Gray, will you please explain to your wolf that it is only for show? A simple illusion to put the guests at ease when they see him?"

Althea played to the ruse she and Faorel had begun at the Durston's and sat in front of Faorel, who stared at her with misgivings in every line of his body, playing along with her.

"Dearest, please," she held the collar in one hand and caressed his furry face with the other. "It is only for the evening. Just a little while. Will you wear it? For me?" She leaned her face close to his, inviting a kiss as though he were a loved pet, and not a wolf.

Faorel licked her nose then bumped the collar with his muzzle. When Daniel reached for the collar, however, Faorel growled once more.

"Perhaps you had better put it on him," he suggested, backing away slowly.

Althea said nothing as she carefully clasped the strap around Faorel's neck. She stood and stepped back, assessing the fit and look of it.

"I will say, it does add something to your overall impression." Then she stepped up and scratched his ears. "Such a good boy."

Faorel sighed.

A great carriage arrived, drawn by six gray horses, all perfectly matched. Faorel stayed well away and downwind of them as he entered the box. Daniel noticed the unnatural caution, but said nothing.

As they pulled up to Lady Barrington's home, Althea spied the fluttering curtains at the house which gave away those curious guests who waited for her appearance.

"Now, don't you fret," Daniel coached her. "I'll do all the talking, and get you and your wolf to the piano forte. Don't say a word. After your performance, if they invite you to join them, us, do so, but say very little, and nothing of consequence. I mean to maintain the distance between you and the nobles. Polite, but distant."

Althea nodded in answer and stepped out of the carriage with all the dignity of a duchess, if not the title. Daniel and Faorel bracketed her to the door where they were announced as Daniel Adams and the Great Gray. As she took in the splendor of the hall they entered, she blinked, her only indication of how stunned she was by the sheer opulence.

The guests approached, eager to make her acquaintance, until Faorel stepped forward, making them pause, uncertain.

"Ladies and gentlemen," Daniel drew their attention away from Faorel. "I am pleased to present The Great Gray. If you will be so kind as to take a seat and allow the Lady and her companion to assume their posts, we shall begin shortly." He looked to Althea, who nodded, and she and Faorel proceeded to the piano. She held her back straight, her chin up, and a ghost of a smile on her lips. Faorel was his natural wary self. A room full of strangers bore watching. He fairly stalked beside her, not bothering to hide his distrust, or his protective instincts.

Althea removed her thick gray gloves, a protection from the cold. She'd practiced shortly before they left, to warm up her hands without inflicting practice techniques on her lofty audience.

She told the story of life with the Wentworths. She began with the grounds, where her best days were spent. Though it was now autumn, she told of spring afternoons. Her right hand hopped through the intervals of the bird calls, mates calling out to one another, while the left throbbed slowly with a world in slumber, just stirring to wakefulness.

She captured the garble of the stream on the grounds, as it tripped and laughed, swelled with snow melt, and delighted at the coming spring.

Lurking beneath it all was a tension, a strange dissonance, her curse, ever present, but easy to ignore when all else sang of hope, joy, renewal. A light tripping of notes as an early spring flower shook with a gentle breeze, shaking loose the water droplets that clung to it. A brief few riffs of the gardener humming his home sick tunes as he cleared the land and readied it for planting.

Mary's laughter broke over the notes, scattering them. Her innocent youthfulness irresistible as she danced and spun in circles, arms held out like the seeds of the of the little fliers the sycamores shed. Althea's protective and indulgent love for Mary added a richness to the chords, warming them, filling them out, where Mary's voice tripped a staccato in the upper register.

Much too soon, the sun began to set, the air grew cool, the individual melodies and riffs slowed, thinned. Mary went inside, her voice calling once for Althea to follow, then fell silent. The gardener, too, clamoured briefly, putting tools away and was gone. All else retreated to slumber through a night still too chill, until all that remained was the gurgle of the stream, the pulse of the earth, and Althea's dissonant curse. She brought them all to a close together, for at that time, all endured.

Althea's audience was still and as she raised her eyes from the keys, she did not see even a glimpse of an elemental, though she'd spun her magic as she played. Her gnome spoke true. They would not reveal themselves in carelessness.

"Daniel," Lady Barrington spoke. "I am all astonishment. I have never heard such a sound in all my life, I assure you." Her tone trod a fine line between accusation and awe, leaving Althea, and indeed, all the room, unsure as to which she meant. Althea placed one calming hand on Faorel, lest he growl his disapproval.

Barrington turned to face Althea. "Lady Gray, you have honoured and amazed us all, won't you please join us?"

Althea bowed her head once, her ghost of a smile reappearing, then gently pushed out the bench and took up Faorel's leash. While she was playing, the servants had silently arranged the seating to allow Faorel room to sit beside her designated chair, without crowding the guests. She crossed the room as a highborn lady, carrying a 'presence' that Daniel wholeheartedly approved of. She took her seat beside Daniel, who was beside Lady Barrington, once again bracketed by both her protectors, and stroked Faorel's head and neck as he sat, but would not lie down, in such unknown company.

"You are a wonder, indeed," praised Barrington, "and I shall be quite proud that ours in the first gathering you've graced."

Althea schooled her expression into quiet thanks, "it was my pleasure, Lady

Barrington, to have so receptive an audience."

Daniel's tiny nod of approval was seen only by Althea as all other eyes in the room were riveted to either her or Faorel.

"And where did you find such a magnificent animal? I am certain he is even larger than those my late husband told tales of."

The warning glance from Daniel was superfluous.

"That, Lady Barrington, is a long tale. I will only say this: I have found no more loyal a companion."

Faorel turned his head to look at her then, and pushed his muzzle into her palm.

Lady Barrington chuckled, "loyal and affectionate. I rather wondered if you might have bespelled him, somehow. He is both tame and savage at once."

The alarm pulsing from Daniel in waves was palpable, at least to Althea.

Althea's expression formed into one of condescension, a silent chiding. "Tales for children and unscrupulous reporters, only. He is a wolf and I a musician. All else is pure speculation."

Daniel sighed in relief, then interjected. "Shall we ask your guests what they thought of the performance, Lady Barrington?"

Althea thought the suggestion gauche. Now that Barrington voiced her approval, her guests had no choice but to agree or risk social suicide. She did not need a room full of sycophants stroking her ego, but that was just what Daniel's suggestion implied. She spared him the same condescending look she'd given their host.

"Oh, I think we can find more suitable topics, Mr. Adams," Althea turned her gaze from him, to the group at large, softening it as she did. "For instance, this season brings a multitude of events, I should like to know what delights are anticipated." Althea targeted a young lady who looked near bursting with wanting to speak, her chaperone presumably a doting father or uncle.

As it turned out, the girl was articulate and perfectly well trained in the art of conversation, sparking others to join in. Their lively participation allowed Althea to divert attention, and more importantly, questions, away from herself, and establish that distance Daniel claimed he sought.

With all of them occupied, Althea leaned over to Daniel and quietly suggested they take their leave. He nodded and moved to have a brief word with Barrington. She nodded and patted his hand, saying only a few unheard words, and they slipped away without disrupting the guests.

If they were minded to gossip, they surely could not do it with Althea present, and she was not truly a guest, and had no right to partake of their company. Besides that, her designated persona grated on her. Nobility and their foolish dancing with words, speaking much, saying little.

Once the carriage pulled away from Barrington's estate, Daniel burst with excitement, until now, tightly contained.

"You played that splendidly, Lady Gray. Such a conundrum for them to place you socially, and you the impeccable snob, observing the protocol of manners flawlessly. A coup, I am certain of it." Daniel went on in that vein for the rest of the journey, making Althea grateful to wave her goodbye's to him when they arrived home.

When they were safely inside, she snapped the collar from Faorel and went straight to the wardrobe to exchange her performance attire for the guild's lounging uniform and then began pulling pins from her hair. The house held no servants, to prevent gossips and leaks of what Lady Gray did when she was not performing. All might assume they had their own army of help, for the size of the house Daniel arranged, but none would come and go to spy on them.

Althea had marked the perimeter of the house when they arrived the night before, and sent a surge of magic into the wards to reinforce them now. Faorel stepped up behind her to help with the hair pins as she struggled, distracted by attempting to purge the unpleasant thoughts chasing each other around in her brain.

"Lovely Lady, allow me to help," he crooned at her.

Althea sighed.

"With my thanks, love." She held still while his deft fingers found, and gently extracted, every pin from within her curls.

"We know, unequivocally, how Mr. Adams feels about tonight's performance. It appears you don't share his enthusiasm." He found the last pin as he spoke and spun her around to face him. He kissed her lightly before she replied.

"I do not."

"I can't say I do either," Faorel made a face. "Such a good boy?" He complained, this being the first opportunity to voice his dislike of being treated like a common house pet.

Althea winced. "I knew it was wrong the moment I said it, but could not apologize in front of Mr. Adams."

"Accepted. Shall we see if we can burn some tea?" he suggested.

Just then a salamander appeared, hovering in the air beside them. It spun in a steady circle.

"Greetings, Earth Master," it hissed, "may we serve?"

It glowed in reds and oranges, bright and solid, and it occurred to Althea that Fire would be the only element to thrive in a city where Earth, Air, and Water were all poisoned to some degree. The offer still surprised her, as she'd made no invitations to them since her arrival.

"Hello indeed, friend. Your offer is kingly, and we should be happy to accept. Thank you." She spun him a quick garland of magic for his trouble and he popped out of sight, presumably to find the kitchen.

Even that tiny morsel drew the wraiths of trapped and weakened earth elementals. Althea saw them, hands and faces pushing through the walls, and pulled Faorel with her as she sat on the floor and began spinning a feast for them.

Faorel held her and they rocked back and forth as she worked. She sent out a general invitation to both Fire and Water, and soon the room was filled with elementals from all three, though only a very few Fire. The opposing elements kept a safe distance from each other. None spoke as all were starved, and Althea too caught up in the moment, wrapped in Faorel's arms and working her magic with a sense of rightness, to spare attention on speech. When she began to falter, Faorel murmured only "Master," softly in her ear as a warning to her.

She tied off the strand and apologized to the horde of creatures in the room.

"I'm afraid I can do no more tonight, my friends. Will you last until I am recovered? Will that hold you for now?"

Every face shone with devotion as they bowed themselves out.

Her head fell back against Faorel's shoulder as a wave of exhaustion passed over her.

He kissed her temple. "Handsomely done, Lady."

"Earth and Water were both sickened. I rather hope they have enough power and sense to get away from this cursed city."

"Let us just hope you have not disrupted some mage's long plans of tempting, trapping, and binding them, else we will have more enemies at the gate." He hauled them both to their feet to help Althea to the kitchen where the fire elementals were working.

☙❧

The next few days Althea and Faorel heard nothing at all about the success or failure of her debut. They spent that time much as they had at the cottage, save for the hunting and socializing. Althea spun offerings for the elementals twice a day and they siphoned off the overflow as she played the house's piano forte. After one such offering, as the fire elementals plied her with food in the kitchen, she commented on their sheer numbers to Faorel.

"I can't tell if it is the same mass as before, or a new group each time. There are just too many of them for me to keep track, and I feel terribly guilty for that. One should be able to tell one's friends apart."

The nearest fire elemental spun in fast circles, a crackly chortle riding on the air.

"You are the first Master in memory with such a problem, Earth Master," the salamander zipped in a quick circle. "Most Masters can only trap a handful of us, and still cannot tell us apart, nor do they care to."

Faorel swelled with affection and pride for his wife. "As you can see, you are forgiven for your imagined trespass. Besides, they are different each time. You cannot be expected to memorize hundreds of new faces every day."

Althea looked at him sideways, "Clearly, you recall them all."

"I am a Guardian."

"Another gift, I suppose?" She arched an eyebrow.

He darted in to kiss her cheek. "Yes, my lady."

Althea shook her head as the salamander nudged her plate, insistent that she resume eating.

"We passed on your thoughts of escaping, Earth Master," the elemental said. "They were good thoughts. No elemental has any great attachment to a place poisoned to him. Each gathering accepts your gifts and flees."

"London will be bereft of any magic save yours," Althea replied.

"Many of my kind will migrate also, Earth Master," the salamander hissed. "Too many of one element disrupts the balance. We prefer balance."

"How many of your kindred will resent me for making this place less hospitable for you?"

"None, Earth Master. Just as seasons and tides cycle, so too do we. More in one place, less in another, until something changes, then we flow again into different areas."

Faorel sat down to ensure Althea ate her fill. "We have a longer view of time, Lady Gray, and a greater sense of entropy."

Althea popped a morsel into her mouth. "Hmm." She swallowed. "I suppose you would."

It was almost a week before Daniel sent word of his arrival, following it a full day later.

"Well, I hope you enjoyed the break, Mrs. Gray, for you shall not have another for some time."

Faorel made a face behind Daniel, 'hardly a holiday' his expression said. Then he sat beside her, nodding his welcome to Daniel.

Daniel resumed. "It took time for word of your performance to make the rounds, and still more for the various hosts to contact me and arrange your performances. Six nights a week we shall have you before audiences."

"Good heavens," Althea exclaimed. "We shall have a very short season at that rate. Surely there cannot be that many highborn in London."

Daniel chuckled. "Fear not, Lady Gray. This will be for a few weeks only, to whet their general appetite. Thereafter, you shall only perform but once or twice a week, and those booked well in advance. Lady Barrington has already requested a repeat performance of you and your wolf." Daniel glanced around. "Where is your wolf, by the way."

"Resting, I believe," Althea temporized.

"Ah," he nodded, dismissing the wolf entirely. "During this marathon run, I should like you to keep completely out of the public eye, excepting the engagements I have booked."

"With pleasure," Althea breathed sincerely. "London does not possess the same appeal for us as it does for some." She locked gazes with Faorel then, both of them recalling their last visit.

"Splendid. I shall return this evening to collect you as I did before." Daniel stood and bowed himself out. Once he was gone, Althea turned to Faorel.

"Will you be able to bear it, my love? Being cooped up inside for weeks?"

Faorel smiled indulgently at his wife and Master. "With you to keep me distracted? Assuredly."

A few weeks became six, straining both Althea and Faorel. She continued her daily offerings to the elementals, draining herself further. By the time the last week arrived, she and Faorel were both snappish.

"I despise that collar," Faorel complained as Althea donned her performance grays.

"Just be grateful you don't have to partake of inane conversation and maneuver around social politics," Althea retorted, dreading the routine of playing The Duchess, as they'd come to call it.

"Yes, your Grace," Faorel snarled at her, bowing then shifting into a wolf.

Althea tensed at that. Only Peter had called her such, and his memory grated on her nerves. She took a deep breath, then turned to face Faorel, who sat staring at her. She knelt down in front of him, heedless of shed hair on her costume, and addressed him.

"My dearest heart, please, if you can help it, don't use that title again. Only one man ever spoke to me so, and he is mercifully gone."

Faorel growled.

"Only five more performances after tonight, and we can retreat to where you can hunt at will and we can both be ourselves again. Until then, just think of the good we may be doing to your younger cousins."

Faorel bowed his head and then bumped her chin with his muzzle, relenting.

That performance, and the remaining ones, went much like those prior, until the last.

During her final performance, one of the guests arrived late, armed with a rifle, unseen by any save Althea, as all eyes were on her. She stood mid-performance and stepped in front of Faorel.

"Lady, step aside," he demanded as the audience turned to see what had startled her so.

"I shall not, sir."

"Manny, for god's sake, put that weapon down. What do you mean by being so tardy and threatening everyone?" The hostess chastised him, as much affronted by his poor manners as his threat of violence.

"That is a savage beast, no matter what the papers say," Manny insisted. "You risk everyone's life having him here."

Faorel fought to move Althea so he could protect her, maul this man, if necessary. Althea side-stepped to block him, making him growl.

"Hush," she hissed. "He's threatening you, not me. Be still." She hated giving him the orders, but could think of no other way to protect him.

"There, you see?" Manny insisted. "Savage."

Their hostess looked at Faorel, obeying Althea's commands.

"I rather think she has disproved your point, Manny."

The standoff stretched through long moments of silence, as Althea held herself still, her chin raised, looking down on Manny imperiously. He lowered his weapon reluctantly. Althea nodded, a dark look on her face, then addressed their host.

"Madam, we shall strain your company no further. If your latest guest will grant us safe passage, we shall depart immediately."

A servant relieved the man of his rifle and Althea took up Faorel's leash. "Come," she commanded, her last order for the evening she vowed silently.

When they arrived back at their lodgings, Althea began packing, leaving Faorel to himself until both their tempers were more certain.

A salamander appeared, hovering over the dresser she was emptying.

"Earth Master?" he asked. "You are vexed. Can we help?"

"If you would be so kind, we should like to leave as soon as possible. Anything you can do to that end would be most welcome."

The elemental bobbed once then disappeared, only to return with a small army of comrades who began folding, wrapping, and packing with a will.

Althea left them to it and went downstairs to write her regrets to Mr. Daniel Adams.

Faorel came to her just as she signed the bottom.

"Lady Gray?" He spoke softly, testing for her temper.

Althea winced, then turned to face him, her apology falling from her lips before she was half way around. Before she could recriminate herself without mercy, Faorel stopped her, by coming to sit at her feet. His subservience broke her heart and stopped her mouth.

"What shall we do, Master?" he asked, still pitching his voice low and careful.

Althea cupped his face in both hands, tilting his face up to look at her. "Unless you have any great desire to stay, I think we would do well to leave this place and go home."

Faorel's face lit with hope. "With pleasure, my lady."

"The elementals are working like fiends, preparing our things, and I've written to Mr. Adams. All that's left is hiring a carriage." She glanced out the window. Full dark.

Faorel followed her gaze. "Allow me to find one," he turned his head to kiss her palm.

While he was out, Althea wrote another quick note to the Durstons, letting them know where to reach her and Faorel at, and begged John to arrange the financial particulars with Mr. Adams. By the time Faorel returned, all was ready.

They departed like thieves in the night.

Epilogue

They arrived home, to their little cottage, in a blizzard. It was all the horse could do to deliver them to their door.

"We haven't a stable, but that," Faorel added more coin to the tip, "should get you a night at the village inn."

The driver touched his hat in thanks, and flicked the reins to get the horse moving again. Faorel grabbed the last trunk and stepped into the house to find Althea fussing with tea and thanking the elementals who flurried about, unpacking and readying food and comfort for the Grays.

Althea's cheeks were flushed by the cold, some glistening drops of melted snow in her hair, as Faorel carried the trunk to the bedroom. He returned to find her seated before the fire, a heavy robe pooled around her. He smiled at how inviting she looked and sat behind her. She leaned back into him, grateful for the comfort and safety of his embrace. Faorel's tension melted away as he sat with her, watching the flames, breathing in the smell of her and home.

"Well," Althea began. "That was an unmitigated disaster."

Faorel chuckled. "So extreme, Althea?"

"Perhaps you are right. But I shan't like to attempt that again." She nestled closer into him.

He kissed her head. "Which part?"

"Most of it, I should think. London. The nobles. Parading you around as a pet. The Duchess routine," she shuddered.

Faorel squeezed her gently. "What of all those elementals, desperate for release?"

"We shall have to find some other guise to travel under. Preferably one that also generates some income."

"Suppose the Lady Gray drops the 'Great' from her name, and the wolf, and the Duchess' airs," Faorel suggested.

"Hmm. And adds the fiddle to her bag of tricks, though how we shall afford another instrument, I'm sure I don't know."

Faorel pulled her to her feet to jar her train of thought. "Best leave that trouble for another day, dearest." He kissed her soundly. "We are for bed."

"Yes, Master Gray," she teased.

When they awoke they were thoroughly snowed in. Not a soul would be moving if they had no pressing need.

"Our water elementals must be delighted," Althea commented, looking out the window. "And our Earth's quite torpid, I should think."

Her favourite gnome broke the surface of the window sill like a swimmer coming up for air.

"Not so, Master," he grinned up at her. "With the permanent wards you set up, we feed well and enjoy the cold as well as the heat."

Althea's face lit up seeing him again. "Glad am I to hear it."

"Fire might have had a bad time of it, but for your hospitality. They come, play in your stove, and leave again to more accommodating places," the gnome explained further. "All are well, Master, thanks to you."

Althea blushed. "I am only too glad to be of service."

"Your Guardian walked the grounds last night. He frolics like a puppy."

"I suppose cold is no never mind to a wolf." She addressed Faorel. He shrugged, a small smile on his lips.

"He told us of your plans."

Althea raised an eyebrow. "Did he?" She glanced between them. "And what think you of them?"

"A fine idea," the gnome agreed.

"How far can a Master lay down wards?" Althea asked her gnome.

"There is no limit, Master. Obstacles are only power and the presence of another Master."

Althea nodded. "Can Masters share wards?"

The gnome laughed his silent laugh. "Such a thing has never been done, Master. Your kind do not share well."

Althea sniffed. "Time enough for that to change, I believe."

Faorel stepped up behind her, wrapping his hands about her waist, and pressing his cheek to hers. "You are no small bit revolutionary, my lady. Tread lightly. Change, even welcome change, is hard. More so for those short lived than those of us who have seen centuries."

Althea grunted, then relented. "At least I can live by example."

Faorel kissed her cheek. "Lady Gray, you do that already."

The season passed uneventfully. The village quiet, the elementals finding rhythm and patterns, and Althea and Faorel resting and renewing their life in the cottage. When spring came, they prepped all of it for a long absence and the elementals presented Althea with a fiddle. Touched beyond words, she could only caress the body of it, her eyes shining with unshed tears.

"Althea, love, play for them," Faorel suggested gently.

She did. The notes trilled and danced up and down the strings, a flurry of emotions with little cohesion until she found a single melody to loop through. It came around in two sections, each leading into the other, or itself again until she wound it down with a final arpeggio.

The elementals accepted her gift, each strewn with an extra garland of magic, woven from the melody, and melted back into the walls, furniture, floors and left.

"Finely done, lady love. Shall we go?" Faorel offered his arm and led her to the door where their packs stood waiting.

"To the open road, and those in need of us," Althea named their journey.

Faorel grinned and shouldered his pack.

"'Tis a fine thing, my Master does, and I am proud to be her Guardian."

Althea glanced at him sideways. "Even if it doesn't keep me safely tucked away from harm?"

"Power calls trouble, Lady Gray. You have much power, so danger will always be near. This way, we face it together, while bringing comfort to my unfortunate cousins."

"Tidings of comfort and joy," she carolled.

Faorel hugged her then, and opened the door. "Tidings they have. Now, to make good on the promise."

Also by Darin Castalds:

Misborn

Visit

www.castalds.com

for more information.

Made in the USA
Charleston, SC
27 February 2015